Praise for
NATIONAL BESTSELLING AUTHOR STEFANIE MATTESON'S *CHARLOTTE GRAHAM MYSTERIES!*

MURDER AT THE SPA

"Clever, original, suspenseful!"
—**David Stout, Edgar Award–winning author of *Carolina Skeletons***

MURDER AT TEATIME

"A gripping mystery, with a splendidly authentic background of the magical Maine coast."
—**Janwillem van de Wetering, author of *Inspector Saito's Small Satori***

MURDER ON THE CLIFF

"Sly . . . an ironic background for murder!"
—**Margaret Maron, author of *Corpus Christmas***

"Delightful." —**Audrey Peterson, author of *Elegy in a Country Graveyard***

MURDER ON THE SILK ROAD

"A very entertaining mystery."
—***Haven't Got a Clue* Book Reviews**

"Reads like a Mrs. Pollifax saga."—***Murder ad lib***

"Matteson's adventure will charm readers."
—***Publishers Weekly***

Charlotte Graham Mysteries
by Stefanie Matteson

MURDER AT THE SPA
MURDER AT TEATIME
MURDER ON THE CLIFF
MURDER ON THE SILK ROAD
MURDER AT THE FALLS

MURDER
AT THE
FALLS

STEFANIE MATTESON

BERKLEY BOOKS, NEW YORK

Excerpts from the poem *Paterson* are from William Carlos Williams: *Paterson*. Copyright 1946 by William Carlos Williams. Reprinted by permission of New Directions Publishing Corp. World rights.

MURDER AT THE FALLS

A Berkley Book / published by arrangement with
the author

PRINTING HISTORY
Berkley edition / December 1993

ISBN: 0-425-14008-3

BERKLEY®
Berkley Books are published by
The Berkley Publishing Group, 200 Madison Avenue,
New York, New York 10016.
BERKLEY and the "B" design are trademarks of
Berkley Publishing Corporation.

PRINTED IN THE UNITED STATES OF AMERICA

10 9 8 7 6 5 4 3 2 1

To Cathy and Ellen
and breakfasts at the Cozy End

From above, higher than the spires, higher
even than the office towers, from oozy fields
abandoned to grey beds of dead grass,
black sumac, withered weed-stalks,
mud and thickets cluttered with dead leaves—
the river comes pouring in above the city
and crashes from the edge of the gorge
in a recoil of spray and rainbow mists—

From *Paterson* by William Carlos Williams

· I ·

"I'VE FOUND IT," said Tom Plummer as he gave their order—two mozzarella and sun-dried tomato sandwiches and two iced coffees—to the Italian waiter who hovered ingratiatingly over their table on the sidewalk outside the small Columbus Avenue trattoria.

Charlotte Graham hadn't seen Tom for a couple of weeks. They had arranged this lunch date to catch up. Tom was what their waiter might have called her *cavaliere servènte*, or serving cavalier. In Italy, many elegant older women enjoyed the special friendship of a younger man who danced attendance on them, and Tom was hers. For the last four years, ever since she had separated from her fourth husband, Jack Lundstrom, Tom had been filling the need for a man in Charlotte's life, serving as companion, escort, chauffeur, confidant—everything in fact but her lover. It was a synergistic relationship. They joked that it was like shark and pilot fish, though who was which they weren't sure. In exchange for being her escort, Tom got to partake of the perquisites that were hers as a veteran of fifty years (this year! it was now 1989, and she had made her first movie in 1939) in front of the cameras and on the stage. For being a star, as her second husband used to say, was like having a first-class ticket to life.

Charlotte didn't need to ask what *it* was. *It* was Tom's Holy Grail, the perfect diner. Though Tom made his living writing books on true crime, his hobby, or, better put, his passion, was diners. He spent his weekends cruising the gritty downtown areas and the rural highways of the Northeast for his model of perfection. This wasn't the first time that he had made such a pronouncement. Ruby's Diner in Schenectady, N.Y.; Rosie's Farmland in Little Ferry, New Jersey; and the Miss Portland in Portland, Maine, were all among the diners that at one time or another been awarded this accolade. But each had been superseded by yet another more worthy.

With Tom, Charlotte had weighed the relative merits—in terms of the perfect diner, that is—of stainless steel versus baked enamel siding, of diners without booths versus diners with booths, of marble counters versus inlaid Formica counters. In the course of doing so, she had sampled house specialties from Atlantic City to Waldoboro, Maine (for it was axiomatic that good diners could only be found in the Northeast, the way good doughnuts could only be found in New England, or good barbecue south of the Mason-Dixon line). She did so somewhat reluctantly, for she didn't share Tom's enthusiasm for diner food, where specialties of the house tended toward the likes of cinnamon buns, macaroni and cheese, and onion rings. She shared the opinion of John Steinbeck, who observed that a diner was a place where you couldn't get a bad breakfast or a good dinner. But she did make an exception for lemon meringue pie, which she had developed as her own area of expertise (in contrast to Tom, whose field was tube steaks and french fries), and about which she had schooled herself in all the subtleties, from the stiffness of the meringue to the consistency and sweetness of the filling.

If the price Tom paid for their arrangement was carrying the bags once in a while, the cost to Charlotte was accompanying Tom on his culinary crusades. Or so she said. Actually, she enjoyed these trips to the hinterlands. More than that—she needed them. Ever since she had split up with Jack, she had felt a peculiar sense of restlessness, an urge to get in a car and go. She was sure that, had she given into her urge to drive west until she hit the Pacific, she would have turned right around and driven back again. That's how bad it was. Her old friend, Kitty Saunders, who was fond of doing readings from Tarot cards, the *I Ching*, the configurations of the stars, and whatever other tools of prognostication that happened to be in vogue at the moment, had defined Charlotte's basic character in terms of the traveler: a person whose creative energies demand the fuel of new experiences. Which was true, but lately she hadn't felt as much like a traveler—who presumably has a destination in mind—as someone who is floating freely through life. The trips with Tom helped satisfy her need to hit the road.

She also suspected that her fondness for these trips had something to do with reliving her youth, which in turn had something to do with her recent birthday, on which she had turned seventy. Sixty-nine hadn't seemed old to her, but the number seventy, with its sharply angled seven and implacable zero seemed to carry a sense of finality that fifty or sixty, or even eighty or ninety, with their sinuous curves, didn't have. Which had nothing to do with how she felt, which was just fine, thank you. Like a girl, in fact—a girl who's just been released from the stifling atmosphere of a New England girls' finishing school. The road trips with Tom gave her the same exhilarating sense of independence that she had felt at the beginning of her career, when, as a cast member in a road company, she had played in one city one night and another the next. The names of those cities reverberated in her memory like the destinations announced over the loudspeaker in a railway station: Waterbury, Allentown, Providence, Hartford, Syracuse. Just thinking about those days brought back that wonderful sense of expecting the unexpected that came from never being quite certain of where she would light next.

She shifted her attention back to the man who sat across the table, his clear, gray eyes dancing with excitement. He had a plain face: honest and straightforward, which was probably responsible, at least in part, for his success. He could talk his way into any milieu from boardroom to barrio and come away with the answers that he needed. She had met him eight years ago when he was writing an article for a New York magazine on her role in solving the murder of her co-star in a Broadway play. He had later expanded the article into a best-selling book entitled *Murder at the Morosco*, after the lovely old theatre at which the murder had taken place, and which had long since been torn down in the name of progress.

"Where?" she asked as the waiter delivered their iced coffees. Though it was mid-September, there wasn't a hint of fall in the air. The temperature over the last few days had climbed into the nineties and stayed there, which made her wonder if winter would make up for this glorious Indian summer.

"Paterson, New Jersey," Tom replied. "The Falls View Diner."

"Paterson, New Jersey," she repeated with a tone of nostalgia. I haven't been in Paterson since I sold war bonds there. At the Fabian Theatre, as I recall. With Lou Costello and Bud Abbott. It was Lou's hometown. I think there's even a park named after him there. Lou Costello . . . and Linc Crawford."

Linc Crawford had been her third husband, and the only one among them who was a movie star. As a result, he was the husband who was best remembered by her public, but she had actually been married to him for the shortest period of time—six months, which had been about five-and-a-half months too long. He had been charming and handsome, but he had also been a womanizer and a drunkard, a fact that was forgotten not only by her public, but even sometimes, by her.

"Aha!" said Tom, his droopy mustache twitching with amusement. "Is that where your legendary romance with the screen hero began?"

"No. I was still happily married to Will then." But it had been the first time she had met Linc, and she remembered the surge of electricity she had felt when she shook his hand (like an electric eel, she now thought). Though she considered the marriage a mistake, it had served one purpose, which was to cure her of any weakness she might have harbored for the blandishments of male charm.

She watched Tom as he sipped his coffee, all the while subtly eyeing the women who passed by their table. He professed to like his bachelor life—though he was close to forty, he had never married—but Charlotte suspected that he would really have liked to settle down. She never discussed this with him—far be it for her to question a lifestyle that was so well-suited to her own needs—but she often wondered how long it would last.

"How did a diner in Paterson ever escape you?" she asked. Not only was New Jersey Tom's home turf—he had been brought up there and had worked for years at New Jersey newspapers—it was also the diner crusader's Holy Land. The diner hadn't been born in New Jersey (that distinction went to the state of Rhode Island), but it was in New Jersey that the diner had reached its artistic peak. New Jersey was to diners what Tuscany was to Renaissance art.

He turned back to face her. "I don't know," he said, shaking his head in amazement that this masterpiece of roadside architecture could have escaped his attention. "Why is it that some New Yorkers have never been to the Empire State Building or some Parisians to the Eiffel Tower? I've lived within a few miles of Paterson almost my entire life, but I've only been there a few times. I'd even heard about the Falls View, but I just never got out there."

New Jersey's ascendacy in the diner world had to do not only with the artistic quality of its diners, but also with their sheer numbers. According to Tom, whose authority on such matters Charlotte considered absolute, New Jersey was home to two thousand of the nation's estimated six thousand diners. At one time, most of the diners in America had been manufactured in New Jersey, which was the location of the Ford, GM, and Chrysler of diner manufacturers.

No one could have grown up in New Jersey, as Tom had, and not love diners, he claimed. It went with the territory, like calling an Italian sandwich a hoagie and body surfing at the Jersey shore. But it had taken a trip to the Museum of Modern Art to transform his native appreciation into an obsession. He spoke about the moment he fell in love with diners with the same kind of nostalgic warmth that is usually reserved for a first love.

The waiter brought their sandwiches. Leaves of fresh basil peeked out from between the edges of the roll. The smell was intoxicating: there was nothing like the aroma of fresh basil on a summer's day, even one in September.

As Charlotte ate her sandwich, enjoying the warmth of the sunshine and the buoyant mood of the city, she recalled Tom telling her about that moment. He had been browsing in the gift shop at the museum when he found himself face to face with an art poster, a photograph of Pal's, in Mahwah, N.J., the diner in which he had spent much of his misspent youth. His first reaction had been incredulity. "Pal's is art?" he asked himself. But then, looking again at the sign that proclaimed "Pal's" in flowing pink neon script and the stainless steel sheathing that gleamed like polished silver, he had realized that Pal's *was* art, part of the rapidly disappearing roadside architecture of the mid-twentieth century.

The framed poster of Pal's now hung in his living room. And Pal's became the first entry in a journal of diner encounters that now extended to four hundred and eleven entries, each described according to make and model, which Tom knew the way others know the makes and models of classic cars. He was now thinking about turning his journal, complete with his collection of photographs, into a book.

Tom set down his sandwich, and looked Charlotte in the eye. "Graham," he said, in an uncharacteristically serious tone, "I know I've said this before, but this time I really mean it. This is the one."

Maybe it wasn't a woman that Tom needed to settle down with, Charlotte thought. Maybe it was a diner. "What's the specialty?" she asked suspiciously, knowing that she would be required to pass judgment on the cuisine.

"Hot Texas wieners."

Charlotte raised a skeptical eyebrow, which was one of her screen trademarks, along with her forthright stride and her clipped Yankee accent. "Hot Texas wieners! In Paterson, New Jersey?"

"I know they sound terrible, but they're really surprisingly good. Take my word for it, Graham. You'll really like them. Local custom calls for them to be served 'all the way'," he added with a mischievous grin.

"Dare I ask what all the way is?"

"With mustard, chopped onions, and chili sauce. And"—he raised a finger for emphasis—"local custom also calls for them to be served with a mug of birch beer and french fries."

"As in 'two all the way with beer and fries?' " said Charlotte, who by now had acquired a certain knack for diner lingo.

"You've got it."

"When are we going?"

"How does Sunday sound? As it turns out, that's the day of the opening of an exhibit at the local museum that I'd like to go to, on the New Jersey diner. The opening reception starts at seven."

"Eat at the diner, then go to the show?"

Tom nodded. "There's an artist who's exhibiting in the show whom I'd like to meet. Maybe we can arrange to have dinner with him. He paints diners," he added. "I thought maybe he could do the cover for my book."

"Sounds fine to me. Remind me to take along the Alka-Seltzer."

· 2 ·

THEY LEFT THE city at about five in Tom's 1962 Buick
Electra 225 convertible, which was named for its overall length
in inches—in other words, a boat—and which was nicknamed
by car buffs the "deuce and a quarter." The Buick wasn't
Tom's only car. He also had a small Japanese car (Charlotte wasn't the kind who could name makes and models,
her descriptions of cars tending to run more to "small red"
or "large gray"), but this luxury liner of an automobile with
real leather seats was Tom's car of choice for diner-hunting
jaunts into the suburbs. Tom said it put him in the mood for
a road trip, as it did Charlotte, especially when she was floating down the highway with the top down on a fine evening
like this one, an old Beach Boys song on the radio. (Tom's
generation, not hers; but the rock and roll oldies stations
seemed to go with the experience of a diner jaunt). Tom kept
the Buick garaged on the West Side, near the entrance to the
Lincoln Tunnel, for quick getaways to prime diner-hunting
territory on the other side of the Hudson.

"So what's so special about the Falls View that it qualifies
for the august rank of the perfect diner?" asked Charlotte, rais-
ing her voice to be heard above the roar of the traffic. They had
just emerged from the Lincoln Tunnel into the land 'o diners,
a landscape that for Tom was delineated not by cities, rivers,
and mountains, but by the locations of roadside eateries.

"Lots of things," he replied. "First, it's a pristine pre-war
diner, circa 1939, which I know you'll recognize as a good
year."

It was the year in which Charlotte had made her first movie.

Ironically, she had played a diner waitress who falls in love with a hobo customer only to find out later that he is a philanthropic millionaire who has assumed the role of a hobo to find out what life on the road is really like. They live happily ever after. Such were the movies of Hollywood's Golden Age. She missed them.

Tom continued: "Stainless steel banding; porcelain enamel exterior; sunburst stainless steel backbars; original menu boards; vintage Seeburg 100 Wallomatic jukebox; original neon sign and exterior clock; curved glass block entryway; open twenty-four hours a day, seven days a week; breakfast at any hour, day or night; plenty of newspapers for the customers . . ."

"Whoa. Slow down. As I understand it, what you've just listed are the basic qualifications for the rank of perfect dinner," Charlotte interrupted. Though it *was* rare to find a diner that had all the basics. Like Miss Americas, even the best had some flaw: an overbite, a regrettable accent, a bustline that hinted at the probability of falsies. "What makes this one extra special?"

"You're right. Those are just the basics. First among the features that makes this one special is the location." He looked over at Charlotte. "I don't think I've ever seen a diner in such a spectacular location. Falls View isn't entirely accurate. You have to walk up the street a little. But when you do, you are overlooking one of the most spectacular waterfalls in America."

"I remember them," she said. "The Great Falls."

"The second special feature is tradition," he continued. "The Falls View is still on its original site. Furthermore, it was built in Paterson. It's a Silk City," he said, naming the Paterson Vehicle Company's famous model. "It isn't often that you find a diner that hasn't been moved, much less one that's located only a few miles from the place where it was built."

Tom was right. Originally built on wheels, diners were designed to be moved from one place to another, and often were.

"And third . . . I guess you'd have to call it local flavor. Lots of diners have a specialty, but it's usually something you could find anywhere, like cherry pie or sticky buns or corned beef hash. If it is a local specialty, it tends to be a regional one, like New England clam chowder. Hot Texas wieners are truly a local specialty, at least the way they're made here."

They rode in silence for a while, enjoying the evening. The air was warm, but it had lost its August heaviness. They were passing the futuristic Meadowlands Sports Complex, with its gigantic football stadium and sports arena. Only fifteen years ago, the air would have been unbreathable. Then this marshland had still been the dumping ground for most of New York's garbage.

"Last but not least, it looks like it's there to stay," Tom added after a while. "Not like—" His glance shifted to the side of the highway, where the Tick Tock Diner stood in all its modern splendor, a stone, steel, and glass structure in the style that Tom called "Greco-glitz." The Tick Tock had once been cloaked in the mantle of greatness now worn by the venerable Falls View.

"*Sic transit gloria dineri*," said Charlotte.

"You said it," Tom replied.

One of Tom's irritating personal idiosyncrasies was tossing out phrases in Latin, the only use to which he was able to put his classics degree from a prestigious institution of higher learning, other than translating the Latin inscriptions on the pediments of museums and banks. Charlotte took great delight in tossing them back at him once in a while.

The sad side of the story of Tom's quest for the perfect diner was that not all of the anointed eateries had been superseded by diners that Tom considered even more perfect. A common fate was to be traded in like a used car and put up on blocks in the back lot of some diner manufacturer in exchange for a new Mediterranean style diner-restaurant, or "dinerant," as Tom called them.

Such had been the sorry fate of the fallen Tick Tock, which, like the Falls View, had once been a classic Silk City. Before it was "renovated," the Tick Tock had been the subject of one of Tom's Diner Alerts. As he had revisited the site of one diner after another only to find the lot vacant and the diner hauled off to a diner graveyard, Tom's crusade had expanded from finding diners to preserving them. He had launched a magazine called *Diner Monthly*, whose Diner Alert column tipped readers off to threatened diners.

A mention in the Diner Alert column was guaranteed to unleash a flurry of protest from impassioned diner devotees. Often their preservation efforts were successful. But the Tick Tock was one of their failures. It had gone from the Diner Alert column to the Sentenced to Death column and finally to the black-bordered Obituaries section. Despite a full parking lot, it was dead as far as fans of the classic diner were concerned.

In the cases of classic diners that were replaced by something more modern, there was at least the hope of reincarnation. Even worse was to be hauled off to some "diner no-man's-land" in Texas or California, and decorated with Elvis posters and old Chevy fenders in some ersatz imitation of what a diner should be. For Tom, such a fate was the equivalent of an art treasure being hauled off by a tribe with no appreciation of its proper history or use.

But one didn't have to go to Texas to find diners that were victims of this retro-diner craze. Tom had once taken Charlotte to a coffee shop on Sixth Avenue that had been assembled from bits and pieces of classic diners. It was decorated with old movie posters, including one of herself with Fred MacMurray in a movie she would rather have forgotten. The diners from which the fittings for this imposter among diners had been salvaged had been given a special listing in *Diner Monthly*: "Cannibalized."

Diners were even being shipped to Europe. There was one in Covent Garden, in London, and even one in Paris. "But," Tom had said, upon telling her this, "The real question is, Can they do rice pudding on the Left Bank?"

The Falls View turned out to be everything that Tom said it would be. It sat on its lot on the bank of the Passaic River just above the famous Falls with the smug comfort of an establishment that had been there for a long time and had no plans to move. *Falls View Diner* was written in pink neon script along the roofline. A neon-ringed clock stood above the name, and "Open 24 Hours," and "Try Our Famous Hot Texas Wieners" were spelled out in smaller letters underneath. The maroon, Broadway-style lettering on the gray porcelain enamel siding read: "Booths for Ladies" and "Gents's Bar" on one side and "Consistently Fine Food Since 1939" on the other. Inside, the mood was one of warm, cozy comfort—a counter of reddish-purple marble, booths of Honduran mahoghany upholstered in maroon leatherette, and the intricate tile designs that were the hallmark of a Silk City. There were no missing tiles, no holes in the upholstery, no Formica panels replacing the damaged woodwork, only the warm patina of surfaces that had been lovingly cleaned and polished day after day, week after week, over the course of fifty years. It was untouched by time: a little slice of life from the late Depression. Charlotte felt right at home—they were both pieces from the same period.

"I see what you mean," she said to Tom as they entered.

But if the Falls View had been overlooked by Tom, it hadn't gone undiscovered. Above the cash register hung a display of T-shirts (one hundred percent cotton, $12.95), coffee mugs ($6), and postcards, all bearing a drawing of the Falls View, and aimed at the diner enthusiast. It was clear that the owner (Greek, judging from the poster of the Acropolis) had no scant appreciation for the commercial possibilities offered by the nostalgic appeal of his dining establishment. It was also axiomatic (and something of a mystery to Charlotte) that all New Jersey diners were owned by Greeks who were usually named Nick, just as all Manhattan vegetable stand proprietors were Korean and umbrella vendors Senegalese.

The diner artist with whom Tom had arranged the meeting was waiting for them next to a sandwich board by the door advertising that the Falls View's famous sauce was available "for that special occasion" by the pint ($2) and by the quart ($3.50). There was no mistaking him. He was dressed as "the artist" for the opening reception: a black dinner jacket and red bow tie worn with blue jeans and high-top black sneakers. His shoulder-length dark blond hair was tied back in a ponytail. Charlotte groaned inwardly at the juvenile pretentiousness, the feeble effort at reverse chic. She could just imagine what his paintings were like.

After he had introduced himself—his name was Randall Goslau—he invited them to sit down in an empty booth near the door—the only empty booth, as a matter of fact. The place was packed.

Once they had taken their seats, Tom introduced Charlotte, thus launching a tiresome discussion in which Randy paraded his knowledge of movie trivia. She could never understand people who wasted their mental energy on such pursuits. If you were going to memorize something, why not poetry? Not these stupid dates and titles, which even she could no longer remember.

He was quite an ugly man, she thought as he spoke: a pale, bloated face pockmarked by old acne scars, gray eyes that were too small, teeth that were too big, and a big nose that was florid with veins. But his intense manner of speaking and small, compact physique exuded a sense of energy that redeemed, at least in part, the unattractiveness of his appearance.

A former commercial artist, he had turned to painting diners as a second career, and become an overnight success. His diner "portraits," executed in painstaking detail from photographs projected directly onto the canvas, were in big demand at the chic Soho galleries that favored the photorealist style. Or so he claimed. He wasn't exactly short on ego.

"Would you like to hear some tunes?" he asked, producing a handful of quarters, which he fed into the wallbox. "They have a great jukebox here, everything from the Andrews Sisters to Springsteen. Not just fifties songs like a lot of classic diners. Not that I don't like fifties songs, but to have just that is to make the place into a museum, you know what I mean?"

Not bothering to wait for a reply, he flipped through the selections at lighting speed, and then punched a bunch of buttons, seemingly at random.

"How did you come by your interest in diners, Mr. Goslau?" asked Charlotte as the mellow voice of Tony Bennett surged out of the speakers. It didn't seem like the kind of music that someone like Randy would have picked, and she wondered if he had even looked at the buttons.

"Not in the same way as most diner enthusiasts, freaks, nuts, maniacs—whatever you want to call us." He elaborated: "Most enthusiasts get hooked on diners in high school. The first thing they want to do when they get their driver's license is to drive to the nearest diner for a cup of coffee. Wouldn't you say that's true, Tom?"

"It was for me. In my case, Pal's, on Route 17 in Mahwah."

"I know it well," said Randy, nodding his head. "In my case, my passion for diners goes back to my earliest youth. You might even say that I was nurtured at the breast of the American diner. My mother died when I was three. My father was a traveling salesman—scientific equipment. After my mother died, I always went with him on trips. We stayed in cheap motels and we ate at diners—his territory was the Northeast. Sometimes he would leave me at one of his favorite eating places while he was making his calls. I came to look on diners as my home away from home and waitresses as surrogate mothers. For me, the diner stood for comfort, warmth, dependability. Then my father remarried and my diner days were over.

He looked up at the waitress, who stood at their table snapping gum. One hand held her notepad, the other rested impatiently on her hip. "It's still impossible for me to look at a diner waitress and not feel a warm rush of filial affection. "Isn't that right, Patty?"

The waitress stopped chewing her gum. "Filial?" she said, her lips curling in a mock sneer. "Give me a break, Randy." Then she smiled, a warm, jolly smile, and resumed chomping.

"Where's the kid?" asked Randy.

"With Grandma," said Patty. "Getting spoiled to death."

Like Randy, she was not an attractive person. In fact, she looked a little like him, except for being dark where he was fair, and for her eyes, which weren't small, but big warm puddles of brown above which her thin, comma-shaped eyebrows were suspended in a perennial expression of amusement.

"Tell him I said Hi," said Randy.

"Sure," she said. "What can I get for you folks today?" she asked, pencil poised over her order pad.

Randy gestured for Tom and Charlotte to order first.

"We'll both have two all the way with beer and fries," said Tom. He stroked his mustache with the smug self-satisfaction of one who has just made himself understood in a foreign language.

"Well done," said Randy in appreciation of Tom's ordering skills. "I'll have the meat loaf special," he said.

"What prompted you to switch from commercial art to diner portraits?" asked Charlotte once the waitress had left.

"It was a who, not a what. Specifically, Don Spiegel, the photorealist painter. At least, that's what other people called him. He hated being called that. Do you know his work?"

"I do," said Charlotte. Though lacking any formal schooling in art, she had a natural appreciation that had been nurtured by frequent visits to museums and galleries and encouraged by Jack, who was a collector of paintings and sculptures.

"Don died last year," Randy continued. "Maybe you read about it. Anyway, I had always painted, but abstract expressionist stuff: you know, angry blobs of paint thrown at the canvas—the derogatory term is vomit art. I thought I was another Jackson Pollack. But it was crap—juvenile, derivative. I had quit my job as a commercial artist to paint, but I was having a tough time making it financially. I could have gone back to work at my old job, but that would have been admitting defeat." Reaching into the pocket of his jacket, he plucked out a pack of cigarettes. As he lit up, he craned his neck to get a better view of the parking lot.

"Are you waiting for someone?" asked Tom.

"Oh," he said, surprised at Tom's inquiry. Then he shook his head. "Naw." Sucking greedily at his cigarette, he continued: "Then somebody told me that Don Spiegel was looking for an assistant. So I applied, and got the job. I worked for him for ten years, doing anything he needed: stretching canvases, mixing paints, balancing his checkbook, doing his grocery shopping. When he found out how crazy I was about diners, he suggested that I paint them, and that was that." He paused for a minute, and then abruptly switched subjects: "I had my first hot Texas wiener here when I was seven," he said. "Do you know the story of the hot Texas wiener?"

"No, tell us," said Tom."

"Well, one would naturally assume that the idea for the hot Texas wiener came from a Texan, or, at the very least, was imported from Texas, but that assumption would be wrong. The idea was actually invented by a Greek named Stavros

Andriopoulis during the Depression to attract customers to his hot dog cart."

Removing a reporter's notebook from the inside pocket of his jacket, Tom started making notes.

"Andriopoulis made it the specialty of the Falls View when he bought the diner in 1939, and it became the standard lunch fare for the mill hands from the surrounding silk mills. The idea has spread to other diners, usually by former Falls View employees, but it's never gone much beyond Paterson. I've been conducting my own little research project on the geographical distribution of the hot Texas wiener. My conclusion is that the Falls View is at the epicenter of the hot Texas wiener phenomenon."

"There may be others, but the Falls View has the best sauce—the original sauce," came a deep voice from behind Charlotte.

She turned around. It belonged to the man sitting in the booth behind her, who proceeded to get up and come over to join them. He must have been six foot four, with hunched-over shoulders and a starched white apron that was spread across his considerable midsection like a sail before the wind.

"Hello, John," said Randy. "Just coming on?"

He nodded. "I'm on the graveyard shift," he said.

"I'd like you to meet John Andriopoulis." Randy said to Charlotte and Tom. "John is the nephew of the originator of the hot Texas wiener." He nodded toward his companions. "I was just telling them the story."

"I heard," the big man interjected with a smile.

"And the owner, with his brother, Nick, of the Falls View."

"As the saying goes, you take two Greeks and you've got a diner," said Andriopoulis. After wiping his beefy hand on his apron, he extended it to Charlotte. "I started out here as a potato peeler when I was ten, and moved up to coleslaw cutter when I was thirteen. My brother, Nick, and I took over from my Uncle Steve when I was twenty-one. Nick's the money person—he works behind the scenes. I'm the people person. I work up front."

"Up front is right. John's the grill man," said Randy.

The thought struck Charlotte that grill men were always tall, and she concluded that it must be the result of a process of self-selection: a short man would feel the heat in his face all the time. Grill men also tended to have bad posture, and gave the impression of having four arms, though only two were in evidence here, one of them bearing a tattoo on the forearm in the form of a heart pierced by an arrow carrying the name "Helen."

"This is Charlotte Graham, whom you may recognize from the movies."

Andriopoulis stared at her through his thick-lensed glasses. Then a wide smile spread over his genial face, which didn't look especially Greek. "Very pleased to meet you, Miss Graham," he said, pumping her hand. "I'm a fan of yours from way back. In fact, I remember when you came to Paterson with Lou Costello to sell war bonds at the Fabian. I was about ten, and it was the thrill of my young life."

"That was the last time I was here," Charlotte said.

"Well, I hope the interval between this visit and your next will be shorter. I'm honored to have you as my guest at the Falls View," he added with proprietary pride. "Is there anything you need?"

"I'm taking care of them, Dad," said the waitress, who had reappeared with five mugs of birch beer, three in one hand and two in the other.

"My daughter, Patricia. This is Charlotte Graham, the movie star."

After giving her father a peck on the cheek, Patty nodded perfunctorily at them, and slid three of the mugs onto the table. Then she headed off to deliver the other two to the next booth.

John shrugged. "She's busy," he explained.

"I'd also like you to meet Tom Plummer," said Randy. "Tom's doing a book on diners. He's here to talk with me about the cover."

Tom passed John a copy of the latest edition of *Diner Monthly*. "I also put out this publication. I'd like to do a write-up on the Falls View, both for *Diner Monthly* and for the book. Do you have a few minutes to answer some questions? I hate to interrupt your dinner."

"No problem," Andriopoulis replied. After grabbing his plate of meat loaf and his mug of birch beer from the adjoining booth, he slid his big frame onto the seat next to Randy. "At your service."

Charlotte noticed that he smelled faintly of grease.

Tom picked up his notebook and pencil. "A 1939 Silk City?"

"Yep. Tag number 3911." Getting up again, he shuffled over to the menu board above the counter, which he slid aside to reveal a metal tag that was fastened to the wall. "Everyone wants to see this," he said. "The original tag." He pointed to the entrance. "There's another one over the door."

As a result of hanging around with Tom, Charlotte knew that most diners bore tags giving the name of the manufacturer, in this case, the Paterson Vehicle Company, and a serial number, which in this case identified the Falls View as the eleventh diner manufactured in 1939.

"Always open?" asked Tom.

"Twenty-four hours a day, seven days a week, three hundred and sixty-five days a year. I don't even have a key. I don't even think there *is* a key."

"Seating?"

"Fifteen at the counter; thirty-two in the booths."

"Original exterior?"

"Nearly original. We've had some work done on the stainless. The interior's original except for the upholstery. We have to replace that every four or five years. We just did it again so it would look shipshape for the advertising people." He paused to take a bite of his meat loaf. "Have you seen the ad for Di-Tabs on TV? Where the guy complains about eating too much?"

"Yeah!" said Tom. "Was that filmed here?"

"That and about a hundred and twelve other commercials. This is a regular little gold mine. They've filmed commercials here for everything from credit cards to lottery tickets to soda. Plus we get free samples. In addition to what they pay us, that is. The best was the ad for Pepsi—they gave us three hundred free cases of Pepsi for that one."

"The art directors probably like the Falls View because it's the quintessential American diner," said Tom.

"I'd like to think it's that, but actually I think it's the location. We're only twenty minutes from the Lincoln Tunnel. I doubt we'd have them beating down our door if we were in

Pittsburgh." He shoveled in some more meat loaf and then went on: "We have this long-standing argument, my brother Nick and I. Nick wants to sell the diner—"

Charlotte saw the look of alarm in Tom's eyes as he mentally listed the Falls View in the Diner Alert column.

"—and replace it with a restaurant. He has big ideas: a maitre d', tablecloths, flower vases. He says we could charge twelve ninety-five instead of six ninety-five for shrimp scampi. But then we wouldn't have the advertising revenue, and I doubt we'd even make as much from the customers. I'll tell you a story." He gestured with his fork. "Eight, maybe ten years ago, we decided to substitute instant mashed potatoes for real. It was cheaper: you don't have to pay somebody to do all that peeling and mashing. 'The customers won't know the difference,' Nick said. Well, I check the plates when they come back. To see what people eat, what they don't eat. The plates started coming back with the potatoes uneaten." He thrust his face toward Tom, and asked: "You would notice the difference, wouldn't you?"

Tom nodded.

Andriopoulis pointed a finger at his enormous chest. "I would notice the difference. Why wouldn't the customers notice the difference? And I'll tell you, it wouldn't have been long before they started going somewhere else, somewhere where they had better potatoes. We switched back. Value— that's what keeps the customers coming back. Yeah, we could charge more for shrimp scampi. But what kind of business would we do?" He waved the tattooed forearm at his surroundings. "Now the place is filled, or damn close to it, eighteen hours a day. There's no way the Saturday-night-out crowd is going to make up for that. I'll tell you something else. People who come to a diner don't even want shrimp scampi. We have it on the menu, but . . ." He waved a hand in dismissal. "What they want is good mashed potatoes, good coleslaw, good meat loaf, good rice pudding."

"That—and the atmosphere," Tom chimed in.

Andriopoulis set down his fork and pointed his forefinger at Tom. "You've got it. There are thousands of mid-price restaurants out there serving shrimp scampi, but there's only one Falls View. They'll come from all over the country for a hot Texas wiener and an art deco diner. We even had a guy in here last year from Michigan. He travels around the country visiting diners, in a van all fitted out like a camper. He said the Falls View was one of the most pristine—that was the word he used, *pristine*—he'd ever seen."

"Kenny Meeker?" asked Tom. "Sells tapes of his diner songs?"

Andriopoulis nodded. "That was the guy. I even bought a tape. I figured that for two bucks I couldn't go wrong. He performed one of his songs for us out in the parking lot: 'The All-Night Diner Blues.' " He laughed at the memory.

"He advertises his tapes in my magazine," Tom said.

"He was a nice guy," said Andriopoulis. "I play the tape sometimes in my car. I like the 'All-Night Diner Blues' one." He started to sing the first line, but was interrupted by the reappearance of his daughter with their orders.

"Tell me," said Andriopoulis, leaning forward to address Tom and Charlotte, as Patty set the plates down. "Have you ever had a hot Texas wiener before?" He pointed his fork at Randy. "I know *you* have."

"I have," said Tom. "I was here last week."

"Aha," Andriopoulis said. "Undercover."

"I asked for the boss, but you weren't around." He looked over at Charlotte. "But Miss Graham hasn't had the pleasure."

"I hope you won't mind if I ask what you think," Andriopoulis said to Charlotte. "Please, go right ahead."

"Not at all," Charlotte replied as she bit into the wiener, which was heaped with a pale orange sauce. To her amazement, she found it quite good. It wasn't hot, but rather a little sweet, with an unusual spice.

"John takes his work very seriously," said Randy as Andriopoulis stared at Charlotte, eagerly awaiting her appraisal. "If the peaks on the lemon meringue pie don't stand up just right, he has the pastry chef do it over."

"Damned right I do. No sense in doing it if you're not going to do it right. But I don't only pay attention to the way a pie looks. A lot of those pies in the cases at other diners look great, but they taste like cardboard. Our pies not only look great, they taste great too." He turned his attention back to Charlotte. "Well?" he said.

"It's delicious," she replied, after swallowing her first bite. "It's like a chili dog," she added. "But it's not really a chili sauce, is it? What's the secret ingredient, cinnamon?"

"Ha! What did I tell you about the customer's ability to detect the subtleties? It *is* cinnamon, as well as other spices that I'm not at liberty to divulge on account of their being a trade secret. Cinnamon isn't exactly a common spice in Tex-Mex cooking, but"—he shrugged—"my daddy came from Athens, not from Amarillo." He shifted his attention to his copy of *Diner Monthly.* "This looks very interesting," he said, tapping the cover. "May I keep it?"

"Sure," said Tom, beaming. "If you want to subscribe, there's a form inside that you can fill out." Reaching in his briefcase, he pulled out a stack of sample issues. "Here, take these for your customers."

As a result of his true-crime books, Tom had become, if not a millionaire, then close to it. He had earned numerous awards, and was much sought after on the talk-show circuit. But it wasn't true-crime reporting that was closest to his heart; it was this modest eight-page periodical, whose circulation was now approaching forty thousand.

"Thanks," said Andriopoulis, rising. "I've got to get to work." He reached out to shake their hands. "It was nice meeting you. Come back again some time." He pointed a finger at Tom. "If you ever get around to doing that book, I'd appreciate your putting us on the cover."

"I'll think about it," said Tom.

"Randy here has done some great paintings of us."

The artist had poked a rift in the wall of the little crater in his mashed potatoes that held the gravy, and was totally absorbed in watching the gravy run out onto his slab of meat loaf.

"Speaking of which . . ." said Tom, as John shuffled off.

"Yeah, let's get down to business," agreed Randy, turning his attention back to his companions. He soaked up the fugitive gravy with a roll, then popped it into his mouth. "Are you sure you want me to do this? Because there are a lot of other artists painting diners these days. Sometimes it seems as if every other gallery in Soho is displaying a diner artist. I'm the best, of course. . . ."

"Yes, I'm sure," Tom put in. "And I can't say I'm not

intrigued by Andriopoulis' suggestion of making it the Falls View."

"I've probably done dozens of paintings of the Falls View. From various angles, under various light conditions, in different seasons. The Falls View is to Randy Goslau what Mont St. Victoire was to Cezanne or ballerinas were to Degas."

Give me a break, thought Charlotte.

"Do you want to use one I've already done, or commission an original?"

"Commission an original, I think."

"Okay. In that case, here's what I think we should do." He craned his neck to look out at the parking lot again, and then continued: "Are you free on Wednesday? If so, you could come out to my studio." He nodded in the direction of the Falls. "It's in the Gryphon Mill, just past the Falls overlook."

"I think so," Tom replied.

"Okay. You come out to my studio, look at slides of my work. I can throw them up on the screen for you. That way you can get a better idea of what it is you're looking for. Just the diner alone, or the diner with its surroundings? Morning light or midday light? Long shot or close-up?"

"I think I get the idea."

Ignoring him, Randy continued: "Oils or watercolors: I do both. Equally well, I might add. Big or small. Then, once you get an idea of what it is you want, we'll talk price. You said you were interested in buying the original for your private collection, right?"

Tom nodded.

Randy sized him up as if he were trying to estimate his bank balance. A layer of sweat had broken out on his forehead, giving him an oily appearance. "I warn you, I don't come cheap. An average-sized oil will run you about thirty grand, plus another twenty-five percent for a commissioned piece. Have you ever seen my work in a gallery?"

"Your show at the Koreman. That's how I tracked you down."

"Damn," said Randy. "Theoretically, if the Koreman referred you to me, they should get a cut. But if you want to keep this visit under your hat, I won't have to pay the gallery a commission and I can give you the painting at a lower price. We'll both make a little on the deal."

Tom shrugged. "Sounds okay by me."

"Once you decide what you want, we'll draw up a letter of agreement: size, medium, date of delivery, amount of the down payment, et cetera. One other thing: I like to be paid in cash."

Tom's eyebrows flew up: "Thirty thousand in cash?"

"Not all at once. Installments are okay. The payment schedule will be spelled out in the letter of agreement." He gestured with a roll for emphasis. "Do you know what a guy who I was talking with last week about a painting asked me. 'Can you give it to me cheaper if you use less paint?' Can you believe it? You'd be amazed at how many assholes are out there."

No, I wouldn't, thought Charlotte, with present company in mind.

"Dessert?" asked Randy.

As Randy signaled to Patty, Charlotte turned around to eye the pie case, where a Black Forest cake, a linzertorte, and an assortment of pies spun slowly under the lights, like the crown jewels in the Tower of London.

"I guess I'll have to try some of that lemon meringue," she said.

Patty arrived, and Randy gave her their dessert orders: lemon meringue for Charlotte, Black Forest cake for Randy, and the inevitable rice pudding for Tom.

She returned with their orders almost immediately. That was another virtue of diners: speedy service. The conversation came to a halt as they devoted their attention to the desserts, which were indeed delicious.

After wolfing down an enormous slab of Black Forest cake with a whipped cream frosting, Randy popped down a couple of antacid tablets (*Di-Tabs*? Charlotte wondered), and abruptly excused himself. "I have to go back to the studio to take care of some last-minute business," he explained.

"I noticed that he didn't offer to pick up his share of the tab," Charlotte said after he had left.

"I noticed that, too. I don't think I like that guy."

"I *know* I don't like that guy. I sure as hell wouldn't give him any cash until he's produced a painting. Are you going to go through with your meeting with him, or are you going to try to get out of it?"

"I'm going to go through with it. I'd still like to see more of his work. But if I do want to get out of the arrangement, I know how to go about it."

"How?" asked Charlotte.

"Ask him to use less paint."

· 3 ·

THE MUSEUM WHERE the art exhibit was located was just down the street from the diner, in one of the historic factories at the foot of the Falls. As they walked along the street paralleling the river, Tom filled Charlotte in on the local history, which he had picked up on a walking tour of the district on his earlier visit. The nation's first industrial city was the dream of Alexander Hamilton, who, while picnicking at the Falls (lacking the convenience of a nearby diner, as Tom put it) with George Washington and Lafayette during the Revolutionary War, envisioned a network of raceways that would harness the waters of the Falls. After the war, Hamilton formed the S.U.M. (Society for the Establishment of Useful Manufactures) corporation and engaged the architect of the nation's capital, Pierre Charles L'Enfant, to lay out a raceway system. Over the next hundred years, Paterson was to become renowned as the nation's foremost industrial city. Among the many products produced in the red brick mills lining the river banks were locomotives, the Colt six-gun, and the beautifully dyed silk that gave the city its sobriquet of Silk City.

Paterson's heyday as an industrial power came to an end in the early twentieth century when a series of crippling strikes organized by the notorious Industrial Workers of the World, or the "Wobblies," led to the demise of the silk industry. Many of the mills fell into disrepair, and the area around the Falls was destined for demolition when a redevelopment movement led by a group of persistent and energetic citizens resulted in its being designated a national historic district. The citizens' vision was to create a "historic Williamsburg of industry," centered around the Falls. With the help of Federal monies, local agencies created a series of parks in the vicinity of the Falls, and restored the scenic network of raceways. One of the goals was to restore the deteriorating mills. This was accomplished in part by providing rent subsidies for loft apartments to artists and musicians fed up with the hassle and expense of living and working in nearby New York. As a result, an artists' colony of New York refugees had grown up—a mini-Soho, as they liked to call it—which had in turn attracted restaurants, boutiques, and galleries. It was a community that was still struggling to survive—as the many still-empty mills, and the winos, crackheads, and lunatics that inhabited them substantiated—but there was no doubt that the artists' presence had injected a much-needed dose of vitality into the blighted city.

None of this was apparent in the neighborhood of the Falls View, which consisted of a series of garages, run-down apartment buildings, and two-family houses lining the river bank. The historic district began about fifty feet up the street, at the bridge that spanned the river just above the Falls. Here, the street was paralleled by the first tier of the three-tiered raceway system that diverted the water to the mills below. Tom said that the water, propelled by turbines, had once rushed through this raceway, but it now flowed languidly between the brownstone retaining walls, which were overhung with willow trees, their pale green leaves now tinged with gold.

Another fifty feet or so down the street, they had their first glimpse of the Falls. In the thirty-odd years since she had seen them, Charlotte had forgotten how magnificent they were, made all the more so by comparison with the urban blight surrounding them. From a wide, still, lakelike expanse, the water plunged over the crest into a narrow gorge in the shape of an inverted V, which was lined by vertical shafts of rock that must have been opened up by an ancient earthquake. Confined by the narrow walls, the spray boiled up into the air like steam from a teakettle. Shining through the mist was a multihued arc that spanned the gorge, like a magical rainbow in a children's storybook.

"The second to Niagara in width and volume in the East," said Tom as they crossed the street to get a better look at the cascade. "Seventy-seven feet high, and two hundred and eighty feet wide."

As Charlotte recalled, she had had difficulty even seeing the Falls from this point on her earlier visit, so overgrown was the area. But the trees and undergrowth had now been cleared to make a lovely park, which gave visitors an unobstructed view. A statue of Alexander Hamilton presided over the park, which was landscaped with Japanese maples whose leaves were beginning to turn a brilliant red.

From this point, the street pitched downward to the heart of the historic district, a 119-acre complex of red-brick mills lining the river bank, and linked by the system of raceways. On this balmy evening it was easy to ignore the garbage, the castoff wine bottles, the beat-up old cars driving by—salsa and rap music blaring from their open windows—and imagine oneself transported to the eighteenth century, when the first of these mills had been built, or even to another country: the willow-lined canals of Burgundy or Provence.

Charlotte was charmed.

Having admired the view, they recrossed the street and headed down an intersecting street toward the museum, which was located in the old Rogers Locomotive Works, where the country's first steam locomotives had been built. A banner outside the museum advertised the show, "The New Jersey Diner."

They entered through enormous wooden doors, through which the newly manufactured locomotives had once passed, and were immediately greeted by the sight of a diner standing in the center of the grand space of the museum floor—not a miniature diner or a replica, but a real diner: the White Manna.

"Look at this!" said Tom with delight as they entered.

It was a small diner, of the kind with no booths, described by diner enthusiasts according to the number of stools, as in "a twelve-stooler." But it was real and it was functioning, judging from the illuminated neon sign and the enticing aroma of fresh coffee.

The White Manna, Tom explained, had stood at the Somerville Traffic Circle in Somerville, New Jersey, for nearly fifty years before being replaced by a modern Mediterranean-style dinerant (another axiom of dinerdom was that every New

Jersey traffic circle has its own diner). "I thought this White Manna had gone to diner heaven," he said. "I listed it in my Obituaries column three years ago."

Tom explained that the White Manna was one of four mini-diners that had been built for the 1939 World's Fair, of which only one was still operating, in Hackensack. The White Mannas had originated the mini-hamburger that had later been made famous by the White Castle chain.

The young woman sitting at the reception desk rose to greet them.

"Hello, my name's Tom Plummer," Tom said, extending his hand. "I publish *Diner Monthly*." He held up the stack of magazines that were cradled in his other arm. "Is it okay if I leave some of these here?" He didn't introduce Charlotte, knowing her preference for anonymity.

"Sure," said the young woman, returning Tom's handshake. "I'm Diana Nelson. I run the Ivanhoe Art Gallery. I'm also the curator of this exhibit. I'm very familiar with your magazine. That's how we located the White Manna, as a matter of fact. Through a classified ad in *Diner Monthly*."

"I remember: 'Wanted: small "dinette" diner to restore.' Why didn't you let me know you had resurrected it?" he asked, miffed.

"We didn't want to publicize it in advance because we weren't entirely sure we could bring it off. In fact, it was touch-and-go until the last minute. It took a lot of work: restoring it—that alone took seven months; getting the proper permits; getting it in here."

"How *did* you get it in here?" asked Charlotte.

"Just." She pointed to the opposite wall, which was lined by a row of huge double doors. "Those doors are fifteen feet high by twelve feet wide—they were meant to accommodate loco-motives—and we had measured carefully, but we weren't sure until the day we moved it in that it would actually fit."

"What would you have done if it hadn't?" asked Tom.

"Our fallback plan was to set it up in the parking lot, but we really wanted it to be part of the exhibit. What do you think?" she asked.

"Terrific. But here's the real question: Are you serving the little hamburgers with the chopped onions? Because to serve anything else at a White Manna would be decidedly less than authentic."

"Not only are we serving them, we brought back the same short-order cook, Swifty, who served them up in Somerville for forty-six years. He came out of retirement especially for the exhibit. Grinds all the meat himself."

"Well done," said Tom, who looked as if he'd gone to diner heaven.

"Why don't you try a couple?" Diana urged.

"Not right now. I just finished a dinner of hot Texas wieners and fries at the Falls View. But give me a few minutes to digest. Then I'll be more than happy to sample some of Swifty's famous burgers."

Charlotte envied Tom his digestive system, which seemed to be able to process countless cups of coffee and endless quantities of fried food without any problem; it would definitely be more than a few minutes for her.

"Here are the programs," said Diana, handing them out. "The exhibit starts on your right and goes counterclockwise around the diner," she said, gesturing toward the exhibition hall, which was already filled with a respectable showing of people.

After Tom had deposited his magazines, they armed themselves with wine and cheese and set off to look at the exhibit. It turned out to be more fascinating than Charlotte would ever have expected. The first section dealt with diner history, including how diners had been made and assembled at the Paterson Vehicle Company. The next dealt with diner memorabilia, and included displays of everything from Hamilton Beach milkshake blenders to vintage jukebox speakers to what people in the antique trade called "ephemera": things like menus, matchbook covers, and postcards.

But the focus of the exhibit was the paintings of New Jersey diners, which were done in the photorealist style that had become popular in the 1970's as a reaction to the domination of abstract expressionism.

"Okay, Graham, interpret," ordered Tom as they approached the first group of paintings, which was by Randy's mentor, Donald Spiegel. Rather than reading the catalogs at art shows, Tom preferred Charlotte's capsule summaries.

"Donald Spiegel, generally considered to be the founder of the photorealist school of painting."

"Why didn't he like the label?" he asked.

"A lot of the photorealists work from photographs by projecting slides directly onto the canvas. Spiegel doesn't, or rather, didn't. He added and subtracted things. He also manipulated perspective to create a certain effect. Look at the parking lot in this one."

The parking lot in the first painting, which was of the Bendix Diner in Hasbrouck Heights, seemed to be tilted toward the viewer, the unnatural angle making it look as if the diner were being served up to the viewer on a platter.

"These paintings are from his early period. Though he was the first to paint diners, he later went on to other things." She eyed Tom: "I guess he figured, Who's going to achieve immortality by painting diners?"

"Hey," Tom warned, jumping to the bait, "I'd be careful about denigrating the subject matter if I were you. There are some people who consider diners as noble a subject as ballerinas. What did he go on to?"

"Urban landscapes, mostly. He started with New York, and then moved on to European cities. His paintings command enormous prices: a million and more. Jack has a couple of them."

Tom whistled.

Charlotte continued: "I don't have much of a taste for photorealism myself, but I always thought Spiegel's paintings were extraordinary. All those layers of reflection force you to ask what's real. Is it the image behind the glass, the image reflected in the glass, or is it the glass itself?"

"Well said," came a voice from behind.

Charlotte turned around. The voice belonged to Randy, who was accompanied by a tall, distinguished-looking man and his younger wife, whose hot-pink hair was sculpted into spikes that stood straight up on her head as if she had stuck her finger into an electric socket.

"Hello," said Randy, "I'd like you to meet some friends of mine. "This is Arthur Lumkin and his wife, Xantha Price. This is the writer, Tom Plummer, who's thinking about buying one of my paintings, and the actress, Charlotte Graham, who I think needs no other introduction."

"Hello, Arthur," said Charlotte, standing on her tiptoes to kiss him on the cheek, and then bending down to kiss the petite Xantha.

"Then you know each other!" said Randy.

"Only for about ten years," said Charlotte.

Arthur and Xantha Lumkin were probably the country's most prominent collectors of contemporary art, and had the distinction of being listed right before Charlotte's fourth husband, Jack Lundstrom, in the "ARTnews 200," the magazine's annual listing of the world's most important art collectors.

Until he met Xantha, a British fashion designer and author of steamy romance novels (and whose name before she changed it had been Geraldine), Arthur had been just another rich investment banker whose idea of a fun evening was studying corporate balance sheets. Xantha's passion for contemporary art had introduced him to an exciting new world in which collectors with deep pockets were courted by artists, dealers, and museums.

Now the darlings of Nouvelle Society, the Lumkins could probably have wallpapered a bathroom with party-page photos and listings in the gossip columns. The fact that his wife called the shots didn't seem to disturb this shy, genteel man in the least, so happy was he to have acquired a purpose in life other than the dull pursuit of money. Nor did he seem disturbed by her outrageous get-ups and her rumored dalliances with aspiring young artists.

"Tell me," said Arthur now. "How is Jack?"

"I hear he's fine," Charlotte replied. "From his daughter, Marsha, with whom I still keep in touch. I really don't see him that often anymore." In fact, she didn't see him at all.

Jack Lundstrom had been the most recent in her life-long history of making mistakes when it came to men. She had thought a successful businessman like Jack wouldn't be threatened by being Mr. Charlotte Graham, which in fact had been the case. The problem was worse: he had wanted a wife. As the widower of a traditional wife, he was accustomed to someone who would accompany him on his business trips, decorate his houses, and host his dinner parties. He had stopped short of asking her to take his suits to the cleaners, but not by much. Worst of all, he had wanted her to live with him in Minneapolis, where his company was headquartered, and where she found, much to her dismay, that he was well-known as a civic leader.

Though it didn't take long for either of them to recognize that they'd made a mistake (in Charlotte's case, the first charity dance at a local hospital), they had limped along pitifully for several years trying to redefine their relationship on the basis of some kind of long-distance friendship. He had finally stopped calling her when he came to New York (after her first encounter, she had never gone back to Minneapolis), and their relationship simply petered out. She had heard from Marsha that he was now courting another woman, the widow of a fellow member of Minneapolis Old Guard.

"What brings you here?" she asked them, thus rescuing Arthur from his obvious discomfort at having asked an awkward question.

"I'll show you," said Randy. He led the the way to the next group of paintings, which were his, and nodded at the label affixed to the wall next to the first one, which read: "'Falls View Diner', by Randall Goslau. From the collection of Mr. and Mrs. Arthur W. Lumkin."

Like Spiegel's, the painting was exact down to the finest detail: the quilting in the stainless steel, the pattern in the Formica tabletops. But unlike Spiegel, whose palette ran to grays and browns, Randy leaned toward colors that looked faded with age.

"Where are the people?" asked Tom.

"I take them out. I call it the neutron-bomb school of painting." He laughed, a high-pitched, nervous cackle. "They detract from the diner. I also take out the electric lines, the adjoining buildings, the automobiles. Just the diner, pure and simple."

"It reminds me of an old postcard," said Tom.

"That's a very astute observation," Randy commented. "I've been collecting postcards of diners all my life; I have over five hundred."

The painting had a folk-artish kind of appeal, and Charlotte could readily see why a diner lover would pay thirty thousand for one. But it lacked intellectual depth. It was like a Norman

Rockwell: a sentimental portrait of a favorite subject.

Her thoughts were interrupted by a greeting from a short, balding man with a warm smile. "Why, Morris!" she said. "What a delightful surprise! I didn't expect to run into anyone I knew here, much less three people."

Morris Finder was another collector of contemporary art, but of a different stripe from the Lumkins. A lifelong employee of the Social Security Administration, he had amassed an astonishing art collection on a salary that was probably less than what Arthur Lumkin made in a day. His fellow collectors joked that his name stood for his ability to "find" new talent before it was generally recognized by the art world. Charlotte liked him and his wife, Evelyn, who worked as a secretary for a brokerage house, enormously. They were simple, unassuming people whose lives were governed by one overriding passion: their love of art.

"What brings you here, Morris?" asked Xantha, after Charlotte had introduced him to Tom and Randy. He was already well-known to the Lumkins.

Xantha's question stemmed from more than just polite curiosity, for Morris's quiet pronouncements regarding the talents of up-and-coming young artists were closely heeded by more affluent but less discriminating collectors like the Lumkins. Like those of many others, the value of the Lumkins' collection had soared as a result of their following Morris Finder's leads.

"I came to see Ed Verre's paintings. Do you know his work?"

"No, I'm afraid we don't," replied Xantha in her cute Cockney accent.

She was wearing a low-cut garment—a playdress, a sunsuit, a romper?—of hot-pink taffeta to match her hair, with a tightly laced bodice that uplifted her ample bosom, and ballooning shorts that buttoned just above the knee. The style might have been called punk bordello.

"But I might ask the same question of you," Morris responded.

"We're here to see Randy's paintings. Arthur and I just love his work. How many of your paintings do we now have, love?" she asked. "Eight, is it?" As she spoke, she grabbed Randy's hand in an intimate gesture that led Charlotte to wonder if he was the latest of her young protégés.

"Nine," he said, "If you count the Short Stop."

"Oh yes, the Short Stop. The Short Stop, of which we have a painting, is the latest addition to Randy's collection of diners," Xantha explained. "He bought it last January. Saved it from the wrecking ball."

"The Short Stop that used to be in Belleville?" asked Tom.

Randy nodded. "I have a collection of diners at my camp out in western Jersey. Five of them, now. When I see a diner for sale, I can't resist buying it. I'm afraid that if I don't, it's going to disappear. I think of it as my contribution to historic preservation."

Intrigued by the idea of a collection of diners, Charlotte asked, "What do you do with them?"

"I live in one, a 1931 Worcester lunch wagon with Haitian mahoghany paneling. I use another, a 1942 Tierney, for a studio and gallery. The other two—a Swingles and an O'Mahoney—are still being restored."

"I'd like to do a write-up on your collection," said Tom.

"You're welcome to come out anytime."

"What about the Short Stop?" he asked.

"I've turned the Short Stop into a guest cottage," Randy replied. "That way my guests get the idea that I don't want them to stay around too long," he joked. "If they do, I just turn on the neon." He raised his hands, opening and closing his fingers in a flashing motion.

They all laughed at the image of guests being reminded that they had overstayed their welcome by a flashing neon sign saying "Short Stop."

"As I recall, the Short Stop is a Paramount, circa 1948," said Tom.

"Good guess," said Randy, "Nineteen forty-seven, to be precise."

"Then you have an example of at least one diner from most of the major manufacturers from the golden age. . . ."

"I don't have a Silk City."

"There are a lot of them around," said Tom. "If you're interested in finding one, you could put an ad in *Diner Monthly*."

"I don't need to," Randy said. "I know which one I want.

"Which one is that, love?" teased Xantha.

They had moved on to the paintings of the third painter in the show, Ed Verre. If Spiegel's paintings could be summed up as intellectual and Randy's as sentimental, then Verre's would be documentary. In fact, it was a testament to the inaccuracy of such labels that these three painters had ever been lumped together under the rubric of photorealism.

Unlike Spiegel's and Randy's paintings, neither of which showed people, Verre's painting not only included identifiable people—John was clearly recognizable from his height and his hunched-over shoulders—but even the specials for the day. The title was "Falls View Diner at Two A.M."

Though there was nothing specific to convey the idea of two in the morning, the painter had nevertheless captured the loneliness of the early morning hours. It was something about the harsh white light and the way the two men at the counter were huddled over their coffee cups, a stool apart—alone, yet together. The presence of the customers added an intriguing narrative element. One had the sense of specific people on a specific night, waiting for something to happen. There was a 1988 calender hanging next to the poster of the Acropolis with the dates crossed off. The date was a year ago last spring.

Randy and Xantha had lingered behind, discussing his paintings. Now they joined the rest of the group in front of the Verre painting.

"It's very good, don't you think, love?" Xantha said to her husband. "But not as good as Randy's work, of course."

As the group's attention shifted to Randy, something very strange happened. Charlotte had the distinct impression that he was disintegrating before her eyes. She could almost see him breaking up into a thousand little glistening shards, like the glass of a shattered windshield.

In reality, his skin was twitching, causing his hands to scramble frantically all over his body as if he were trying to stop it. His head was swiveling from side to side in wide-eyed terror. Charlotte had often heard the phrase "made my skin crawl"; now she knew exactly what it meant.

As she watched him, it dawned on her this was a drug reaction, and that his appealing aura of energy had been drug-induced. Turned up by several degrees—or rather, all the way—it was no longer very pretty.

"I think I know what he had to go back to his studio for," Tom whispered.

"What is it, love?" asked a concerned Xantha. She hovered next to Randy like a protective fairy, her magenta-rimmed eyes wide with alarm.

"I see them," he said, staring at the painting. "This time I'm certain I see them." Then he moaned, a low moan, like an animal in pain, and stuck his right arm out stiffly at the painting. "They're under the counter." Beads of sweat had popped out on his temples. "Don't you see them?"

"*What* do you see, love?"

By this time, Randy's behavior had attracted the attention of the other guests, who stood around in silence, plastic wineglasses in hand, staring discreetly out of the corners of their eyes.

"What's happening?" asked Diana, appearing at Charlotte's side.

"Randy's going off the deep end again," came the bored, cynical voice of the woman behind her. "Somebody had better go get Patty."

Suddenly Randy shouted: "I've got to get out of here." Then he lifted his forearms, as if he was trying to shield his face from attack, and backed slowly away. "Where can I go?" he cried out. Then his knees buckled and he crumpled to the floor, sobbing.

As the guests stood around trying to figure what to do— it had all happened so fast—a woman appeared at Randy's side. Charlotte recognized her as Patty Andriopoulis. She had shed her black polyester waitress's uniform for a simple black cocktail dress.

Randy looked up at her. "Australia: that's where I'll go," he said, answering his own question. "He won't be able to find me there."

"Patty, thank God you're here," said Diana. Reaching into her pocketbook, she discreetly handed Patty a long white business envelope. "Here," she whispered. "Give him this. Tell him it's his ticket for Australia."

Patty nodded and grabbed the envelope. "I have your plane ticket right here, Ran," she said in a soft, soothing voice. "Your flight's at one A.M." She gently took hold of his arm. "C'mon. Let's go get a drink. Then we'll go back to your place and pack your suitcase."

She gestured for one of the bystanders to help her, and together they pulled Randy up to a standing position. Holding him firmly by one elbow, Patty slowly guided him toward the door.

Randy meekly let her push him along, relief flowing over his pale, sweat-drenched face.

Charlotte and Tom happened to be on the scene when the police recovered Randy's body three days later.

They had come to Paterson to talk with him about the painting, or rather, Tom had. Charlotte had been planning to take the self-guided walking tour of the historic district, using the map she had picked up at the museum on the evening of the opening. They had just parked in the lot across the street from the Gryphon Mill when a string of four police cars came racing by, gumballs flashing. They were trailed by a rescue squad truck. When the vehicles came to a screeching halt next to a vacant lot fifty feet down the street, Charlotte knew from the gleam in Tom's eye that there was no way they were going to miss out on whatever it was that was going on. He was hardly one to ignore a police emergency, especially when they were a few minutes early for their appointment anyway.

The vacant lot where the police cars had pulled over was bordered by a raceway, which ran under the street and behind a row of mills on the other side. Joining the cluster of onlookers which had gathered on the bridge over the raceway, they immediately saw the cause of the commotion: it was a body floating in the water. Or rather, a set of shoulders and a head with long, flowing blond hair. The rest of the body had been carried into the culvert, where it had become lodged in the mud. The body looked strangely romantic, Charlotte thought, perhaps because of the long, flowing hair. That and the murky, yellow-green water with its reflections of the overhanging willows; the spikes of blue-flowered pickerel weed and the path that meandered along the grassy bank reminded her of a romantic painting by one of the Pre-Raphaelites (was it Burne-Jones's painting of Ophelia?) in which a drowned girl floats on her back, her flower-bedecked hair spread out over the surface of the water.

But this corpse wasn't floating on its back; it was on its stomach, a condition that a pair of fire department rescue workers were now trying to rectify. Wearing rubber fishing boots, they had waded into the shallow water and were prodding the body with a hook affixed to a pole. A third rescue worker stood nearby, steadying a floating stretcher.

But the body wasn't cooperating. Bloated from decomposition, it was as resistant to their prodding as a waterlogged plank. After a third helper had been called in, they finally succeeded in turning it over.

A low murmur of shock coursed through the gathering of onlookers as they caught sight of the victim's face, which looked like some horror-movie makeup man's idea of a ghoul. It was pale and swollen to twice its natural size, and its nose, chin, and lips were studded with little red wounds where chunks of flesh were missing.

"Turtles," said the man next to them to no one in particular. Though he was dressed in plain clothes, it was clear from the orders he was giving the uniformed police officers that he was the one in charge.

Repulsed by the horrible sight, some of the onlookers moved back, allowing Charlotte her first clear view of the corpse. She knew immediately who it was. There was no mistaking the large, protruding teeth, which, seen through lips that had been drawn back in death, gave the body a rodent-like appearance.

"It's Randy!" she said with a little gasp as she turned to Tom, who was right behind her. Then she felt her knees begin to buckle.

The plainclothes officer, who was standing at the balustrade next to her, reached out to grab her elbow. "Steady, there," he said. He waited a moment for the shock to pass, and then asked: "You know this guy?"

She looked again at the corpse. The body had been wrapped, mummy-like, in white fabric—a bedsheet, perhaps—but if she had any doubts, they were put to rest by the clothing that was visible. He was still wearing the red bow tie and the high-top sneakers.

"His name is Randall Goslau," she said.

The officer holding her elbow was in his mid-fifties, and nearly bald. With his broad shoulders and pot belly, he gave the impression of physical power. Despite his bulk, however, he had a certain grace. She would have guessed him to be a good dancer.

"He's an artist," Tom offered. "He lives and works in that mill over there." He nodded at the building to their right.

The officer looked over at the red brick mill, one of a line of three or four, and then back at Tom. "How do you know him?"

"I was going to buy one of his paintings. That's why we came out here today. We had an appointment with him at ten."

"Too late now," the officer said, with a glance at the corpse, which was being loaded onto the stretcher. He had taken a pen and notepad out of his pocket. He pointed the end of the pen at Tom. "Lieutenant Marty Voorhees. Criminal Investigation Division. Who are you?" he asked.

"Tom Plummer."

"Hey, I know you," he said, pointing the pen at Tom again. "You're the guy who writes the true-crime books."

Tom nodded.

"Pleased to meet you," the detective said.

Tom was the darling of police officers. In his books, the cops were always the heroes, the victim always the wronged party, and the murderer always the villain. Cops were always happy to meet an author who didn't tell the story from the murderer's point of view, which so many of them now seemed to do.

After taking down Tom's name and number, he turned to Charlotte. "And who do we have here?" he said with the brazen look which comes from years of sizing up women in terms of their sexual availability, a habit so ingrained it couldn't be turned off, even for a seventy-year-old woman.

"Charlotte Graham," she replied.

The cop suddenly stopped writing, and gave her the once-over again.

"Well, how do I look?" asked Charlotte sharply. She hated

being scrutinized like this. She could hear him telling his wife: *she must be seventy, if she's a day.*

"Pretty damned good for an old warhorse," he said.

Charlotte had to smile. It was one of her life's little benisons that she had aged well. Her black hair was worn pulled back into a chignon now rather than in her famous pageboy and she had gained a few pounds, but her skin had held up, partly because it was so pale that she had always taken pains to protect it.

"I read *Murder at the Morosco*, by the way. Not only are you a helluva actress, Miss Graham, you're also a helluva detective. Now, about our friend here," he said, nodding down at the corpse. "When did you last see him? Alive, I mean," he added with a smile that revealed a gap between his front teeth.

Tom explained about the incident at the opening, which the other guests had also attributed to drugs. It had come out afterward that Randy had been a cocaine user, and that his behavior of late was becoming increasingly bizarre.

"How long has he been dead?" Tom asked.

"At least a couple of days by the looks of him," said the detective. He looked down at the bloated body, which was being removed to the morgue wagon that had just pulled into the vacant lot. "We'll find out when we get the medical examiner's report."

"A homicide?" asked Tom.

Did Charlotte detect a hopeful note in his voice? After all, he had just finished a book, and was scouting around for a new subject.

"Got to be—unless he wrapped himself up in that sheet. Which might very well have been the case. I've seen suicides do stranger things."

"How would he have killed himself?" asked Charlotte.

"Jumped. We get a lot of suicides. The observation bridge is almost as popular as the Golden Gate. But he would have had to jump in above the Falls to end up in the raceway system. The intake valve's just up river from the Spruce Street Bridge."

"Why the sheet, then?" asked Charlotte.

"Maybe he wanted to keep himself from changing his mind. With his arms pinned to his sides like that, he wouldn't have

been able to swim." The burly detective shrugged. "Just speculation."

"It wouldn't have been easy to wrap himself up like that,"
said Tom.

"You're right," said Voorhees. He pointed the end of his pen
once again at Tom and Charlotte. "I'll tell you one thing . . ."

"What's that?" asked Tom.

"If it's a homicide, you'll be hearing from me."

· 4 ·

VOORHEES CALLED CHARLOTTE at nine the next morning.
She had just finished a leisurely breakfast in bed at her
townhouse in the Turtle Bay section of Manhattan when the
phone rang. She welcomed the interruption. Not long ago, she
had signed a contract with a publisher to write her memoirs.
Over the years, she had often been approached about doing an
autobiography, but she had always resisted. She rarely even
gave interviews, so jealously did she guard her privacy. So
why write a book? But Tom had finally convinced her that she
owed her life story to an adoring public who had supported
her for half a century with their loyalty and love. What had
finally won her over was his argument that writing her memoirs
needn't necessarily require laying bare her life, nor need it be a
boring chronicle of dates. It could simply be a sharing of her
wisdom, knowledge, and experiences. Put this way, it didn't
sound quite so daunting. And, as her friends had died, her movies had crumbled into dust, and the studio system disappeared,
she had also come to realize that, like the Falls View, she was
a slice of the past, with a history that was worth preserving.

Tom's fellow campaigner in this crusade was Charlotte's
personal secretary, Vivian Smith, who had made it her mission
to keep a portable tape recorder within Charlotte's reach at all
times in case she should suddenly be overcome by the need
to record a particular memory. So far, Vivian's ploy hadn't
worked: the mere sight of a tape recorder was enough to send
Charlotte out the door and hurtling across the countryside.

One of the half dozen or so recorders that Vivian had purchased and scattered around the house was now resting on

Charlotte's bedside table, where it had been for the last several weeks. Never one to give into defeat, Vivian had set up this morning's tableau—breakfast tray with flower vase and silver tea service, scrapbooks from Charlotte's early career on the side—in hopes that it would inspire her to take the first step.

Cradling the telephone against her ear, Charlotte removed the breakfast tray to the bedside table, and rearranged her pillows so that she could sit up straight against the headboard.

It was definitely murder, Voorhees said. Toxicology had found large amounts of cocaine in Randy's organs, but the cocaine wasn't what had killed him. He had still been alive when he was dumped in the river. Probably unconscious—it was hard to say whether he'd come to or not—but definitely still alive. The medical examiner had found microscopic algae in his organs, which meant that he'd still been breathing when he was thrown in the water.

With her free hand, Charlotte closed the scrapbook on her lap, and moved it over to the other bedside table. "What about the possibility of suicide?"

"It would have been impossible for him to have tied himself up in that way," said the deep voice on the other end of the line. Voorhees explained: "That wasn't a sheet he was wrapped up in; it was aprons."

"Aprons!" she exclaimed.

"Two of them. Long, white, restaurant-type aprons. The first was worn in the usual way, except that the belt was used to bind the upper legs together. The other was worn upside down, with neckband wrapped around the feet and the belt tied around the upper arms."

Charlotte shuddered at the thought of awakening from a drug-induced stupor to find oneself floating in a river, unable to move one's arms or legs. "Do you have a time of death?" she asked.

"Between twelve and two A.M. on Sunday, September ninth."

"The night of the opening reception."

"Right. Which makes you and Plummer among the last people to have seen Goslau alive. And which is why I'd like you both to come down to headquarters. I'd like to ask you some questions."

"Certainly. When would you like us to come?"

"Plummer said he could come right away." (Not too eager, Charlotte thought.) "He also said he thought you could probably come with him, but he suggested I check with you. How does that sound?"

Charlotte thought for a millisecond. Apart from reliving her life, which she had no desire to do, she didn't have anything planned for that day. A little shopping and a few errands, but they could wait.

"Sounds fine," she said as she stuck her tongue out at the tape recorder.

They were to meet Voorhees at police headquarters, which was located not far from the historic district, in a new public safety complex. "You can't miss it," Voorhees had said. Well, they could, and they did. But getting lost had its advantages in that it gave them a better sense of the city. The first thing to strike Charlotte was that it hadn't changed since she'd last been there. The nearly complete absence of modern buildings meant that the gracious turn-of-the-century landmarks had not been eclipsed by modern glass and steel towers. With the exception of the church spires and the smokestacks, the highest structures were the public ones. The aura of importance vested in these buildings by their physical dominance gave the city a sense of order that was missing from many cities—American cities, that is; European cities seemed to do better at preserving some kind of architectural sense. Charlotte marveled at the wonderful old architecture as they drove by (in several cases, more than once): the elegant Beaux Arts City Hall, with its shining white clock tower; the neoclassical county courthouse, with its cool, gray dome; the old Flemish-style post office, now a court building, with its stepped red brick gables. Even the old Fabian Theatre, where she had sold war bonds, was still there, though it was now divided into five movie theaters. What had happened to the marvelous vaulted lobby with its showpiece chandelier? she wondered. And, although many of the historic mills had been abandoned, a surprising number were still in operation, the signs above their entrances proclaiming that they made shirts or silk thread or machine parts. Between the mills, the quiet streets were lined with squat clapboard four-family houses of the type that used to be called cheeseboxes when cheese still came in boxes. Children played on the streets while mothers watched from the stoops or from the open first-story windows. Though the ethnic identity of the inhabitants might have changed—they were now Spanish, Portuguese, and even Lebanese and Syrian instead of Irish, Italian, and German—the ambiance remained the same. It was a city in which people still lived within walking distance of where they worked. It was a city of neighborhoods.

The other thing that struck her was the city's sense of being fortified against the outside world, like a frontier garrison. Unlike most eastern cities, it lacked a river or ocean port. Its *raison d'être* was the Falls, not its access to the wider world. The closed-in feeling that came from the absence of a port was reinforced by the fact that the city was bounded on three sides by the great arc of the meandering river, which insulated it from the surrounding suburbs like a castle moat, and on the fourth by the craggy summit of Garrett Rock, which loomed over it like an ancient watchtower.

It was a city encapsulated not only in time, but in space; a city living in its own cozy little world, and pulsing to a primordial rhythm that had been established long before the beat of commerce was added to the score: the rhythm of the heavy waters of the river plunging into the narrow gorge and crashing onto the sharp-edged rocks below.

At last they found the public safety complex. It was a giant concrete fortress that took up several blocks, the exception to Charlotte's observation that Paterson had no modern buildings. Voorhees was right. How could they have missed it? A cop at a reception desk directed them to the Criminal Investigation Division on the second floor, where Voorhees met them at another reception desk and escorted them into an office cubicle. After inviting them to sit down on a couple of the folding chairs that were ranged against one wall (he must not have wanted the people he interrogated to sit too close, Charlotte thought), Voorhees took a seat in the swivel chair behind his desk and leaned back with his hands folded over his paunch. A blow-up of a photograph of a girl poised on the end of a diving board hung on the wall behind his desk, the only decoration in an otherwise sterile office.

"Someone you know?" asked Charlotte, nodding at the photograph. It had obviously been taken at a competition of some kind; the background was a crowded grandstand.

Voorhees swiveled his chair around to face the photo. "My daughter. She's a diver. She's also my second job. Every weekend there's another meet. The plane fares alone are enough to break me, to say nothing of the coach and the motels. I was spending so much time in Fort Lauderdale that I finally bought a condominium there. It was cheaper than paying for accommodations, and I figure I'll be able to retire there in a few years."

"She's very pretty," said Charlotte.

"Yes, she is," he agreed with quiet pride. He shrugged. "What are you going to do? She loves it, and she's good at it too." He swiveled the chair back around to face them. "Okay, tell me what happened that night." He nodded at Tom. "Plummer first."

Tom recounted their meeting with Randy, and their visit to the museum. In response to Voorhees' instructions not to leave out any details, he included their meeting the Lumkins and Morris Finder, and mentioned Charlotte's connection with them through Jack Lundstrom. He concluded with Randy's attack of paranoia, if that's what it was.

"Well, as the old saying goes," said Voorhees when Tom had finished, " 'Just because you're paranoid doesn't mean that somebody isn't out to get you.' " He turned to Charlotte: "Do you have anything to add, Miss Graham?"

"Only that it was the painting—it was a painting of the Falls View Diner by the artist Ed Verre—that seemed to have set him off."

Removing his hands from his belly, Voorhees leaned forward and toyed with his pen. "The police department is at a disadvantage in this case. The artists' community here is a tight little group. If the victim had been a numbers runner or a drug dealer, we'd have informants to help us out—to tell us who wanted him dead. But we don't have informants in the artists' community, and"—he waved the pen in the direction of the bank of desks where the rank and file of detectives sat— "not being highly cultured types ourselves, this leaves us in something of a bind. A bind that you might be able to help us out of."

"By becoming your informants?" asked Tom.

"Something like that, yes. Goslau's death might have been a random thing. He might have been thrown in the river by a crackhead for no reason at all. That sort of thing is always happening around here. But then again, maybe it had something to do with the artists' community. And a little birdie tells me that finding out whether or not it did might be right up your alley." He leaned back and smiled. He had a wide mouth, and teeth that were stained from smoking. But it was a pleasant smile.

"Did your little birdie also tell you that we don't know anything about the Paterson artists' community?" asked Charlotte.

"You'd met Goslau. Plummer here was going to buy one of his paintings. Your husband is a well-known art collector, which makes me assume that you know something about art. That's an entrée, which is more than we have."

"What do you want us to find out?" she asked.

"The gossip. These people must have some theories about why Goslau was killed. I want you to find out what they are. Naturally, I'd like you to be discreet."

"Just satisfying our natural curiosity," said Tom.

"Exactly. I'll fill you in on our progress as we go along. So far we only know that Goslau left the museum with Patty Andriopoulis, as you already know. Did you meet Patty at the Falls View?"

They nodded.

"Everybody who eats at the Falls View gets to know Patty eventually. She took him back there, and gave him a couple of stiff drinks to bring him down. She said he was pretty coked up."

"Were she and Randy lovers?" asked Tom.

"I don't think so. I think he was just one of her strays. She tends to take in people the same way she takes in dogs and cats. But that's the kind of thing I want you to find out. He stayed for a while at the party. . . ."

"Party?" interrupted Charlotte.

"The museum had hired the diner for it—it was a post-opening thing for the organizers and the artists—and then he left. That was sometime around eleven. He never slept in his bed. Besides that, we know exactly zip."

*   *   *

They decided to talk with Diana Nelson first. Or rather, Tom decided to talk with Diana Nelson first. As a local art dealer—the only local art dealer, as far as Charlotte could tell—she would have the inside scoop, Tom said. In reality, Charlotte suspected that he had other motives; she had recognized Diana right away as being Tom's type. He had a weakness for tall, slim brunettes. Diana was a little less dramatic in appearance than his usual type—with her long neck, lovely smile, and wide blue eyes, she had the all-American prettiness of a beauty pageant contestant—but she fit the general mold. In fact, except for the color of her eyes and her hair, which was cut very short, she was almost a dead ringer for Daria Henderson, who had been Tom's most serious love interest to date. They had met several years ago in Maine in the course of another murder investigation in which Daria had almost become the second victim, and split up last year over nothing, at least in Charlotte's opinion. But she was hardly one to talk. With four marriages and more affairs than she cared to admit to on her record, she wasn't in a position to comment on other people's relationships.

After parking in the museum lot, they walked up to the Ivanhoe Gallery, which was located in an old mill, the Ivanhoe Wheelhouse, at the head of Spruce Street. The Ivanhoe sat at the foot of an escarpment next to the tailrace of the Upper Raceway, which ran along the base of the hill, and into which the spent water from the millwheels had once been discharged. The headrace, which delivered water to the mills through a series of water troughs, ran across the upper part of the hillside. The head and tailraces were linked by a man-made waterfall, or spillway, which fell into a lily-studded pool adjoining the Ivanhoe. From this pool, the Middle Raceway carried the water under Spruce Street to a line of mills on the other side, of which the Gryphon, where Randy had lived, was one.

Given that it was nearly five, they half expected the gallery to be closed, but the wide double doors here still swung open to the warm afternoon. They found Diana inside, talking with a customer about the current show, which featured a Paterson ceramic artist named Louise Sicca.

While they waited for Diana to finish with her customer,

they looked at the ceramic sculptures that were displayed on pedestals. The sculptures also had a diner theme, planned no doubt to coordinate with the museum's show, but the subject was diner food rather than diners themselves. They might have been called photorealism in ceramics: one pedestal displayed a glazed ring cake, complete with cake stand and plastic cover; another displayed a still life of a jar of Heinz ketchup, a napkin holder, and a pair of salt and pepper shakers.

"Here's your lemon meringue pie," said Tom, who'd been browsing among the paintings hanging on the brick walls, and had stopped at a ceramic work displayed on one of the pedestals. He gestured for Charlotte to join him. "Look at those peaks!" he said. "Andriopoulis would definitely approve."

The pie was realistic right down to the beads of moisture that had congealed on the surface of the meringue. Charlotte had never seen anything quite like it.

Having finished with her customer, Diana wandered over.

"This stuff is great," said Tom. "What do you call it?"

"Well, I would call it *trompe l'oeil* ceramics, but the artist prefers the term material illusionism."

"It makes you think you've never really looked at a pie before," Tom said.

"That's the idea," said Diana with a smile. "The artist's goal, to quote her, is to reawaken the dormant joys of observation." She cocked her pretty head and asked: "What can I do for you?"

"We just came in to chat about Randy," Charlotte said, after introducing herself. "Tom wants to do an article on him. Randy told us a little about himself the other evening, but we wondered if you could fill us in."

"Would you like to sit outside?" asked Diana. She gestured at the table and chairs on the flagstone patio just beyond the open doors. "Go ahead," she directed them. "I'll just get us something to drink."

Stepping outside, they took seats at the table, which was shaded by a huge old sycamore. The cool rush of the waterfall was delightful on this hot afternoon. The setting reminded Charlotte of one of her favorite places: the vest-pocket park, with its refreshing waterfall, on New York City's West Forty-fifth street.

"What was this building used for?" Charlotte asked Tom, her authority on the history and lore of Paterson.

"It housed the wheelhouse for the Ivanhoe Papermill Complex. The wheel was there," he said, pointing to the taller section of the building, "and the egress for the water was down there." He pointed to an archway at water level.

Leaning back, Charlotte studied the elegant brickwork of the wall looming over them. It was studded with wildflowers that had found niches in the moist nooks and crannies between the old bricks.

Diana reappeared momentarily with a tray on which sat three glasses, a bottle of Pernod, and a small bowl of green olives.

Not only did Charlotte not feel as if she was in the heart of a deteriorating American industrial city, she didn't feel as if she was in an American city at all. With the Pernod and olives, she could have been sitting at an outdoor café in Cannes or Nice.

"How's business?" asked Tom after Diana had poured the yellow, anise-flavored aperitif and handed the glasses around.

"In a word, it stinks. Do you see any customers?" she asked, waving an arm at her surroundings. "It's bad. So bad, in fact, that I may not be in business much longer. At this point, it's only my income as a curator that's keeping the wolf from the door. I had big hopes when I came here. I thought I would be the Paula Cooper of the Great Falls Historic District."

"Who's Paula Cooper?" asked Tom, popping on olive in his mouth.

"She was the first art dealer to open a gallery in Soho, in 1967. Now there are a hundred and forty of them. She followed the artists, who were lured there by the cheap rents. Back in the seventies, I thought the same thing was going to happen here. There was nowhere to go but up, or so we thought. Paterson had been rated the most depressed city in America. For a while, it looked good: the historic district and all that. There was a lot of energy, a lot of enthusiasm. They were calling Paterson 'the Venice of America,' because of the raceways. What a joke." She laughed bitterly. "Then it all just fizzled out. The odds were too overwhelming. Not only did the new people not come, the pioneers started leaving. Once they started having children, they moved to the suburbs, where there are safe streets, good schools. I don't blame them."

"People talk as if there's a thriving community here," said Charlotte.

"We talk a good game. Or maybe it should be called wishful thinking. The much-vaunted renaissance of the historic district is a fraud. I've got a crack den across the street." She pointed to a picturesque little brick building that was perched on the bank of the raceway behind the Gryphon Mill. "I've got winos sleeping in my doorway. It seems like another mill goes up in smoke every few weeks."

"The owners are torching them?"

"They deny it. They say it's squatters setting fires to keep warm. But most of the fires have been in the summer. Who needs to keep warm in summer? You tell me. The developers bought these mills during the good years, with high hopes of restoring them, and then the economy soured. A lot of them didn't realize how expensive it is to restore these buildings. There are all sorts of restrictions that go with historic district status. See those windows?" She turned around to nod at the huge windows on the first floor of the gallery. "Each one is a slightly different size, which means a custom replacement, or close to it, for every single one."

"Sounds like the voice of experience speaking," said Charlotte.

"You bet," she said. "Costly experience." She sipped her drink thoughtfully. "Our last ray of hope was Don Spiegel. He was a Paterson native who had come home to roost. When he renovated the Gryphon Mill we all thought he would pull us back from the edge, and he nearly did. Our white knight; the big-name artist. But then he had the audacity to jump off the bridge and ruin it for us all."

"The observation bridge over the chasm?" asked Tom.

Diana nodded. "It's a popular jumping spot; very picturesque. New Jersey's answer to the Golden Gate." She looked up toward the bridge as if she were considering jumping herself. "His body didn't come up for four months. That often happens. The bodies get tangled up in the old construction debris from the hydrolectric plant at the bottom. Being where I am, I have front row seats for the retrieval of corpses. The rescue squad lowers the boat into the river right up there." She gestured toward the head of the street. "Though I didn't have the pleasure of being a witness to that one, thank God."

Charlotte thought of the amount of decomposition that had taken place in Randy's corpse after just three days, and shuddered at the thought of what Spiegel's body must have looked like after four months.

"But you wanted to know about Randy. Speaking of drowning victims," she added with an ironic little laugh. "I used to represent him. When he was starting out. After he became successful, he abandoned me. Moved to the Koreman Gallery, on West Broadway in Soho."

"That's where I originally saw his work," said Tom.

"Tell me, when you were talking with him about buying a painting, did he ever mention giving a commission to the gallery?"

Tom shook his head.

"I didn't think so. If you keep quiet, he'll charge you a reduced price, and you'll both make out, right? Wrong. He would have charged you full freight anyway. He pulled the same stunt with my customers. Cheated me, and cheated them. After all I had done to promote his work. It takes a lot of energy to shape the reputation of a young artist, and he was an unknown when he came to me. Then he decided he didn't want to be represented by a small-time gallery anymore. Actually, I shouldn't complain. What he did to me is nothing compared to what he was doing to Mary Catherine Koreman."

"You mean by cheating her out of her commission?" asked Charlotte.

"No. I mean by shaking her down. Extortion is the word, I believe."

"Extortion?"

"Randy got a kickback for every painting the Lumkins bought from Koreman. The deal was this: if Mary Catherine didn't fork over, he would use his influence with Xantha"—she contorted her face in an expression of repugnance—"to get the Lumkins to take their business elsewhere."

"Where they *were* willing to pay."

"You've got it. If you wanted to sell a painting to the Lumkins, you had to go through Randy. Mary Catherine has probably paid him tens of thousands of dollars over the past few years. I'll tell you—the only person who ever made out in a deal with Randy Goslau was Randy Goslau." She shrugged her lovely shoulders, which were set off by a gauzy sleeveless dress. "As you can tell, I'm not exactly brokenhearted that the conniving little creep is dead."

Recognizing his cue, Tom stepped in: "Who *else* do you think might have wanted to kill him?" he asked with a charming grin.

Diana smiled. "Besides me, you mean? Believe me, if it had been me who killed him, I wouldn't have just thrown him in the river. I'd have thought of a much more painful way to do him in. Having him keelhauled or drawn and quartered are two means that spring to mind." She thought about the question for a minute. "Well, there are a lot of suspects. Randy managed to offend just about everyone he knew at one time or another."

"For example?" prompted Tom.

"Mary Catherine Koreman, for starters. She'll save a lot of money with Randy out of the picture. By killing him off, she would be eliminating the middleman, so to speak. But then, she *has* a lot of money, so maybe she doesn't really have that much of a motive." She paused to think again, and then continued: "Bernice, of course. Everyone is already saying that Bernice did it, or hired someone to do it."

"Bernice who?" asked Charlotte.

Diana seemed astonished that they didn't know who she was talking about. "Bernice Spiegel, of course."

"The wife of the artist?"

She shook her head. "The sister of the artist, and the heir to his estate. Do you mean to tell me that you haven't read about Bernice's legal battle with Randy? It's been written up *ad nauseum* in the art journals, to say nothing of the newspapers. I think there was even an article about it in *People*."

Charlotte and Tom both looked at her blankly.

"Well, I can see I have a lot of filling in to do. Living in such a hermetic little world here, we sometimes forget that everyone else doesn't have the same interests we have."

"I think you'd better start at Square One," Charlotte said.

"Okay. Square One. Bernice Spiegel is, or rather was, Don Spiegel's business manager. She is also the self-appointed keeper of the flame, guardian of the grave, whatever."

"A Cerberus," said Tom, the classics scholar.

"I guess you could call her that." She looked over at Tom. "Was Cerberus a pit bull?" she joked. "Anyway, Bernice was president of the corporation, the Gryphon Corporation, which managed Don's business affairs. He was a salaried employee. It was a tax shelter, also a convenience for Don. With Bernice in charge of his money he could devote himself entirely to his painting. He didn't have to worry about monitoring his investments or paying his bills."

Charlotte was familiar with the arrangement. Though she herself was too suspicious to trust somebody else with her money, she knew that many of her acting colleagues did. In fact, there were businesses that provided a similar service for Hollywood celebrities.

Diana continued: "The dispute arose over Don's will, which stipulated that, apart from a substantial trust that had been set aside for his son, the remainder of his estate, including his property holdings—namely the Gryphon Mill—and all of his paintings would go to the Gryphon Corporation. In other words, to Bernice. The value of the residuary estate has been estimated at anywhere from forty to sixty million dollars."

"Gulp!" said Tom.

"Don was one of the most financially successful painters of his generation. Now, to backtrack a little: Randy was Don's assistant. He had worked for Don for ten years or so. He was hired a year or two before Don split up with his wife, Louise. Not only did Randy mix paints and stretch canvases, he also did all the cooking—Don never cooked—the cleaning, the grocery shopping, the errands. He was the household manager."

"He became the wife. . . ." said Charlotte.

"Exactly. In all fairness, I have to say that he worked like a dog. It was a twenty-four-hour-a-day job. He wasn't paid much—two fifty a week, he once told me—but to talk about his pay is misleading because Don, or rather the Gryphon Corporation, also covered all of Randy's expenses: rent, food, dry cleaning, airport limos—you name it. There were other benefits too. It was Don who started Randy painting diners, who introduced him to high rollers like the Lumkins, and who promoted his career in general. The dispute between Bernice and Randy arose over another of these perks: an agreement that upon Don's death, Randy would take possession of a collection of twelve paintings which Don had loaned to him over the years, and which hung in Randy's studio at the mill. The gift agreement was Don's way of providing for Randy's long-term security. It was a formal agreement, drawn up by a lawyer and including detailed descriptions of the paintings. The value of the paintings at the time of Don's death was estimated at eight to ten million dollars."

"Whew!" said Tom. "A million a year isn't bad long-term security."

"Yeah," said Diana. "Don was a generous guy, extravagantly so. It was just as well that Bernice was managing his money. He probably would have pissed it all away otherwise. Anyway, this document was drawn up, oh, maybe three or four years ago. To continue the story: as Randy became more and more successful, he began to resent his position as Don's vassal, however well-treated he might have been. He started neglecting his duties: not showing up, throwing temper tantrums when he was asked to do something he considered beneath him. That sort of thing. He also developed a serious cocaine habit. I'm not talking party coke here. I once found him passed out in my doorway when I got here in the morning. He must have been hanging out with the winos. Anyway, he and Don began to quarrel. Then came the *ARTnews* incident. In an article on artists' assistants, Randy claimed that he had actually painted some of Don's paintings himself, paintings that were signed 'DS.' Don always signed his work with his initials, which were hidden somewhere in the painting. Randy made it sound as if Don's paintings were like the products of one of those Renaissance workshops in which the only parts actually executed by the signatory artist were the finishing touches and the signature."

"Was it true?" Charlotte asked.

"Let me tell you about the Gryphon Mill. The mill was an ongoing house party. If the art community of Paterson could be said to have had a clubhouse, the mill was it. Artists, would-be artists, dealers, collectors, sycophants, jazz musicians, groupies, poets, writers—you name it. People like the Lumkins thought it was great, a safe little taste of Bohemia.

There were people going in and out of Don's studio all day, every day. Rare was the night when there weren't a dozen people for dinner. Part of the reason that Louise left Don was that she couldn't stand living in a goldfish bowl. In all the times that I was there—and I was there three or four times a week over the course of twelve years—I never saw anyone but Don put a brush to one of his canvases. Besides, it would have shown. Don had a magic touch: he was very precise. He could create an effect with one stroke. Randy's technique is entirely different."

"I gather the article didn't make Spiegel very happy," Charlotte commented.

Diana nodded emphatically. "He was crushed. He felt that Randy had betrayed him, and everyone else pretty much agreed. Bernice was especially angry. She and her brother were very close, and I think she had always resented Randy's status with Don. She had been nagging Don to fire Randy, but he always refused. When Don died, the first thing that Bernice did was to start eviction proceedings against Randy. The second thing she did was sue him for the return of the paintings Don had given him. She claimed that the paintings belonged to the Gryphon Corporation, and that Don had never intended to give them to Randy, especially after their falling out."

"Sounds like it got pretty ugly," said Tom.

"It got worse than that. We're talking brass knuckles stuff. Randy not only turned around and countersued the Gryphon Corporation for compensatory damages for the mental anguish Bernice's suit had caused him, he threatened to sue for palimony."

"Palimony!" exclaimed Charlotte. "Were he and Spiegel lovers?"

"No. Don liked women, as any number of them, myself included"—she smiled—"could readily attest. But, as it later came out, the courts do not necessarily define such a relationship as involving sex, and Randy wasn't saying that it did. But the mere mention of the word was enough to raise the suspicion that he and Don had been lovers, which was Randy's intent. He knew that any blemish on the reputation of her beloved brother would drive Bernice nuts—nuts enough to settle."

"What about *his* reputation?" asked Tom.

"He didn't give a damn about his reputation. He went either way when it came to sex. I hesitate to call him a bisexual only because it wasn't a matter of sexual identity. It was a matter of self-aggrandizement: he'd have sex with anyone if there was something in it for him. To see him in action was a lesson in how to hustle. He had a way of sniffing people out—male or female—to get a sense of how much money they had or how well-connected they were."

"Did the police know about this dispute?" asked Charlotte.

"Everybody knew about it. It was the talk of the town I think Bernice is their main suspect at this point, at least that's what I gathered from the questions they were asking me about her."

"Who was asking you?" said Charlotte.

"The police. Specifically, a detective named Voorhees and his young henchman. I'm surprised they haven't gotten around to you yet. He said they would be talking with everyone who was at the opening. I had to give them a list of names and addresses."

Charlotte exchanged glances with Tom. So much for Voorhees knowing "exactly zip." She should have known better. His strategy must have been to see what details they came up with on their own. She couldn't blame him: it was usually the details that solved the case.

"Did Bernice back down as a result of the palimony threat?"

"Not immediately. I think she would have settled eventually, but of course that's all irrelevant now."

"I wonder if it is," said Charlotte, looking out at the pool.

"What do you mean?" asked Diana.

She returned her gaze to Diana. "If the gift agreement is valid—and it seems to me that if it was drawn up by a lawyer and signed by Spiegel it would be, despite Spiegel's intentions—then wouldn't Randy's heirs inherit the paintings?"

"Randy's heirs," said Diana. "Now there's an interesting question. I never heard him mention any family. His father is dead, and he doesn't have any siblings. I think there may be a stepmother, but if there is, he isn't close to her."

"Who has physical custody of the paintings?" asked Tom.

"Randy did. They were hanging in his studio the last I knew."

"Then Bernice hadn't succeeded in evicting him."

"Not yet. But it was just a matter of time: the Gryphon Corporation owned the building. She *had* succeeded in confining him to his studio. She had a steel door installed between his studio and the rest of the building. It looks like I imagine the door to Hitler's Berlin bunker to have looked. She also changed the locks on all the outside doors. She was afraid he might rip off some of Don's other paintings, or trash them. I don't blame her. His behavior had become so bizarre that it was becoming difficult to predict just what he *would* do."

"His behavior certainly was bizarre at the opening," said Charlotte. "Do you have any idea what he was talking about when he was looking at Verre's painting?" She couldn't help thinking that his behavior that night was linked to his death.

"Your guess is as good as mine," said Diana as she sipped her drink.

"Had you ever seen him like that before?" asked Tom.

"I haven't, no. But a friend of mine has seen him freak out twice before, both times in connection with a photorealist painting. Funny, isn't it? Maybe there's something about photorealism that sets him off, the way the vibrating colors in a Vasarely can induce a seizure in an epileptic."

"Did he freak out in the same way?"

"I don't know any more about it than that. But if you're interested, you can ask my friend. His name is Jason Armentrout. He did the paintings you saw inside. He can also tell you more about Randy. They were good buddies. Though Randy was even starting to grate on his nerves toward the end."

Tom looked up. "It looks like you have a visitor," he said.

· 5 ·

A HUNCHBACKED OLD woman clad in a long skirt and a shawl was descending the steps to the patio. Her face was nearly covered by a kerchief, and her feet were incongruously shod in new white running shoes. She couldn't have been much more than four feet tall, so bent over was she by old age. Coming up to Charlotte, she gestured with a gnarled hand toward the shopping cart that she pulled behind her, which was filled with crumpled newspapers, and muttered something in a language that sounded like Italian. Gesturing again at the cart, she said in English, "One dollar."

Curious, Charlotte reached into the cart and withdrew one of the crumpled newspapers. To her delight, she found that it was filled with a bouquet of autumn wildflowers: black-eyed Susans, Queen Anne's lace, and wild asters. "How lovely!" she exclaimed. Taking out her wallet, she paid the woman, who responded with a toothless smile.

Handing another bill to the old woman, Diana said: "I'll buy one too," explaining to her guests that the old woman had been around before. "Sometimes she has violets, sometimes mushrooms, sometimes wild herbs." She nodded at the mountain that loomed over the city. "I think she picks them up in the reservation."

"Excuse me," said Diana as the old woman mounted the steps back up to Spruce Street, "I'm just going to get a vase for these."

She returned momentarily with a small ceramic vase filled with the wildflowers, which she placed in the center of the table. "Here are some damp paper towels for yours," she said to Charlotte as she handed them to her. "To keep them fresh until you get home."

"Thank you," Charlotte said.

"That's the magic of Paterson," Diana continued as they watched the woman make her way down Spruce Street, pulling her cart behind her. "Magical little things like that old woman appearing with her wildflowers are always happening here. Have you read the poem *Paterson* by William Carlos Williams?"

They shook their heads.

"Allen Ginsberg sometimes does readings of it here. He's a Paterson native son. Ginsberg, I mean. Williams was a doctor in Rutherford. Anyway, there's a line in that poem: 'The mystery of streets and back rooms—' That mystery is why I hang on here, despite it all. That, and the wonderful buildings."

They stayed a few more minutes, asking questions about Randy, to support the charade about the article. Though Diana clearly didn't believe their story, Charlotte doubted that she suspected their real motive. As an inveterate gossip herself, she probably thought they wanted an excuse to get the lowdown.

"Where can we find your friend Jason?" Charlotte asked as they were preparing to leave.

Diana consulted her watch. "Let's see. At this hour, he'll probably still be at his studio, which is in the old Columbia Bank building, downtown. Nine Colt Street. If you're facing City Hall, Colt Street is to your right."

Tom nodded. They had gone by City Hall several times in their search for the public safety complex.

"If he's not at his studio, he'll be at Le Club Parisienne, which is right around the corner.

"Is that a restaurant?" asked Tom. "I'm starving."

"Of sorts," she replied.

The Columbia Bank was one of those wonderful old Beaux Arts buildings that Charlotte had admired as they were driving around downtown Paterson. Adjacent to City Hall, it, like the other banks in the vicinity, had been built in the same ornate style, with wrought-iron grillwork at the enormous windows, pilasters crowned with lions head capitals, and corbels in the form of baskets overflowing with fruit. It was a six-story monument to the days when Paterson had still been a mighty industrial power. No longer a bank, it now appeared to be occupied by offices and studios. In the directory, Charlotte had noticed the names of several photographers and commercial artists. The name JASON ARMENTROUT was followed by two room numbers, both on the fourth floor.

A creaky old elevator deposited them at a dingy, poorly lit hallway lined by doors with windows of wire-mesh safety glass, and smelling sharply of cleaning powder. After a bit of a search, they finally located the first room, where no one responded to their knock. They had better luck at the second room. The door was opened by a thin man with a black ponytail going to gray. He was very handsome, with an intense face of sharply-angled planes, and heavy black brows overhanging penetrating, deeply set blue eyes. He wore a navy blue T-shirt, and a faded blue plaid flannel shirt that brought out the color of his eyes.

Tom introduced himself and Charlotte, and explained that they had been sent over by Diana Nelson.

"Come in, come in," said Jason. "Diana just called. She said you would be coming over. "Jason Armentrout," he said, extending his hand.

Charlotte and Tom entered the room, which had enormous windows overlooking City Hall. A beat-up old couch stood against one wall, a stack of canvases against the other. Several works-in-progress were propped up on easels.

"This is a beautiful building," offered Charlotte by way of an opening.

"It was at one time," Jason replied. "I'm afraid it's going to wrack and ruin." He pointed to a hole in the ceiling where the plaster had fallen down. "It's for sale: two hundred and fifty thousand dollars."

"Two hundred and fifty thousand for this entire building!" exclaimed Tom. "There are lots of places you couldn't buy a house for that."

"That's right. Gives you an idea of the sorry state of Paterson commercial real estate, doesn't it? It means cheap rent for artists, though. I understand that you want to know about Randy. Doing an article or something."

Tom pulled out a copy of *Diner Monthly*. "I put out this magazine. I'd like to do something on him for it."

Jason studied the magazine for a minute, and then checked

his watch. "I'd like to help you. But I was just on my way out—to le Club Parisienne. It's right downstairs. I'm working on a painting there. Have you eaten lunch yet?"

"No, and we're starving, or at least I am," said Tom.

"Good. Then you can eat while I work."

Le Club Parisienne was a go-go bar. It was also in the Columbia Bank building, but around the corner from the Colt Street entrance. For a go-go bar, it was quite respectable-looking, with a red canvas marquee that stretched out to the curb, and a heavy wooden door with polished brass trim. On the wall next to the door hung a sign advertising the luncheon specials: boeuf bourguignon, breaded veal cutlet, braised calamari Provençale, and, as a sop to the locals, Great Falls Salad. On the opposite side of the door was a sign with a martini glass, the words "Girls, girls, girls," and three framed black-and-white head and bust shots of the girls in their costumes. Their names were written in flowing script underneath, along with the themes of their acts. Not content with being mere topless dancers, these go-go girls had developed acts reflecting their native cultures. Chantal, a black woman in a leopard pelt, represented Africa; Yolanda, an Hispanic woman in a feathered serpent headdress, represented Central America; and Mariette, who wore a rhinestone choker and a bonnet with an enormous brim, represented France. At last! Ethnic pride had come to the go-go lounge.

"I now see what Diana meant when she said 'of sorts,' " said Tom as they stood in front of the door, through which they could hear the muffled pounding of a jungle beat. He looked at Charlotte. "Are you ready for this?"

She nodded. "Sounds like Chantal must be on," she said. Reaching into her pocketbook, she pulled out a scarf and some dark glasses. This was not the kind of place in which she wanted to be recognized.

"The food's great," said Jason with a smile, which revealed a handsome set of straight, white teeth.

After holding the door open for them, he followed them in, and was greeted by a mustachioed maitre d'. "Hello, Louie," Jason said, embracing him warmly. Then he turned to Charlotte and Tom: "I'd like a table for my friends here."

Nodding assent, Louie led them past a long bar to a dining room at the back. At one side was a mirrored stage, which was separated from the audience by a brass rail. On stage was a not-so-young woman with dyed blond hair whom Charlotte recognized from her photograph as Yolanda. She was naked except for a G-string and the headdress, which would have done Quetzalcoatl proud. As she rotated her breasts in time to the music, the loose flesh swinging around like the balls on a gaucho's bola, the patrons watched with jaded detachment. They were mostly businessmen, with a few blue-collar types thrown in. There were even a couple of tables of secretaries, neatly made-up Hispanic girls who were doing their best to ignore the entertainment.

Charlotte's acquaintanceship with go-go establishments was limited, but she suspected this place could have been worse. It clearly aspired to some degree of refinement. Actually, it must have been quite elegant in the days when its customers were Paterson's bankers and business leaders. The theme was Second Empire, with the decor running to intricately carved walnut woodwork and oversized mirrors with ornate gilded frames. And although the woodwork was scarred and the burgundy paint was flaking, the crisply starched tablecloths and vases of fresh flowers showed that someone still cared.

The maitre d' showed them to their table, which was in the row farthest away from the stage, in deference to her age and sex, Charlotte suspected. Jason had lingered behind to talk with one of the customers at the bar.

"Is this your first visit to Le Club Parisienne?" Louie asked. He pulled out a chair for Charlotte, and then spread her napkin on her lap, clearly pleased at the novelty of serving someone he sensed was a lady of the old school.

"Yes," Tom replied, "Has the club been here long?"

"Sixty-five years. Le Club Parisienne was once famous. Frank Sinatra used to sing here, Tony Bennett. They both sang here when they were starting out—Sinatra was a Hoboken boy, you know—but they kept coming back, even after they became famous. Ed McNamara. You would be too young to remember Ed McNamara," he said to Tom. He turned to Charlotte: "But maybe the lady would."

"Of course I remember Ed McNamara," she said. "The Singing Cop."

"See?" he said with a broad smile. "He was from Paterson. The great American contralto, Madame Schumann-Heink, who lived here, discovered him. She brought him to the attention of Enrico Caruso, who took him on as a pupil. He was the only pupil Caruso ever had."

"Is that so?" said Tom, making the obligatory comment.

"Those were the good old days," the maitre d' continued. "The movie premieres at the Fabian: the klieg lights, the hoopla, the stars. All the stars came to Paterson back then: Bette Davis, Rosalind Russell, Gary Cooper, Linc Crawford, Charlotte Graham . . ."

"Charlotte Graham," interjected Tom with a devilish grin. "She was my favorite. I wonder what she's doing these days?"

"My favorite too," said the maitre d'. He rolled his eyes to the ceiling. "Those legs, ooh la la."

At that moment, Charlotte was using one of them to kick Tom.

"She's still working," Louie continued. "I saw her in a TV movie not long ago. She looked great. Unfortunately, Paterson doesn't attract that kind of talent anymore," he added with a rueful smile. "Now we have"—he cast a sidelong glance at the stage, and rolled his eyes—"a different kind of attraction."

As a holdover from the old days, Louie clearly didn't approve.

"Your waiter will be with you in a moment to take your order," he announced with a little bow. Then he departed to fuss over another customer.

The waiter arrived momentarily: a young man in a white apron that reached almost to the ground, in the style of waiters in French brasseries.

Jason arrived right behind him, taking the seat next to Charlotte, which faced the stage. "We'd like a bowl of olives," Jason told the young man. "And I'd like to buy my guests a drink. What will you have?" he asked.

After they had given the waiter their orders, Tom turned to Jason. "I guess you're a regular here," he said.

"I'm here every day, or close to it. This place is my muse, the way the Falls View was Randy's." He pointed at the easel that stood at one side of the stage. "Now that I think about it, they both appeal to a sense of fantasy: a go-go bar to a fantasy about sex; a diner to a fantasy about security."

"We saw your paintings at the Ivanhoe, but I confess that I didn't really look at them that closely," said Charlotte. They had left her with a Moulin Rouge impression, reminding her of Toulouse-Lautrec's cancan dancers. "We were really there just to talk with Diana. Are you a photorealist too?"

"You didn't look? Tsk. Tsk." He shook his head in mock disapproval. "A realist, but not a photorealist. In the great tradition of American realists like Edward Hopper and George Bellows." He raised a hand in demurral. "Not that I put myself in the same league."

After rotating her breasts at a dizzying speed to a musical finale that sounded like an accordion rendition of the "Flight of the Bumblebee," Miss Quetzalcoatl retreated backstage. Louie, who also served as master of ceremonies, announced a break before the next act.

"Would you like to see the painting I'm working on now?" Jason asked. "Now's a good time. Before Mariette comes on."

Charlotte and Tom said that they would.

He led them over to his easel, on which a large canvas was propped. In the foreground were the dark, looming silhouettes of the customers. In the rear, bathed in a warm, rosy glow, was the dancer with the rhinestone choker and the enormous bonnet, wearing several layers of black crinolines and little else.

The painting was executed competently enough, but Charlotte was more taken with the way in which the rich texture had transformed the down-at-the-heels atmosphere of this seedy go-go bar into something warm and filled with promise.

"I'm calling it 'La Vie en Rose,' " Jason said.

"After the Edith Piaf song?" asked Charlotte.

Jason nodded. "The life through rose-colored glasses," he said, translating the title. "Do you like it?"

"Very much," she replied. "Who would have expected to find a little slice of Montmartre in downtown Paterson?"

"Paterson is a very interesting place. You can find a little slice of just about anything here. I know that's what they say about New York too. But in New York, it's more diffuse: New

York must have hundreds of go-go bars with pretentions, but Paterson has only one. Do you know the poem *Paterson*?"

Charlotte and Tom shook their heads, again.

"There's a line in that poem that captures the special feeling of Paterson." He proceeded to recite the line: " 'The mystery of streets and back rooms—wiping the nose on sleeves, come here to dream . . . ' "

It was the same line that Diana had quoted.

"How did you get into painting go-go bars?" asked Charlotte as they threaded their way back to their table, where their drinks were waiting: a beer for Tom, a Manhattan for Charlotte, and a Pernod for Jason. There was also a small bowl filled with Spanish olives.

"By painting the girls, literally. When I was starting out years ago, I worked at a topless bar called Mickey's Paint Factory, where the girls' breasts were painted with cartoon figures: Mickey Mouse, Donald Duck. I was the one who painted them." He chuckled at the memory. "I needed a job, and they needed an artist." He paused to take a packet of cigarettes out of his shirt pocket. They were unfiltered French Gauloises.

Charlotte noticed that the blue of the packet exactly matched the blue of his eyes. Which may have been the idea.

"Anyway, that's when I first got into the scene. After that, I'd hang out in topless bars sometimes. Then, when I took my studio here, I discovered this place. I've been coming here ever since. Look at this"—he fingered the fringe of the red-silk moire lamp on their table—"you could be in Paris."

The waiter reappeared with menus, which he set in front of them, along with a basket of fresh French bread, which smelled delicious.

"The dancers here are different too," said Jason. He broke a piece of bread off for himself, and passed the basket. "Most of them date from the days of burlesque. They can remember when dancing was an art form. They make an effort; they aren't here just to push drinks."

Charlotte hadn't noticed that the last performance was particularly artful, but she supposed the feathered headdress counted for something.

"Take Mariette, the dancer who's the subject of my current series. She teaches exotic dancing at an adult school. She takes what she does very seriously." He took a sip of the yellow-colored aperitif. "Anyway, you didn't want to know about me; you wanted to know about Randy. What can I tell you?"

For a few minutes, they chatted about Randy—the same sort of information that Diana had given them, and then the conversation drifted, or rather, was directed by Tom, to the murder.

"A lot of people didn't like Randy," Jason said. "They were turned off by his ego. But I discounted that as coming from the lonely, scared little boy inside. And, like a little boy, he could be very loyal and loving. I don't understand why anyone would kill him. Even to those who didn't like him, he was just a minor annoyance. On the order of a hangnail or a mosquito bite."

"Diana told us that you considered him your friend," said Charlotte. "But she also said that even you were losing patience with him."

"Yeah, I was. He kept borrowing money and never paid it back. It wasn't that he didn't have it—he had a lot more than I do—but he was so strung out that he couldn't keep his finances straight. Once I found a six-month-old check for twenty-eight thousand dollars lying around his studio. Finally it got to the point where I told him I wasn't going to loan him money anymore."

"What about Bernice Spiegel?" asked Charlotte. "Would you say that he was only a minor annoyance to her."

"Most of all to Bernice. Bernice is about to inherit sixty million dollars. Not only will she be sitting pretty financially, but she can also look forward to lifetime employment in the job she loves: the keeper of the eternal flame at the grave of Donald Edgar Spiegel. It's hard to imagine that she'd jeopardize all that by having a pest like Randy thrown in the drink."

Then Tom asked him about Randy's behavior in recent months.

"Very strange," said Jason as he lit a cigarette. "I attributed it to the drugs. Or else he was just plain losing his mind."

The fragrance of the rich tobacco drifted across the table. It smelled almost as good as the bread, and Charlotte had to fight down the urge to bum a cigarette. Though she didn't smoke much—she had cut back to half a pack a day years ago—she was now trying to quit completely.

"Diana said you saw him freak out on a couple of occasions."

"Yeah. The first time was last January at a show at the Koreman Gallery. He started twitching all over. It reminded me of the way a horse twitches its skin to shake loose a horse fly. The men in the white coats ended up taking him away to Bellevue. The diagnosis was cocaine-induced paranoia."

"Why paranoia?" asked Tom as he popped an olive into his mouth.

"Because he kept talking about someone from the past coming back to get him. The second time was also at a show. At the Montclair Art Museum. The same thing: the heebie-jeebies, the fear that someone was after him. He'd been talking about going into rehab, but . . ." He shrugged, and took a long puff on his cigarette.

"Do you know what it was exactly that set off the attack? Did he see something, or someone perhaps?" Charlotte asked.

Jason shrugged again. "I don't know," he said. "The paintings? But why would anything in a painting cause someone to react like that? Believe me, I've thought about it. Especially since I found out that he'd been murdered."

"What do you mean?"

"That maybe someone *was* out to get him."

As Jason had informed them, the food was delicious. Charlotte and Tom both chose the breaded veal cutlet, which could have matched that served at any top-notch French bistro (and which was light years away from hot Texas wieners). But Jason's judgment when it came to the entertainment was not on as firm a footing. The Magnificent Mariette, as she was billed, did a Folies-Bergère act that consisted of a lot of high kicking while wearing only a black G-string and a black garter belt attached to black stockings under her voluminous black crinolines. It was tame enough stuff (the notorious crotch shots of Busby Berkeley, the premier Hollywood musical director of the thirties, had been only slightly less titillating) but it was hardly high art, despite Mariette's qualifications as an adult-school authority on exotic dancing.

Charlotte emerged into the bright glare of early afternoon convinced that Jason's fascination for the Bohemian subculture of Paris during la Belle Epoque belonged in the same psychological niche as Randy's for classic diners of the nineteen thirties and forties, and wondering if Jason's father had been a salesman who left him in go-go bars while he called on customers.

"Well, that was interesting," said Tom with a little smirk as they paused on the sidewalk outside the building to study the photographs. " 'Straight from Paris,' " he read. " 'The Magnificent Mariette.' I wonder what Diana thinks of Jason's little hobby?"

"So you caught that too: the Pernod and the olives."

"And the quote from William Carlos Williams," added Tom.

"I think it's pretty safe to conclude they're an item." She looked over at him. "Which is too bad for you."

"It's true, she's my type," he said. Then he smiled. "But there's always Yolanda." He checked his watch. "It's going on two. What do you want to do now? Go back to see Voorhees, or head back to the city?"

"I'd like to see him, but not to tell him what we've found out. He already knows about Bernice, and I don't want to tell him what Jason just told us about Randy going berserk at the other art shows until we check it out. But I would like to see him: to see what he can tell *us*."

"You mean, to find out what 'exactly zip,' is."

Charlotte nodded.

"Maybe we should call first to see if he's in." Tom went back inside to call, and returned a moment later: "He says to meet him at the Gryphon Mill. He's on his way over there now." Then he added, nodding toward the inside: "If you thought Yolanda was a hoot, you should see the one who's on now."

Charlotte looked at the publicity still. "It must be Chantal," she said. " 'Straight from the jungles of East Africa.' "

"Of the leopard headdress and clawed mittens," said Tom. "And the tail with the pompon," he added. "She looks like the Cowardly Lion in drag."

"I'm so sorry I'm going to miss her act."

Except for being only two stories instead of three or four, the Gryphon was a typical Paterson mill: a red brick structure pierced with rows of enormous windows that had allowed mill workers to take advantage of the natural light and ventilation. Except for the relief sculpture of the gryphon, a creature with the head and wings of an eagle and the body of a lion, over the front door, the building was devoid of ornament. But the love, understanding, and skill of the craftsmen who had built it had resulted in a structure with great eloquence.

After parking once again in the lot across the street, which was meant for overflow parking for visitors to the Falls, they crossed the street and waited for Voorhees out in front.

He pulled up a minute later in an unmarked police car, followed by a police cruiser driven by an officer whom Voorhees introduced a few minutes later as his assistant, Bill Martinez. He was a young man in his early twenties with a pleasant face and a small William Powell-type mustache.

"You've been holding out on us," said Charlotte good-naturedly once the introductions had been dispensed with.

"Who me?" said Voorhees, a meaty hand spread over his chest.

"You didn't tell us a word about the dispute between Randy and Bernice Spiegel," she said accusingly.

"I wanted to see what you would find out. What did you find out?"

Charlotte proceeded to recap what Diana had told them, leaving out their trip to le Club Parisienne. Though she thought Randy's death might have been linked to his attack of nerves, she doubted that Voorhees did, and she didn't want her theory dismissed before she'd had a chance to pursue it.

"Now, what do you know that you haven't told us?" she asked.

"Only that we think the victim was thrown in the river behind the Falls View. There was a particular kind of vegetation caught in the aprons that he was tied up with and in the backs of his sneakers, which only grows in a few places along the river, one of them being behind the Falls View." He consulted his notes: "*Polygonum cuspidatum*, commonly known as Japanese knotweed."

Charlotte was familiar with it: a tall weed, reaching a height of eight or ten feet, with hollow, jointed stems, and a pale, greenish-white flower. It was common in New England, where she had grown up. Cultivated by the early settlers, it had become a vicious weed that was practically impossible to eradicate, as she had once discovered. "I know it," she said. "But we always called it bamboo."

"Another name for it is Japanese bamboo," Voorhees said. "It's native to Japan. The medical examiner theorized that the victim had been dragged shoulders-first through this bamboo before he was tossed in. We found the probable site this morning: a path from the parking lot to the river bank where the stalks had been laid flat. The intake for the raceway system is only fifty feet down river from there."

"Any other evidence at the site?" asked Tom

"Only some vomitus at the edge of the parking lot. We figured the victim may have thrown up before he passed out. Unless he'd eaten something really distinctive like blueberry pie, which he didn't, there's no way to tell if it was his vomitus. But it's a good bet that it was his puke and that the place where the bamboo was flattened was where he went in. The nearest place this bamboo stuff grows is three-quarters of a mile up river."

"Do we know who else was at the diner?" asked Charlotte.

"We're working on that. But suffice it to say that we'll have no shortage of suspects. The guest list for the post-opening party runs to about twenty-five people. Plus there's the diner staff."

As he spoke, another car drove up and parked behind the police cruiser. A woman got out and headed down the street toward them. She was a middle-aged woman, carefully made-up and with straight black hair in a Cleopatra cut. She wore a simple, expensively cut black suit, and a white silk blouse.

"Bernice Spiegel," Voorhees explained. "She's why we're here. She claims that the paintings that her brother gave to Goslau—the ones that were the subject of the legal dispute— have been stolen." He looked over at his assistant. "Brace yourself, Martinez. I think we're about to catch some shit."

Bernice was walking very fast, with her hands clenched at her sides. Her head, which was square in shape, was thrust forward, and the skin on her forehead was pinched in a frown. Charlotte was reminded of Diana's reference to a pit bull. Had she been on a leash, she would have broken it.

"My paintings are missing," she shrieked as she drew near. "They are worth eight million dollars." By now, she was face to face with Voorhees. "Did you hear me?" she said, thrusting her face into his and pointing her forefinger at his chest. "Eight million dollars. You were supposed to be guarding them."

Now that she was closer, Charlotte recognized her as the woman who had made the remark at the opening about Randy going off the deep end again.

"If you don't recover them," she threatened. "I am going to sue the city of Paterson for every last cent of their value."

Taking her gently by the arm, Voorhees steered her to a bench on the brick sidewalk. "Now, Ms. Spiegel," he said quietly as he took a seat next to her, "Why don't you tell us all about it?"

Bernice glared at him.

"Well, if you're not going to cooperate, we might as well go home." He looked up. "What do you say, Martinez? We have better things to do."

Martinez made a move toward the car.

"Okay," said Bernice. She took a deep breath, and then spoke. "I know that you told me that the studio would be protected, but I was worried about the paintings. All those people going in and out; somebody could so easily have walked off with one of them. So this afternoon I came over . . ."

"When was that?" asked Voorhees.

"Just a little while ago. I asked the police officer who was guarding the door if I could just take a peek. When I looked in, none of the paintings was there." She clenched her eyes shut for a second, as if reliving the painful experience, and then sighed. "I couldn't believe it."

"Ms. Spiegel, there are paintings there. I saw them myself."

"Those are Randy's paintings. I'm talking about my brother's paintings. There were twelve of them: they were hanging on the back wall. Lieutenant, those paintings are worth eight million dollars."

"I know," he said. "You already told me." He sighed, and stood up. Then he introduced her first to Martinez, and then to Charlotte and Tom. She was too upset to question what

Charlotte and Tom were doing there. Finally he said: "Why don't we go take a look?"

He then led them down an alley between the mill and the neighboring building, a small brick Victorian house. At the rear of the mill, a cop was sitting on a chair next to a door. At the sight of Voorhees, he sprang to attention. "Hello, Lieutenant," he said. He eyed Bernice warily; she must have given him a piece of her mind too.

Voorhees proceeded to grill the cop on the arrangements for guarding the premises. According to the cop, the building had been "secured at all times" since the discovery of the body. Then they entered the building. The door opened onto a stairwell, at one end of which was a thick metal door—the door that Bernice had had installed to keep Randy out of the rest of the building. Then they went upstairs to Randy's second-floor studio apartment.

The first thing to strike Charlotte's eye was the yellowing eviction notice hanging on the door. The next was the TV monitor whose lens was aimed at the door. There was also a burglar alarm system, which Martinez deactivated. Randy must have been very afraid of break-ins. The door opened onto a large space that ran the full width of the back of the building. To their right was a small kitchen and living area, and at the far end was the door to a bedroom.

"The paintings were here," said Bernice. She led them over to the interior wall, and pointed to a series of hooks surrounded by faded rectangles marking the spots where the paintings had once hung.

"And those?" said Voorhees, nodding at the paintings on the far wall.

"Those are Randy's diner paintings," she replied icily.

Voorhees sauntered down to the end of the studio, and stuck his head in the bedroom door. "Those are Randy's paintings in there, too," said Bernice. "I looked everywhere," she added as he wandered around, peeking in closets and behind couches and bookshelves.

"We'll have to go through all of these papers," said Voorhees as he passed a desk in the living area. He nodded to Martinez, who made a note. Then he pulled out an album from a rack of half a dozen on the desk, and opened it. "Will you look at these!" he said, as he leafed through the pages.

"That's his collection of old diner postcards," said Bernice.

"Is that right?" said Tom casually as he flew to Voorhees' side.

"How about the rest of the building?" asked Voorhees as he idly riffled through the rest of the papers on the desk, leaving Tom to the postcard albums. "Or in your brother's house. Could he have hung them somewhere else?"

"I don't know." The police officer wouldn't let me look. He couldn't have put them downstairs after I installed the steel door, but he might have done it before."

"Can you describe some of the missing paintings?"

"Yes. The biggest was 'Horn & Hardart.' It was of the interior: a close-up of the shiny little stainless steel doors with the windows for viewing the food. Then there was one of the W. R. Grace Building, and one of the towers of the Brooklyn Bridge . . ."

"Okay," said Voorhees, "We'll go take a look."

Led by Bernice, the four of them toured the rest of the building, which was divided into a large living area, a cavernous studio, and a second-story mezzanine, which overlooked the studio. None of the missing paintings was hanging on the walls, nor were they in the storage rooms.

Next they toured Spiegel's house, the little brick Victorian that had formerly been the mill superintendent's residence. The living area in the mill had been Spiegel's public living space—the scene of the ongoing party that Diana had described—but this little house was where he had actually lived. The paintings weren't there, either.

"Okay," said Voorhees after they had completed their tour. "I think we can conclude that the paintings aren't here. Which means one of two things: either Goslau disposed of them before his death, or someone broke into his studio and stole them."

They were standing on a small patio at the rear of Spiegel's house. It reminded Charlotte of the garden of her own townhouse: a little oasis of green in the midst of the urban congestion.

"Since the studio has been guarded since his death, we'll work on the first assumption," said Voorhees. He had taken a seat on one of the patio chairs. Leaning back, he rubbed his neck. Then he asked, "Is there anywhere else that Goslau might have stored the paintings?"

"Out at his camp," said Bernice, who had finally calmed down. "It's out in Warren County, near the Pennsylvania line. I doubt he would have displayed them there—they were too valuable to hang in a place that was unoccupied most of the time—but he might have hidden them out there."

"Why would he have hidden them?" asked Voorhees.

"He might have been afraid that I was going to take them."

"Had you threatened to?"

"Yes. They're mine. My brother was planning to rescind the gift agreement under which he had given Randy the paintings. He told me so."

"But he hadn't done so at the time of his death," said Voorhees, adopting a chastising tone. "Moreover, they were the subject of a legal dispute."

"No, he hadn't," replied Bernice, subdued.

"Is there anywhere else that Goslau might have hidden the paintings?"

"Not that I know of."

"Is there a possibility that he may have sold them?"

"The court ruled that they weren't to be sold until after the settlement," said Bernice, "But he might have sold them anyway. In recent months, there was no predicting what he might do."

"Okay," said Voorhees. "Here's what we're going to do. I presume that a detailed description of the works in question was drawn up in connection with the lawsuit: title, size, description, and so on."

Bernice nodded.

"Do you have a copy of it?"

She nodded again.

"Martinez here will follow you home, and you'll give him a copy. We'll notify the art squad in New York that the paintings are missing. Once we get the list, we'll send it along, and they can notify galleries to be on the lookout for the missing pieces."

"What if they went overseas? Don had collectors in Europe and Japan."

"The art squad will also notify the FBI, which will notify Interpol. Meanwhile, I'll go out to Goslau's country place and look for the paintings. I was thinking about going out there anyway. I'll let you know as soon as I get back what I've found."

After a few more minutes of discussion, Bernice got into her car to leave. After closing the door for her, Voorhees handed her his business card through the window and said: "If you think of anywhere else the paintings could be, give me a call."

Seemingly satisfied, Bernice took the card with an effort at a smile.

Charlotte was impressed at how well he had handled her, but she supposed he'd had years of training in dealing with irate people.

After Bernice had driven off, followed by Martinez in the police cruiser, Voorhees rejoined Charlotte and Tom in front of the mill. Stretching out his arms, and sniffing the sweet air, he said: "Anyone for a ride out to the country?" He looked over at Tom. "Maybe we'll find a good diner along the way."

Charlotte didn't need to check first with Tom to see what his answer would be. She could already sense a new book in the works.

"Where exactly is Randy's country place?" Tom asked.

"Blairstown," Voorhees replied. "Out near the Water Gap."

Tom's eyes gleamed. "I know just the one."

· 6 ·

TOM AND CHARLOTTE followed Voorhees in the Buick. It took them a little over an hour to get to Randy's camp, which was at the end of a long, winding dirt road on the wooded banks of the Beaver River—in western New Jersey. What had once been a fishing camp—the kind of weekend retreat where New York stockbrokers used to go to drink and spit to their heart's content—had been transformed into a rustic trailer park for old diners. As Randy had already told them, there were five of them, arrayed in a semicircle around the original building, a log cabin lodge with a fieldstone chimney that looked as if it dated from the twenties. There were two diners on one side, these set fairly high above the water, and two on the other side, lower down. The fifth, the diminutive Short Stop, was set on a small island in the river, which was reached by a wooden bridge. Neatly manicured gravel paths led from one building to the other, and the woodsy grounds were beautifully land-scaped with plantings of native trees and shrubs interspersed with flower beds of zinnias and marigolds. The effect was peculiar in the extreme: it reminded Charlotte of the tourist courts, the predecessors of modern motels, that could still be found on old highways, except that these structures were sided with stainless steel and porcelain enamel instead of clapboard or rough-hewn logs.

"This is my idea of a summer place!" Tom exclaimed as they got out of the car and studied the shining buildings. "The neon must look wonderful at night against the leaves. Look at that one," he said, pointing at the sign for one of the diners on their left: the RED ROBIN. The name was followed by three robins that probably lit up in succession to give the image of a robin bob, bob, bobbing along. "I wonder if they all work."

Charlotte looked up. "There are electric lines running to all of them."

"We'll have to ask Voorhees if we can come back at night."

Voorhees was standing with his hands on his hips, looking around. Then he turned and walked over to them. He walked with a rolling gait, like a sailor who isn't entirely comfortable on dry land. "I thought I'd seen it all, but this is a new one on me."

"I think it's great," said Tom.

"Each to his own," said Voorhees, shaking his head.

"I know some of these diners," Tom announced with the pleasure of someone who's accidentally come across an old friend. "That one, the C & E, used to be in Pawtucket, Rhode Island. And that one, the Silver Spoon, used to be in Burlington, Vermont. They were listed for sale in *Diner Monthly*. I guess that's how Randy found out about them."

Voorhees was studying the ring of keys he held in his hand.

"Where do we start?" asked Charlotte.

"They're all labeled. Let's see," he said, picking out two of the keys. "Plummer, why don't you take the two on the right." He handed Tom the keys to the Silver Spoon and the Tastee. "Miss Graham can take the C & E, the Red Robin, and the Short Stop," he added, handing Charlotte three more keys, "and I'll take the lodge."

"Do you think there's an alarm system?" asked Charlotte.

"I was just getting to that." He fished around in his coat pocket. "Martinez got the code from the alarm company." He pulled out a scrap of paper. "It's 2031. The panels should be just inside each of the doors."

Charlotte chose to visit the C & E first. She liked the looks of it. It was a small, shiny, jewel-like diner with a barrel roof.

It turned out to be Randy's living quarters, and she could readily see why he had chosen it for this purpose. It had a J-shaped counter, the area beyond the curve of the J making a natural space for a bed. The rest had been remodeled into a living area, with a banquette under the front windows, and shelving under the counters.

Although it was fascinating as a study of adaptive reuse—who would have thought of using a mirrored pie case for a bookshelf?—it didn't tell her much. Most of the possessions were practical ones: a TV and a stereo system, a blender and some other kitchen gadgets; some fishing gear. The only art was an old photo of the C & E.

As she was leaving, Charlotte noticed an area nearby that had been recently cleared by a bulldozer. Inspecting it, she found that a road had been bulldozed through the woods. Remembering that Randy had talked about having a particular diner in mind to add to his collection, she concluded that this must be its future site.

Next she checked out the Red Robin, which was one of the diners that Randy had described as undergoing restoration. It was a mess: half the stools were missing, the interior stainless was pitted and rusted, and the woodwork looked like someone had used it as a punching bag. Seeing it, Charlotte was struck by how much work must have gone into restoring the C & E.

The third diner, the Short Stop, was a dinette, one of the mini-diners that had been built after the war for ex-GI's who had learned to cook in the Army, and who didn't have the money to invest in something bigger. The stainless steel bands on the exterior alternated with bands of pink enamel to match the color of the sign, which featured an arrow pointing downward at the entrance.

The C & E and the Red Robin had yielded nothing in terms of clues, but at the Short Stop, she struck pay dirt.

The Short Stop was the diner that Randy said he'd just acquired for a guest house. It was a guest house all right, but for a particular guest: a guest whose taste for hot-pink matched the neon sign and the enameled stripes between the stainless steel banding. In short, the Short Stop was Xantha and Randy's love nest. Xan and Ran, how cute.

"The Short Stop," Charlotte repeated, laughing to herself at the aptness of the name. Taking a seat in a chair covered in imitation zebra skin, she studied the interior. It was a sight to behold.

Unlike that of the C & E, the interior of the Short Stop had been gutted to make one big bedroom whose decor, in both color and style, matched the pink-on-white cloud pattern of the Formica walls. It was all fifties high-camp, with a ruffled pink satin bedspread, an elaborate dressing table whose mirrored surface was covered with makeup containers and perfume bottles, and lamps in the shape of French poodles with pink tulle shades.

Swallowing her qualms about the propriety of snooping around, Charlotte boldly peeked into the closet. Any uncertainty about the identity of the occupant was erased by a glance at its contents. Almost all of the garments bore the Xantha Price label.

Hearing a step behind her, she turned around. It was Voorhees: he was standing in the glass-block entryway, an expression of astonishment on his broad face. "Holy moly," he said. "What the hell have we got here?"

"I think it's what you'd call a love nest," she said.

"The Short Stop," he said. "He couldn't have picked a diner with a more suitable name. Maybe we can add it to the nooner and the quickie as a slang expression for the hasty sex act."

"He could have chosen the Tastee," she joked.

Voorhees chuckled.

"Look at this," she said. She gestured for him to join her at the closet, where she showed him the label in a beaded sweater dress. "I wonder what Arthur Lumkin would think about this."

" 'Xantha Price,' " he read. He looked over at her, and then raised his hands in an expression of bafflement. "Okay, I give up. Who is Arthur Lumkin and what does he have to do with the label in a dress?"

"Arthur Lumkin is a prominent investment banker who is very, very rich," she explained. "Xantha Price is a British fashion designer. She is also Lumkin's wife, and, it most certainly appears, Randy's lover."

"I remember now," he said, nodding his bald head. "They were at the opening; you and Plummer met them there."

"They're art collectors. They had loaned a painting to the museum for the diner exhibit—one of Randy's, I might add. Randy told me at the opening that they owned nine of his paintings."

"I knew there was a reason I asked you to help out in this

investigation. Well, at least we now have one suspect: the husband." He scanned the interior: "No paintings, I presume."

"Not that I've found. Either here or at the C & E or the Red Robin."

"None at the lodge, either." He looked at his watch. "It's going on six. What do you say to some dinner?"

Charlotte agreed, and they joined Tom outside the lodge. He had found paintings—one of the diners he had checked out was being used by Randy as a studio—but they were all Randy's own.

After checking out the C & E again—Tom just had to see it—they regrouped in the parking area. "Where's that diner you were talking about?" asked Voorhees. "I'm getting hungry."

"Follow me," Tom responded.

Their destination was the Sunrise Diner in Blairstown, whose sign boasted "Great Coffee." It was a classic diner that had been ruined, at least as far as Tom was concerned, by the addition of a dining room on the back. Though it had never actually achieved the august rank of perfect diner, it had—prior to the addition of the dining room—been a contender for that title, and it still ranked among the best in Tom's estimation. Among the features that elevated the Sunrise above the ordinary were the hand-lettered sign above the grill, which said: "There are only two places to eat breakfast: here and at home"; the homey note provided by the blue- and white-checked tieback curtains; the view overlooking the municipal ball field; and the specialty of the house, a simple roast chicken.

Last but not least among the diner's winning features was the waitress, Lorraine Kelly. Lorraine was the subject of one of Tom's diner stories, which he regaled them with once they were comfortably settled in a booth with a view of the Little League game-in-progress.

"Her husband was an interstate truck driver, and she used to go along on trips with him sometimes," he said. "They lived in the Midwest. Dubuque, I think. Anyway, they were eating here when he excused himself to go to the bathroom. He never came back."

"What do you mean?" asked Voorhees. "Somebody offed him in the john?"

"No. He got in his truck and took off for parts unknown. Lorraine was stranded here. She didn't even have her pocketbook. She'd left it on the front seat of the truck. All she had was a plate of lasagna and a cup of coffee."

"What did she do?"

"Nick, the owner, took pity on her. Put her up at his house. She waited for her husband to come back, but he never did. She tried to track him down, with no success. So she went to work for Nick. She figured she didn't have anything to go back to Dubuque for."

"How did you find all this out?" asked Voorhees.

It was a question Charlotte didn't need to ask. Tom was always finding out things like this. Complete strangers would tell him their life stories. He said it was simple: he just asked.

"Lorraine and I had a long talk one day. She's been working here now for seventeen years." He added: "Every diner has a story."

"And Tom can tell you four hundred and eleven of them," said Charlotte. "Show the lieutenant your diner log book," she urged him.

Tom obliged by pulling out a small notebook, and handing it to Voorhees.

"Four hundred and fourteen," he corrected. "These are my field notes. I write the information down in here: the name; the location; the specialty; the former names, if any; the date that I visited; and whether it was operating, defunct, for sale, or what. Then I put the data in my computer. It's an obsession," he confessed. "I like to think of myself as a normal person, but in reality"—he grinned good-naturedly—"I'm a sickie."

"If a week goes by in which Tom hasn't visited a diner, he starts getting separation anxiety," said Charlotte, "which is expressed in the form of an overwhelming craving for tube steaks and french fries."

"Speaking of which . . ." said Tom, looking up at the waitress.

She was a middle-aged woman with long, dyed-black hair; black penciled-on eyebrows; and a smile as warm and sweet as a slice of hot apple pie. Her husband must have been a real cad to have left her.

"Hello, Tom," she said. "Nice to see you again." She took her order pad out of her apron pocket. "What can I get for you?"

They gave her their orders—three beers (the Sunrise was fortunate in being a diner with a liquor license) and three roast chicken dinners, and then returned to the conversation about diners.

"Right now I'm suffering from another diner-related malady," Tom said. "A case of diner-envy. I confess to having a deep desire to possess the C & E. It's a fantasy of mine to live in a diner."

"What do you mean! You're already halfway there," said Charlotte. She explained to Voorhees how the kitchen table in Tom's apartment was a diner booth, complete with a wallbox and a large EAT sign in red, white, and yellow neon mounted on the wall above it.

Voorhees, who had been leafing through Tom's log book, proceeded to read an entry: " 'The Orange Diner. Main Street, West Orange.' Hey, I know that diner. It's a nice little place." He went on: "I must admit that I have a soft spot for diners myself. I spend a lot of time on the road with my daughter. We eat in diners whenever we can."

"Aha," said Tom. "Another closet diner freak. They're all over the place. I had a suspicion that you might be a fellow traveler when I saw your interest in Randy's postcard collection. Here's my stock question," he said. "I ask it of everyone who admits to a weakness for diners. What specifically is it about diners that you love?"

"Well, they're cheap and the food's usually pretty good. But that's not entirely it." Voorhees thought for a moment, and then said: "The food, the service, the sense of comfort. But most of all it's this." He ran his big hand over a place where a tear in the upholstery had been patched, and then over a spot in the Formica tabletop where the pattern had been worn away.

"The sense of humanity," said Tom.

"Yeah, I guess that's it," he said. "These worn places make me think of all the people who've been here before me: the warmth, the laughs, the confidences." He thought for a minute. "A diner booth is like an old shoe or an easy chair: it has a sense of history."

"Well-said," pronounced Tom as Lorraine delivered their beers. Picking up his mug, he hoisted it in a toast: "To diners everywhere!"

After they had drunk to diners and their devotees, Voorhees asked Charlotte to fill him in on the Lumkins.

Charlotte and Tom had just been discussing them in the car. She now repeated what she had just told him. "They've been married for ten or twelve years. He was married once before, she twice. Her real name is Geraldine; she only became Xantha shortly before she married Arthur."

"The name's sort of a wash, isn't it?" said Tom. "Whatever she gained by becoming a Xantha she lost when she became a Lumkin."

Charlotte smiled, and then continued: "Xantha changed Arthur's life. Before he met her, he was a millionaire without a purpose in life."

"A millionaire without a purpose in life," Voorhees repeated. "I really feel for the guy, you know what I mean?"

"He had been interested in buying art," Charlotte went on, "but he didn't know how to go about it. What to buy, who to buy it from, how much to pay. Xantha opened up a new world to him. She was a collector of contemporary art. Have you ever seen a picture of her?"

Voorhees shook his head as he sipped the head off his beer.

"Hot-pink spiked hair; dramatic eye makeup; four-inch heels; low-cut dresses that show off her décolletage."

"Not exactly the shy and retiring type."

"But the perfect match for a shy, insecure millionaire. I'll tell you a story I once heard about Arthur. This took place before he married Xantha. He himself told it to a friend of mine. He wanted to buy some paintings, so he had his driver take him to a well-known gallery. But once he got there, he couldn't get out of the car. He was too insecure. He didn't know how to behave, what questions to ask. He was afraid of looking stupid, or being cheated, or—worst of all—being snubbed. After sitting in the car for half an hour, he finally ordered the driver to take him home. Xantha changed all that for him. Meeting her gave him a mission in life other than making money."

"Meeting him gave her a mission, too: spending it," said Tom.

"Right. And since there was a lot of it, they quickly became well-known collectors. Their collection, in turn, gave them social prominence. Suddenly Arthur was being asked to serve on the boards of high-powered cultural organizations, and Xantha was being asked to chair their fund-raising functions."

Tom elaborated: "Not just the downtown stuff that she had been doing before she married Lumkin—Ethiopian relief, and that sort of thing. We're talking status institutions, like the Museum of Modern Art and the Whitney." He turned back to Charlotte. "Now we get to the interesting part."

"What's the interesting part?" asked Voorhees.

"Her lovers," Charlotte replied. "The price that Arthur paid for Xantha's lighting up his dreary existence was to put up with a succession of young lovers, most of them artists, of which it appears Randy was the most recent."

"And did he put up with them?"

"To all appearances, yes. The charade was that these young men served as escorts for Xantha when Arthur was occupied at board meetings or corporate functions. But the scuttlebutt was that, apart from the fact that he loved Xantha, he didn't want to risk a costly divorce. He had a reputation for being, if not tightfisted, then mindful of his money. And his divorce from his first wife had cost him sixteen million, or something like that. Now . . ." she went on, "we get to the *very* interesting part, which is the death of Xantha's last lover, a young Brazilian artist by the name of Louria—Victor, I think. The rumor was that his death wasn't an accident."

"What happened to him?" asked Voorhees.

"He fell, or jumped, or was pushed out of the fourteenth-floor window of a midtown apartment that was the Manhattan *pied-à-terre* of a friend, a Brazilian socialite. He landed on the roof of a delivery truck, wearing only red jockey undershorts and a gold chain with a gold cross. His death was written off as suicide, but there was no note."

"I remember that case now," Voorhees said. "His pants and T-shirt had been neatly folded up on a chair just inside the window."

"That's why the police called it a suicide. Suicides often do things like that, but not murderers. In any case, Arthur Lumkin wasn't sorry to see him dead. He chartered a jet to ship the coffin back to Rio. It cost him a hundred and seventy-five thousand dollars, which he was said to have described as 'well worth the money.' "

"What do you think?" asked Voorhees.

"I think Louria threw himself out of the window. He was said to have been distraught because Xantha had dumped him for someone else. Randy, maybe. Which is not to say that his death might not have put some ideas in Arthur's head about convenient methods of disposing of his wife's lovers."

"Was Lumkin at the post-opening party?" asked Tom.

"I don't know," Voorhees replied. "But Martinez should have the list of guests by now. Diana Nelson was going to drop it off today."

"I would imagine that he was," said Charlotte. "He and Xantha had loaned some paintings from their collection to the museum for the exhibit. It would have been customary to invite them."

Their roast chicken dinners had arrived, and they started to eat. As Tom had said, the food was very good: fresh mashed potatoes, delicious homemade giblet gravy, green beans that hadn't been boiled to death. One of the virtues of a good diner was the ability to do simple food very well.

As they ate, they discussed aspects of the case. If Arthur Lumkin had killed Randy because he knew Xantha's relationship with him was more than just a fling, he must have been aware of her set-up at the Short Stop. Which meant that he must have been out there. Which in turn meant that the neighbors might have seen him.

"Do you know where we can get a photo of Lumkin?" Voorhees asked. "Without going directly to him, I mean. A magazine, or something?"

Charlotte thought for a minute. "Yes. I think I have one at home. His picture was in this year's 'ARTnews 200,' the list of the two hundred most prominent art collectors. I remember the picture because my husband was complaining that Arthur rated a picture and he didn't."

"Do you still have it around?"

"I think so. If not, I could get it at the library. His photo also appears in business magazines from time to time."

"Okay," said Voorhees. For a minute, he stared out at the ball field, which glowed with the golden hues of late summer. "Here's what we'll do. Provided that you're still willing to take part in this investigation, that is."

They nodded.

"Miss Graham will get us a couple of copies of a photograph of Lumkin." He looked inquiringly at Charlotte, who nodded again. "Meanwhile, I'll find out what kind of car he drives. Are you free tomorrow?"

Charlotte said she was, but Tom had an appointment he couldn't break: a talk on true-crime writing at a college of criminal justice.

Voorhees continued: "If it's okay with you, Miss Graham, I'd like you to come back out here tomorrow with Martinez and show the picture around: the neighbors, the convenience store, and so on. You can do the talking: people are more likely to open up to a woman. Martinez will let you know about Lumkin's car."

"I would guess that he has a driver," said Charlotte.

"Good. That would make him more conspicuous. We'll also find out if there's a caretaker. I assume there is. Martinez will get you the name and address. Check out the same thing with him. Meanwhile, I'll make the rounds of the historic district."

Charlotte thought that she had the best chance of coming up with something. It would have been brazen in the extreme for Xantha to have moved in with Randy at the mill. But to set up a love nest at his isolated country place was another story.

Voorhees continued: "Ask about strangers in the neighborhood, too. If Goslau did move the paintings out here, someone might have stolen them."

Charlotte nodded. She had almost forgotten about the paintings.

"This is great coffee," said Voorhees. "I always judge a diner by its coffee. That, and the number of calendars: if there are old ones hanging on the wall, it means that they're too busy to change them."

"There you go," said Tom. "Not only an enthusiast, but a connoisseur."

*   *   *

Charlotte had no trouble finding the issue of *ARTnews* with
the photo of Arthur Lumkin. It was in a stack of old magazines in her library. He was posing, in black tie, with Xantha,
who was wearing one of her outrageous get-ups and smiling
widely for the *paparazzi*. She had Vivian make some copies
for her the next morning at the local copy shop. The copies
weren't great, but Lumkin was distinctive enough, with his
bald pate, horn-rimmed glasses, and long, aquiline nose, that
anyone who had seen him would recognize him from the
photo. As she ate her breakfast, she pondered what to do
with her day. She and Martinez weren't scheduled to go out
to the camp until three, which left her morning free. There
were a lot of things she should be doing—sitting down with
Vivian to answer her mail, looking at scripts (having just
completed a movie, she had to start thinking about what she
was going to do next), or getting down to work on her memoirs. One of Vivian's damned tape recorders was now sitting
on the kitchen counter right next to the toaster, where she
couldn't miss it. Why was it that she couldn't bring herself to get started on this? she wondered. Was it perhaps
the number of her marriages? She had always thought of
herself as a conventional person who would marry for life,
and the fact that she'd been married four times was something of an embarrassment to her. But she'd been living with
that for years. It was something else. And then it dawned on
her what was at the bottom of the unsettled feeling that had
been plaguing her. It was the unfinished chapter in her life,
namely, her relationship with Jack. They had been separated
now for more than a year—really separated, as opposed to
the charade they had been keeping up for a couple of years
prior to that. She knew what had to be done: one of them
had to file for divorce. She also knew why she didn't want
to be the one to do it. It would be an admission that she
had failed once again. "Hope springs eternal in the human
breast," the poet had said, and she supposed that she still
nurtured a faint hope that something of her marriage could
be salvaged, despite Marsha's news that Jack now had someone else.

No. She was definitely not ready to start talking into that

damned black box. What she *was* ready to do was go down to the Koreman Gallery and nose around. She wanted to find out what it was about the photorealist show that had made Randy Goslau go off the deep end.

· 7 ·

BY TEN, SHE was on her way. After retrieving her car from her garage, she drove down to Soho. Miraculously, she found a parking spot right in front of the old cast-iron fronted loft on West Broadway that housed the Koreman Gallery. West Broadway, so-called because it was west of the other Broadway, was the main north-south artery of the artists' community that Soho had become, and the site of its most prestigious galleries and boutiques. The Koreman Gallery was one of these. With a vast space that could accommodate three shows at once, it was one of Soho's biggest galleries.

Charlotte had been there before with Jack, and ascended the steps to the door, marked only with a small plaque that read KOREMAN, with the confidence of someone who is familiar with the territory. If you hadn't known it was there, you would never have noticed it. There were no windows or signs, apart from the inconspicuous plaque on the door. The lack of identifying features was a not-so-subtle form of intimidation typical of art galleries that thought themselves to be better than they were. The message was: we don't want your business unless you're already well-enough informed to know who we are.

Voorhees had been right in soliciting her aid. As Arthur Lumkin had discovered, the art community was a closed little world that was often hostile to outsiders, no matter how much money they had.

The receptionist behind the front desk treated her with the usual indifference. It was remarkable to Charlotte that many of these galleries stayed in business, so seemingly unresponsive were they to prospective customers.

"Excuse me," she said. "My name is Charlotte Graham. I'd like to see Ms. Koreman, please."

Mary Catherine Koreman was the owner. Though the gallery was technically owned by her and her husband—a quiet man named Robert Fein—it was Mary Catherine who ran the business, with Bob helping out with the framing, hanging, and staging of shows.

The receptionist looked Charlotte over as if she were a bag lady asking for a handout. "Do you have an appointment?" she asked. She wore her hair in what used to be called a crew cut, a style that showed off ears that were pierced in half-a-dozen places.

Charlotte replied that she didn't.

"I don't know if she's in."

"Could you check please?" said Charlotte icily. Elusive owners were another hallmark of the gallery with pretensions. "Tell her Miss Charlotte Graham is here to see her."

The receptionist got up resentfully and shuffled off to the back in her jack boots, leaving Charlotte to admire an exhibit of colorfully painted furniture. She returned a minute later, followed by Mary Catherine.

"Miss Graham," Mary Catherine said with a smile, extending a welcoming hand, "So very nice to see you again. How is your husband? We haven't seen him in a while." When she smiled, her protruding front teeth gave her round, dimpled face an endearing chipmunky expression.

She was a heavy woman, whose gray hair was parted in the middle and pulled back into a bun at the nape of her neck. She wore a caftan of hand-woven cotton, and oversized eyeglass frames in a checkerboard pattern that matched the pink and lavender of her dress.

Charlotte had always liked Mary Catherine, and thought her an astute businesswoman, despite the inconspicuous sign and the sullen receptionist. But perhaps that was only the regard of one professional woman for another. "He's very well, I hear," she replied. "I don't see him much anymore.

"Oh, I'm sorry to hear that. Well, then, what can we do for you?"

"I'm here on a personal matter. A friend of mine is a friend of the painter, Randy Goslau, who drowned last week. Perhaps you heard about it?"

Mary Catherine nodded. She stood with her hands folded expectantly in front her, like a nun who has just asked the class a difficult question. She was clearly waiting to see what this had to do with her, or with her gallery.

"On the evening of the night he drowned he attended an opening reception for the Paterson Museum's show on New Jersey diners. While he was there, he had a kind of"—she groped for the right words—"nervous attack. . . ."

"He freaked out."

"You heard," said Charlotte.

"I was there. Bob and I went because some of the paintings in the exhibit were on loan from our inventory. We got there just after Randy had been taken away. But everyone was still talking about it."

"That explains why I didn't see you. I was there too, but I must have left before you got there. Anyway, a friend of Randy's told my friend that he'd experienced a couple of these episodes before, one of them at a show here."

Mary Catherine nodded. "Last January," she said. "The photorealist show."

Charlotte continued: "My friend thinks these episodes might be linked to his death. When he heard that I knew you, he asked me to do him the favor of looking into what happened here."

The sizable bosom beneath the hand-woven fabric of Mary Catherine's caftan seemed to visibly deflate. She had been tense from holding her breath, but Charlotte had failed to ask whatever unpleasant question it was that she had been anticipating. "Looking into it?" she repeated innocently.

"Did you see it happen?" asked Charlotte.

Mary Catherine nodded again.

"What exactly did he do?"

"Oh, I don't know. He moaned, he waved his arms around, he acted crazy. We're used to strange behavior here, but his was exceptionally strange. I attributed it to the drugs. I think everybody did. The rescue squad ended up taking him to the psych ward at Bellevue. He was okay once he came down."

"Do you know what triggered it?"

"I would guess it was the painting he was looking at. He was staring at it as if it were going to jump off the wall and bite him. Though it didn't happen right away. He had been looking at it for a while before he freaked out."

"Do you remember which painting it was?" Charlotte asked.

"It was a painting of a diner by Ed Verre. It was also a diner painting by Verre that triggered his attack at the Montclair Art Museum, from what I understand."

Charlotte took a sharp breath.

"What is it?" asked Mary Catherine, clearly unaware that it was also a Verre painting of a diner which had triggered the latest attack.

"Nothing," said Charlotte. "Listen, do you by any chance have a slide of that painting that I could look at?"

"Better than that, I have a catalog. We don't usually do catalogs—as you know, they're very expensive—but we did one for this show. We anticipated some big buyers." She turned to the receptionist. "Jackie, will you please get Ms. Graham a catalog from the photorealist show?"

The receptionist shuffled off toward the back again.

"Tell me"—Mary Catherine nodded toward the receptionist—"was she pleasant when you came in? Or did she give you the cold shoulder?"

"The latter," said Charlotte.

"I hate that. She came to me from another gallery, where they think the more attitude a receptionist gives, the better. I've instructed her that that's not the way we do business here, but she doesn't listen. I may have to get rid of her. But it's hard to find experienced people."

Charlotte tried to look sympathetic.

The receptionist returned momentarily with the catalog, which she handed to Mary Catherine. Leafing through the pages, she opened it to the painting in question. "This is the one," she said.

It was a painting of the Falls View Diner—an exterior view, as opposed to the Verre in the museum show, which depicted the interior. The title was "Falls View Diner on a Rainy Spring Night."

"Can you tell me anything about the artist?" asked Charlotte.

"Not much. He sent in his slides about a year ago, and I immediately recognized a major talent. He came out of nowhere, had only just started painting. This was his first exhibit. It was as if he had sprung full-blown like Venus from the head of Jupiter."

"What about his personal life?" she asked.

"He lives in Paterson. I can give you the address." She turned to the receptionist again, and asked her to write down Verre's address. "Beyond that, I don't know much. I've never actually met him. He's kind of reclusive—he didn't even show up for the opening."

"What about the painting?" asked Charlotte. "Did anyone buy it?"

"Yes. Morris and Evelyn Finder. They got a bargain, too. In a few years, Verre's paintings are going to be worth ten times their present value. We get young painters in here all the time who think that because they can paint in the photorealist style their paintings are going to bring the same prices as a Spiegel. Often, they do command good prices—for a while. Randy Goslau was a good example of what I'm talking about. But they don't last. The only reason Randy had any continuing success was the popularity of his subject matter. And, of course, his connection with Don Spiegel. But if diner art were to have gone out of fashion, he would have had to hang up his paintbrush. These young painters don't understand that copying isn't what it's all about. They have to have the technical skill, yes; but they also have to have a vision. The Finders could spot that right away about Verre: the difference between a copyist and an artist. That's what makes them such great collectors. Do you know them?"

"A little. My husband knows them very well, of course."

"They're very nice people. Maybe they'll let you take a look at the painting. It's really quite magnificent."

Charlotte thanked her for the suggestion. "May I pay for this?" she asked, holding up the catalog.

"Of course not," Mary Catherine replied.

"Thank you very much," said Charlotte, adding: "I don't see my husband much anymore, but I do still see his daughter, Marsha Lundstrom. Next time I do, I'll ask her to tell him that you've been inquiring about him."

"Thank you," said Mary Catherine.

*   *   *

Charlotte was on her way to lunch at a neighborhood café where she used to eat with Jack, when she passed the Bellinger Gallery. The downtown branch of the uptown gallery of the same name, the Bellinger was the most prestigious gallery in Soho. Its founder, Winston Bellinger, had made a name for himself as an early supporter of the works of the abstract expressionists, and these now-established artists still comprised the bulk of the works at his uptown gallery. The newer, downtown gallery was devoted to younger, more experimental artists. Jack had bought paintings from both galleries, but more so in recent years from the downtown gallery, the prices for the works of the early abstract expressionists having soared out of reach for all but the wealthiest collectors. In the course of his collecting, Charlotte and Jack had become quite friendly with Bellinger's daughter, Ellen, who managed the downtown branch.

Diana Nelson had named Mary Catherine Koreman as one person who might have had a motive for killing Randy. If there was anyone who could shed further light on the relationship between Randy and the gallery owner, it was Ellen Bellinger.

Charlotte was still thinking about dropping in at the Bellinger when she nearly collided with Ellen, who was just on her way out. She was a young woman, full of energy and enthusiasm for her work.

Within minutes, Ellen had ushered Charlotte into her office, and was treating her to a cup of coffee and the lowdown on the Koreman. Yes, it was true that Randy had been shaking down the Koreman for the Lumkins' business, Ellen told her. "From what I understand, Mary Catherine paid him a kickback of twenty percent on every painting that the Lumkins bought," she said.

"How much do you estimate the Lumkins spent there in a year?"

"Oh, I have no idea. But it must have been in the hundreds of thousands, maybe even a million or more, which meant a pretty penny for Randy." She went on: "At least, however, Randy limited his extortion activities to the Koreman Gallery. If on occasion the Lumkins bought something from our gallery, he didn't hassle us. Which is not the case with Mary Catherine Koreman."

"What do you mean?" asked Charlotte.

"Now that Randy's dead, Mary Catherine isn't content with getting most of the Lumkins' business. She wants a cut of the business they do with other galleries too. We had a little visit yesterday from her husband, who informed us that if we wanted to continue doing business with the Lumkins, we had to go through them."

"Which means that they take a commission."

Ellen nodded. "Twenty percent. Not only are they saving the twenty percent they used to pay Randy, they're getting twenty percent on everyone else's paintings too."

"Do they need the money?" Charlotte asked.

"I don't think so. As far as I know, they're doing very well. But that has nothing to do with what drives people to accumulate more. Did Michael Milken need more money?" she asked, referring to the stockbroker who had recently been indicted for insider trading.

"True," said Charlotte.

"Then there's the label scam," Ellen continued.

"What's that?"

"A painting generally has a card on the back giving its provenance: who owned it before, and when. The savvy buyer will peek at the back to see if the painting came from another gallery. If it did, he can then call the other gallery and ask, 'Do you by any chance have a Spiegel?' "

"Thereby sidestepping the consignment markup."

"Exactly. It's a little game we all play. But Mary Catherine routinely takes the cards off the back of her consignment pieces and replaces them with phony cards. Which is strictly *verboten*."

So it was questions about her less-than-kosher business practices that Mary Catherine had been anticipating, thought Charlotte. She was a much sharper businesswoman than Charlotte had believed.

Ellen looked at her watch. "I'm really sorry, but I have to get going. I have an appointment in fifteen minutes."

"These are just the kinds of things that I wanted to find out about," said Charlotte. "I really appreciate your help."

"Good luck," Ellen replied. "If there's anything else I can do . . ."

"As a matter of fact, there is," said Charlotte. As they headed out to the street, she explained about the disappearance of the twelve paintings that Don Spiegel had given to Randy.

"The same paintings that were claimed by Bernice Spiegel?"

"Yes. If you hear anything about them, will you let me know?"

Ellen agreed, and they parted in front of the building.

Charlotte continued on in the direction of the café, and then changed her mind when she saw a sign on the side of a building that read: WORLD'S GREATEST DINER RIGHT AROUND THE CORNER. She was catching Tom's disease, she thought as she followed the painted arrow to the Moondance, a tiny diner that stood in a lot at the corner of Grand Street and Sixth Avenue, and whose slogan was "It's a wonderful night for a moondance."

Though Tom would have sneered at the chef's diploma from the Culinary Institute of America hanging over the soda dispenser; the signs advertising champagne, cappuccino, and the "mineral water of the week"; and the self-conscious retro chic of the renovation, Charlotte found it charming. After placing her order for the daily breakfast specialty, banana pancakes with Dutch cream, and a cup of coffee—she settled in at the counter with her catalog from the Koreman.

Unlike Verre's painting of the Falls View in the museum show, which gave the impression that the artist had set up his easel right behind the two men at the counter, this painting was a long shot. It might have been painted from across the street. The diner sat squarely in the middle of the canvas surrounded by the parking lot, which was complete with cars: a couple of nondescript sedans, an enormous truck, and an old van with Michigan license plates. There were seven or eight customers: three men sitting at the counter, and several others in the booths. The grill man was busy at the grill, his back turned to the viewer. As the title said, it was a rainy spring night. The leaves on the trees growing on the river bank behind the diner were only just beginning to come out. The magnificence that Mary Catherine had spoken of came from the technical challenge of painting a rainy night scene. The painting seemed to shimmer with reflections: in the wet glass of the diner's windows, in the puddles in the parking lot, on the chrome bumpers of the cars. There was also the rain itself, which the glowing pink of the diner's neon sign turned to colored mist.

The painting told her exactly nothing, except that Verre was a far better painter than Randy could ever have been. She could see why Mary Catherine had called him a major talent. The painting reminded her of Edward Hopper's famous painting, "Nighthawks." It had a haunting, dreamlike beauty, capturing perfectly the ambivalent mood—a strange combination of the cozy and the alienating—of the wee hours at a diner on a rainy spring night.

Could it be that Randy's reaction had been a magnified form of *angst*? she wondered: a recognition that despite the substantial prices collectors paid for his paintings, he, as Mary Catherine had said, was a painter of little talent whose work wouldn't stand the test of time.

Finishing her banana pancakes, which were delicious (as far as she was concerned, a diploma from the Culinary Institute could do nothing but improve the quality of diner food), she headed back to her car for the trip out to Paterson.

Charlotte and Martinez struck pay dirt—in the form of the neighborhood busybody—at the first house they visited, a split level directly opposite the spot where the access road to Randy's camp joined the main road. The owner was a tall, thin woman in her sixties, with a giraffe-like face to match. Although it was nearly four, her hair was still in curlers, which were covered by a souvenir scarf from the Statue of Liberty, and she was wearing a pink-flowered housecoat. Holding the chained door open a crack, she peered out at them suspiciously over the tops of her reading glasses. But once Martinez had showed her his badge and explained what they were there for, her expression changed to one of rapt interest. And when he followed this with the photo of Arthur Lumkin, she hastily unchained the door and ushered them in.

"What took you so long?" she complained as they entered. "I've been expecting you ever since I heard that that Goslau man had been murdered. If I didn't hear from you soon, I was going to march myself right on down to the police station, and give you the dirt. You can call off your investigation," she announced. "I can tell you who did it. That man." She waved a long, bony finger at the photograph. "I even predicted it. I told my neighbor, Mrs. Anderson"—she waved an arm in the direction of the neighboring house—"that no good was going to come from his hanging around here like that. He's the husband." She peered at Martinez over the tops of her glasses again. "Am I right?"

"Yes, you're right," said Martinez. He pulled a notebook out of his pocket. "Can you tell me your name, please?" he asked.

Charlotte now knew why Voorhees had wanted her help. Martinez had said hardly a word on their hour-long journey out, and he was barely doing much better now. He was as silent as Voorhees was garrulous.

"Marion Blakely," she replied. "Sit down," she added, directing them across a plastic runner to easy chairs that were also covered with plastic. "I'll tell you all about it."

As Charlotte crossed the room, Mrs. Blakely stared at her curiously. "Do I know you?" she asked.

"I don't think so," said Charlotte.

"That's funny. You look very familiar. Maybe I knew you in another life." She laughed, a kind of rumbling cackle. "Anyway, you want to know the who, what, when, where, and why." She looked at Martinez. "Right?"

Martinez nodded.

"Well, I'm the one who can give it to you. He started coming around here last December. Just after Goslau took up with that strumpet. The outfits that woman wore would shock the britches off the devil himself. Shortly after that—February maybe, Goslau brought in that diner just for her: the Short Stop. Felix—he's the caretaker—told me about it. It's all done up in ruffles and pink satin. . . ."

"What did he do when he came out here?" asked Charlotte.

"He didn't drive himself. He had a chauffeur. Usually, but not always. A gray Mercedes Benz, it was. New York plates. The chauffeur parked the car under the street light right across the street." She waved an arm at the picture window. "Then he would get out and walk down the road. He always carried binoculars with him."

"He was spying on them, then?"

"Well, I assume he was. He wasn't bird-watching, I can tell you that. And quite an eyeful I imagine it was that he got. That diner Goslau bought for her, the Short Stop"—she smiled at the name—"was all windows. And there weren't any curtains on them, either." She studied Lumkin's picture again. "Quite a distinguished-looking man. I imagine he's quite rich. Who is he, anyway?"

"We'd prefer to keep that confidential," said Charlotte.

"Of course," she agreed readily, puffed up with the thrill of being involved in a police investigation.

"How often did he come out here?"

"He was here a lot. Always at night. I imagine he could see more then. Also, there was less likelihood that they would see him. He only came when she was here, of course. She was here at least one evening a week, usually Wednesdays. He came maybe every other Wednesday."

"Did she come out here at other times as well?"

"Oh yes. She often came out during the day. Once she stayed for a whole week. That's when she decorated the place. I didn't see him at all then. I figured he must have been away." She paused for a moment and then went on: "I can't say that I'm terribly sorry that that Goslau man is dead," she said. "When he had all those neon signs turned on, it looked like the carnival had come to town. I always thought there must be a law against signs like that, but I never got around to looking into it. Won't need to now," she added brightly. "Can I get you a cup of coffee?"

"I don't think so, thank you," said Martinez. He looked over at Charlotte. "Is there anything else you wanted to ask?"

She said, no, and they thanked Mrs. Blakely, and left.

"Yeah, Lumkin was hanging around the Gryphon Mill too," said Voorhees. He was standing behind his desk, holding the telephone to his ear. "Spying on his wife. The jealous husband bit. But we're forgetting about him for the moment."

Charlotte and Martinez had just finished relating the tale of their excursion, which had included a subsequent visit to the caretaker, who had confirmed everything that Mrs. Blakely had said.

"Why forgetting him?" asked Charlotte once Voorhees had

hung up the phone, apparently giving up on whoever it was he had been holding for.

"We've got another suspect with a stronger motive." He picked up a piece of paper and handed it to Charlotte. "We found this when we went through the papers in Goslau's desk."

It was a Contract of Sale agreement between Nikos Andriopoulis and Randall Goslau for the sale of the Falls View Diner, for two hundred and seventy-five thousand dollars.

"I don't get it," Charlotte said. "Who's the suspect and what's the motive?"

"The suspect is John Andriopoulis, and the motive is the preservation of the Falls View. Here's a guy who started working at the Falls View when he was ten. Since his brother bought it out from the uncle forty years ago, he's worked there seven days a week, three hundred and sixty-five days a year."

"It's his life," offered Martinez.

"Exactly. He'd always dreamed of leaving it to his daughter. But his brother, Nick, had a different dream. Nick's dream was to get rid of the old diner, and open up a tablecloth restaurant on the site. Then Goslau comes along and offers Nick two hundred and seventy-five grand for it."

"Wait a minute," said Charlotte. "Didn't John own a share?"

"Yes, but his brother owned the controlling interest. As the older brother, he had bankrolled the buy-out from the uncle." Voorhees continued: "It was an offer that Nick couldn't refuse. He signed the Contract of Sale agreement. Then John found out, and hit the roof."

"*When* did John find out?"

"On Sunday night, just before the party. John was furious that Nick hadn't discussed it with him first. There was an argument: a lot of yelling, some of it in Greek, some pushing and shoving. Finally Nick walked out. Everybody in the diner saw it."

"But what would be the point of killing Randy?" Charlotte asked. "If Randy was willing to pay two hundred and seventy-five grand for the diner, then somebody else would eventually have been willing to pay that too. It would only have been a matter of time."

"Wrong. I've checked this out with your friend Plummer.

The diner was only worth twenty, maybe thirty thou. If the right buyer happened to come along. The reason that Goslau was willing to pay the inflated price was that he wasn't footing the bill."

"Who was, then?"

"Xantha Price. Nick Andriopoulis said she was buying it as a present for him. It was going to be the showpiece of his collection." He shook his head in amazement. "I'd like to know what that guy did for her to earn himself that kind of present."

Charlotte remembered Randy talking at the opening about having a Silk City in mind for his collection. "That explains the freshly cleared lot at Randy's camp," she said.

Voorhees nodded. "Anyway, to continue with my story. Randy leaves the diner at about eleven. He throws up in the bamboo, then passes out. John leaves a few minutes later for a break before reopening the diner to the regular trade at twelve. He's gone for about forty-five minutes. I figure it happened this way: John comes across Randy lying unconscious in the bamboo, and figures, here's his chance. If he tosses Randy in the drink, who's going to know? He goes back to the diner for the aprons. Then he wraps Randy up to keep him from swimming if he regains consciousness, and tosses him in. But he doesn't count on one thing—that the body wouldn't go over the Falls, as he had planned. Instead, it ends up in the raceway system."

"Why John, though?" she asked. "Couldn't it have been anyone who tossed Randy in? There were enough people who didn't like him. And most of them were at the diner that night."

Voorhees picked up two brown paper bags that were sitting on a chair. "Here are the aprons that were wrapped around the body," he said, pulling two aprons out of the first bag. "We just got them back from the drying room." He spread them out on the surface of his desk.

They were stiff and dirty from the mud of the raceway, and smelled of algae. Or was it putrefaction? Charlotte wondered.

Lifting the edge of one of them, Voorhees showed them the spot at the waist where the laundry service's logo had been stamped in indelible blue ink, like the USDA stamp on a cut of beef. "See this?" he said, pointing to an S in a circle, with the words "Supreme Linen Service" in another circle around it.

Charlotte and Martinez nodded.

Then Voorhees reached into the second bag and pulled out another apron, this one washed, starched, and folded, and pointed out the identical laundry service logo. "This one comes from the Falls View," he said. "They were kept just inside the back door. Nobody would have seen John come back to get them."

"But how do you know that the aprons used for wrapping up Randy's body were from the Falls View?" Charlotte protested. "The same linen service must supply aprons to dozens of restaurants. They might have come from any one of them."

"They might have," Voorhees admitted. "But it's unlikely. We've already checked with them. They said that they supply aprons to nine other restaurants in Paterson. The one that's closest to the Falls View is the Madison Four, which is on the border of South Paterson."

"Is that far?" she asked.

Voorhees nodded.

Charlotte sighed. It just didn't add up to her. "Why would John tie the body up in his own aprons?" she asked. "He isn't stupid. He must have realized that the aprons would link the body to the diner, and therefore to him."

"He probably thought the body would end up in Newark Bay. In any case, far enough away not to be linked to the Falls View. He'd had enough experience with rescue squad searches to know that bodies don't always come up where they go down."

"But could he have counted on that? After all, a lot of bodies—if not most of them—*do* come up where they went down, or pretty close to it. Wouldn't it have been smarter to weight the body down so that it wouldn't have come up at all?"

"Yes, but murderers aren't always the clearest thinkers in the world, especially if they're taking advantage of a chance opportunity. Remember, we're not talking about a premeditated murder here."

Charlotte leaned back in her chair, deeply disturbed by Voorhees' revelations. They didn't add up, mainly because she couldn't imagine John Andriopoulis as a killer. "Have you confronted him?" she asked.

Voorhees nodded. "He says the aprons probably came from the laundry bin, which he had put out back for the linen service collection on Monday morning—that anyone could have come along and taken them out of the bin."

His tone indicated that he thought John's explanation was a feeble one. But Charlotte thought otherwise.

Tom came over to Charlotte's house that evening, and they sat in Charlotte's library, talking about the investigation. Voorhees' case against John rested on the aprons; that, and his forty-five minute absence. But if the aprons had really been in the laundry bin out back, then anyone could have taken them, as John claimed. Arthur Lumkin, for one. It seemed to them that Arthur was another person who wasn't likely to be happy about Xantha's plan to buy the Falls View. Especially if he was footing the bill. Which they imagined he was. Though Xantha's work as a boutique fashion designer probably brought in a tidy income, Charlotte guessed that it wasn't enough to go tossing money around in hundred-thousand-dollar increments. And she was familiar enough with Xantha's background to know that she didn't have any family money. As Xantha herself readily admitted, she had worked herself up from the bottom, her Cockney accent, which to her credit she had never tried to alter, testimony to her East End origins. Finally there was the question of exactly why Xantha had decided to buy the Falls View. Was it just to demonstrate her love? Or, was she planning to use it for a bigger and better love nest? Even perhaps a more permanent country residence? Any of these reasons might have served to inflame Arthur's already considerable jealousies.

As a murder suspect, they concluded, Arthur seemed to be an all-around better bet than John. Not only was John's motive too slim, his constant presence at the diner made him entirely too obvious as a suspect.

· 8 ·

TWO EVENTS OF the next morning only served to confirm Charlotte's belief in the weakness of Voorhees' case against John. The first occurred as she was sitting at her kitchen table, eating her customary cinnamon toast, and drinking her customary cup of coffee. She was reading a week-old *New York Post* that Vivian had left lying around. The *Post* wasn't her usual breakfast fare, much less a week-old one, but the *Times* hadn't been delivered that morning, and her morning routine demanded newsprint, however dated, as much as it did caffeine. It was an item on "Page Six," the gossip page, that caught her eye. Sandwiched between a snippet about the pregnancy of a television sitcom star and the driving-while-intoxicated arrest of a talk show host, was an article featuring the names of Xantha Price and Arthur Lumkin in boldface type:

> Our trusty Page Six spy spotted Wall Street investment banker, **Arthur Lumkin** at the office of divorce attorney, **Marvin Margulies**. "Everyone is saying that their marriage is on the rocks," said our source, of Lumkin's marriage to British fashion designer, **Xantha Price**. Our source noted that Ms. Price had been seen wearing a new emerald ring. She has been keeping steady company with a young photorealist painter. Could it be that wedding bells are about to ring for the third time for the fuchsia-haired dynamo?"

After reading this, Charlotte set her coffee cup down with a clunk. If Arthur was as jealous as his spying activities seemed to indicate, the fact that Xantha was planning on dumping him for Randy would certainly have been sufficient to drive him over the edge. To say nothing of the notoriety of a much-publicized divorce, which, as a gentleman of the old school, he would have abhorred. Adding to his discomfiture would be the expense of a divorce. He wasn't likely to be thrilled about shelling out another ten or fifteen million in alimony, and Xantha didn't strike her as the type who was willing to walk away from a marriage to a rich man without any pecuniary demands.

The second event was the telephone call from Patty Andriopoulis.

The phone rang just as Charlotte was finishing her breakfast. Patty's story was punctuated by sharp, wracking sobs: John had been arrested for the murder of Randy Goslau. He was being arraigned now, and would be taken immediately afterward to the bail unit.

"We're all afraid that this is going to kill him," Patty said, her voice even more raspy than usual. "He has a bad heart. He had a triple bypass three years ago. I know he didn't do it. He wouldn't hurt a flea."

Charlotte had heard that before, but she tended to believe it of John. She wondered why Patty was calling, to raise bail money, perhaps?

Then she revealed the purpose of her call: "Bill Martinez told me the other day that you'd been helping him and Marty. Bill's the one who gave me your phone number. We went to Kennedy High together."

Charlotte had wondered how Patty had gotten her number.

"I have some information that may help Daddy out. I wonder if I could talk with you. I know I should probably go to Marty, but I just can't bring myself to do that. Right now, I hate the man."

"I understand," said Charlotte. "Would you like me to come to the diner?"

"Could you?" Patty replied, pleadingly.

"I'll be there in forty-five minutes."

Though the diner wasn't crowded with customers—it was the lull after the breakfast rush—it was crowded with people, all of them Greek and all of them men. It appeared as if every male Andriopoulis within a hundred miles had rallied to John's cause. They were huddled together at one end of the diner with grim expressions on their swarthy faces, talking earnestly in Greek.

Patty stood waiting for Charlotte just inside the door; a cute little boy with eyes like shiny brown buttons was at her side. She introduced him as her son, Johnny. After setting him up at the quiet end of the counter with a coloring book and a box of crayons, she escorted Charlotte to a nearby booth.

"He's taking Randy's death really hard, poor lamb," she said. "He and Randy were good buddies. So am I, for that matter. I just came back from his funeral. What there was of it. Not many people were there. Can I get you a cup of coffee or something?"

"Sure," said Charlotte. "But you're not on duty."

She was dressed in jeans and a T-shirt, over which she wore a blue denim jacket with a picture of Mickey Mouse appliquéd in sequins and satin thread on the back. It reminded Charlotte of Jason's job painting breasts at Mickey's Paint Factory.

"I'm always on duty," she said. Getting up, she poured two cups of coffee from a pot on the hot plate behind the counter, and delivered them to the table with the casual efficiency of the experienced waitress. "I brought a plate of Danish too," she said, setting the plate in front of Charlotte.

"Don't you want any?" asked Charlotte as she took one.

"No thanks," she said, resuming her seat. "My stomach is in knots." As she took a swig of coffee, her eye caught the plaque on the wall above them. "See that?" she said. She read the inscription: "To John Andriopoulis, in appreciation of continued service to the Paterson Fire Department."

"Is your father a volunteer firefighter?" asked Charlotte.

"No, he serves the rescue squad food and coffee when they're up the street fishing bodies out of the river, as they often are. The city gives him a plaque, and then they arrest him. Do you believe it?" Tears welled in her big brown eyes, and she blinked them away.

Charlotte handed her a Kleenex, and she blew her nose.

"Okay, down to business," she said, once she had finished blowing. "I wanted to tell you about Randy. Maybe there's something in the story that will help Daddy." She paused, and then began: "Randy is—was—a good friend of mine. The Falls View has been an artists' hangout, and that's how we originally met. He became a sort of surrogate father to Johnny, whose real father took off for parts unknown shortly after I told him I was pregnant. Randy used to take him to ball games, or fishing out at his camp—that kind of thing. Despite what everybody is probably saying, Randy used to be a nice guy. I think he saw a lot of himself in Johnny: as a boy, Randy also spent a lot of time in diners."

"He told me," said Charlotte.

"I'm giving you this background to make the point that I knew him very well, probably better than anyone else." Seeing the inquiring look on Charlotte's face, Patty answered her unspoken question: "No, we weren't lovers. Nor did I ever expect that of him. He only had sex with people from whom he had something to gain—something more than two hots all the way and a mug of birch beer, that is." Her attempt at a smile came out more like a grimace.

"That doesn't sound like such a nice guy to me," said Charlotte.

"You had to understand Randy. Underneath the braggart was an insecure, love-starved little boy. We shared a lot. Randy was raised in diners, so was I. How could someone like me whose life has been devoted to a diner not like someone who thinks diners are the greatest thing since sliced bread? You should have seen his postcard collection. He had postcards of diners from all over the country. He'd been collecting since he was seven.

"As you probably know, Randy used drugs—cocaine. He already had a habit before Don Spiegel died—they quarreled over it a number of times—but after Don's suicide it got worse. He'd go on sprees—stay awake for two, three, even four days on end. Wouldn't shave, get dressed, talk to anyone. Then he'd drink to bring himself down, or take Quaaludes. He had what he called his good weeks and his bad weeks. On his good weeks, he didn't do anything. That's why he didn't think he had a problem. Even with his habit, though, I would still have called him normal. He was prone to exaggerating his own importance in order to pump up his ego, but so are a lot of people." She paused and said, "Maybe I will have a Danish after all."

Charlotte passed her the plate.

She picked out a pastry, took a bite, and then put it down. "Okay," she said, taking a deep breath. "Then things changed—very suddenly, almost overnight in fact. His behavior became very bizarre."

"In what way?" asked Charlotte.

"A paranoid way. For instance, he thought his studio was bugged. If you wanted to talk with him, he'd drag you into the bathroom and turn on the faucets. Then he'd sit on the toilet, and keep flushing it while you talked. He thought his phone was tapped. He'd make all his calls from pay phones." She nodded at the pay phone in the corner. "He spent thousands on motion detectors, TV monitors, you name it."

Charlotte remembered seeing the TV monitor outside his door.

"Oh, countersurveillance equipment too: gizmos to tell if your apartment is bugged or your phone is tapped. At one point, he even hired a countersurveillance consultant who came in with about a hundred thousand dollars worth of fancy electronic equipment and swept the studio for bugs."

"Did he find anything?"

Patty shook her head. "But that didn't convince Randy. He still thought the place was bugged. He said there were so many ways of bugging that it was impossible to have swept for them all."

"When did all this start?"

"Right after he freaked out at the Koreman show. Maybe you heard about it. It was just like what happened the other night. That's also when the good weeks stopped. From there on out, there were only bad weeks."

"Then it wasn't the drugs that induced his reaction at the Koreman show; it was whatever happened at the show that induced the drug use."

Patty nodded. "The rescue squad took him to Bellevue. The diagnosis was cocaine-induced paranoia. But, as I said, up until then, he hadn't been doing that much coke." She took another swig of coffee, and then went on. "To continue on the subject of his bizarre behavior: he thought he was being followed. He would enter and leave his studio through a back entrance. He changed the locks on his doors every other day. He thought his food was poisoned. He talked constantly about being surrounded by informants, about not being able to trust anyone. Every stranger walking down the street was a tail; every car that slowed down was an unmarked vehicle that had been sent to spy on him. He said that I was the only one he could trust, and that the diner was the only place where he felt safe. He was talking about going to Australia to get away, as you know from the incident at the museum."

Charlotte now remembered how he insisted on sitting facing the door at the diner, and how he kept looking out the window.

"Everyone attributed the paranoia to the drugs. Even Randy himself sometimes. He had a little saying he used to recite: 'Snort coke, get paranoid, drink to mellow out, fall down.' Which was about how it happened that night. The worse his paranoia got, the more drugs he took. It was a vicious cycle. He said he felt like one of those lab rats who keeps pushing the lever to get more cocaine, despite the fact that it's getting zapped each time by an electric shock. It was getting very scary. It finally got so bad that he started talking about checking himself into Straight and Narrow. . . ."

"Straight and Narrow?"

"It's a drug rehab clinic—on the corner of Straight Street and Narrow Street. What a name, huh? It's one of Paterson's claims to fame—it's in *Ripley's Believe it or Not*. Would you believe that the Salvation Army's alcohol rehab clinic overlooks Temperance Island? Paterson is a quirky place. Anyway, he was talking about checking himself into Straight and Narrow, but it was just a joke. He never would have gone to Straight and Narrow—it's for hard-core junkies. He had actually been looking into a private clinic—Don had even offered to pay for it—but he never followed through. Okay, get to the point, Patty," she said to herself. "The point is that I believe that Randy's paranoia wasn't all drug-induced. I believe that there really *was* somebody out to get him."

"What makes you think that?"

"I was a party to some of it."

"Some of what?"

"The harassment Randy claimed to have been experiencing. One of the things that he raved about was the telephone calls he said he'd get all night long. Whoever it was would call and hang up, call and hang up. He couldn't sleep. He changed his number, but the calls kept coming. Then he switched to an unlisted number. That didn't work either. I thought the phone thing was one of his paranoid delusions, until he had his phone disconnected. Then he started getting the calls here." She nodded again at the pay phone. "It would happen whenever he was at the diner. The caller, who was a man, would ask for Randy, but when Randy answered, he would hang up. No sooner would Randy get back to his seat—by the way, he always sat facing the door. . . ."

"I noticed that," said Charlotte.

"No sooner would he get back to his seat than the phone would ring again. It got so we didn't answer the phone when he was here. The ringing drove the other customers crazy. Then there were the bumping incidents. Randy would complain that these Hispanic kids were always bumping into him on the street. He thought they were doing it deliberately. Again, I thought it was his imagination. But then one day we went to the market on lower Main Street. We were walking back when this young Hispanic kid comes up to Randy, and knocks him over. Not accidentally, deliberately. The grocery bags went flying. Randy said it was the same kid who had done it before."

"Did he have any idea who was harassing him?"

She nodded. "He had the calls traced. But he wouldn't tell me who it was. He said that if that person found out I knew, he might come after me too. He wanted to protect me." She stopped to look up at a woman who had come over to their booth. "Oh hi, Mom," she said.

Patty's mother was still pretty in spite of her age, which must have been around sixty. She had a round face with a wide smile that was filled with warmth, and lovely hazel eyes now reddened from weeping. She looked more Irish than Greek, and may very well have been.

"Hello," she said, extending her hand. "I'm Helen Andriopoulis. My daughter says that maybe you can help us." She looked down at Patty with love, and sadness. "My husband didn't think much of Randy Goslau, as Patty may have told you, but he never would have killed him."

Charlotte now recognized her as the woman who was usually behind the cash register. "I know," said Charlotte. "I'll do my best."

"Is there anything I can do?" Mrs. Andriopoulis asked. "Do you need anything?"

"No, Ma," Patty said. "We're fine. We'll be finished here in a few minutes." Once her mother had returned to her post, Patty went on. "As Mom said, Daddy didn't approve of Randy—the drugs and all. He said he was just another stray that I had picked up. I have this weakness for stray animals. . . ." She nodded at the dog pen that adjoined the house across the street.

Charlotte turned around to look at the enclosure, in which she could see several dogs. "How many do you have?" she asked.

"At the moment, eleven cats and four dogs."

"For a person with a weakness for strays, that's not bad."

"It's been worse. The pen's been full at times. Thank goodness I don't have to bear the expense of feeding them. They eat the leftovers from here. That's my parents' house," she explained. "Johnny and I live upstairs in the apartment where my grandmother used to live before she died. My mom and dad live downstairs with my younger sister." She shrugged. "It's convenient."

Charlotte looked out at the house, which had imitation brick siding on the lower story, aluminum siding on the upper story, and identical picture windows up and down. It was sandwiched between a recycling warehouse for glass, cans, and paper, whose raw materials stood around in heaps on the lot, and a "Monumental Works," whose gravestones were displayed out front.

"I try to find homes for the animals, and I do pretty well at it. I put the signs up here. If the customers are interested, they can just walk across the street and take a look."

Charlotte had noticed one of these signs when she came in: "Loving golden retriever needs a home. For information, see Patty."

"Anyway, I tell Daddy that I got it from him. If I have a weakness for stray animals, it's because he has a weakness for stray humans. Any wino on the west side knows he can get a handout from John Andriopoulis." She nodded at a bum who was sitting at the counter. "Like Roger Barry. He comes in every morning at ten. You could set your clock by him. Where were we?" she asked.

"On who it was. Could it have been Arthur Lumkin?"

Patty shook her head emphatically. "No. I thought that too. But Randy said it was someone else."

"He had been spying on Xantha and Randy."

"Randy knew about that. Arthur wasn't subtle about it. Randy told me that he and Xantha made a little game out of spotting him. They called him Waldo, after that kids' book *Where's Waldo?*, where you have to find this geeky guy named Waldo among the people in the crowd. It's a favorite of Johnny's. Randy used to look at it with him. Once Randy found Arthur's car out in the parking lot. It looked like it was empty, but when Randy opened the door, there was Arthur crouched down on the floor. Randy told me that Xantha had discussed Arthur's spying with their marriage counselor, who said that his behavior was due to his inability to face his mother's rejection of him." She shrugged. "The counselor told Xantha that he only did it because he wanted to be a part of her life. Isn't that pathetic? A rich, important man like him. All he ever wanted out of life, he told Xantha, was to make her happy. I wish I could find a man whose only mission in life was to make me happy."

"Was he here that night?"

"Only briefly. He and Xantha came in separate cars. He had to leave early to take care of some kind of telephone business in Sydney before the Australian stock market closed. I overheard him talking about it with one of the guests. Xantha stayed until about eleven."

"I wonder why she didn't go home with Randy."

"I think she was a little horrified by Randy's behavior. I suspect she had thought up until then that he only did party coke. It looked to me as if she was avoiding him, but it could have been the other way around: he was snuggling up pretty close to his bottle of Jack Daniels."

"Wouldn't she have heard about his drug use?"

"Probably. But we believe what we want to, don't we? He was always on his best behavior with her. She never saw him coked up to the eyeballs the way I have. Ranting about the powerful telescopes that could pierce the walls of his studio, and the little white snakes that were crawling all over the floor."

"Were there other episodes as bad as that night?"

"The time at the Montclair Art Museum was worse. That was the only other time I've seen him with the coke bugs. That's what they call them: the coke bugs. A tactile delusion, the doctor told me. Randy described it as feeling as if he had broken out in an unbearable case of poison ivy. This time they stopped, thank God."

"What about the other time?"

"He scratched himself until his skin was raw. It took weeks to heal—he had these ugly scabs all over his arms and legs. He ended up in the hospital that time, and the previous time too."

"Were he and Xantha going to get married?"

"Ah, you saw the piece in the *Post*."

Charlotte nodded.

"That's all I know. I looked for a ring on Xantha's finger at the party that night. There was one there—with a green stone—but I couldn't say whether it had been there before or not."

"What about the painting at the show?" asked Charlotte. "Did you notice anything about it that might have set Randy off?"

"No. But I didn't look at it that closely. I had just walked in when it happened. I just wanted to get him out of there as quickly as possible. Thank God Diana thought up the tickets thing."

"It was by an artist named Ed Verre. Does that name ring any bells?"

"Not a one," said Patty.

The meeting at the other end of the diner appeared to be breaking up, and they watched as three of the men departed.

"My uncles. They're probably going down to the court-house. Some of the others are from the church: St. George Greek Orthodox. My father's on the parish council. But most

of them are relatives. They're here because of family honor."
She said the word in Greek: "*Philotimo*. It's a big deal with
Greeks."

"Do you speak Greek?" asked Charlotte.

"Unfortunately, yes," she said, making a face.

"Why unfortunately?"

"Sixteen years of after-school Greek lessons. Other kids got
to run and play, I got to study Greek. Talk about boring." She
smiled. "I'm only going to make Johnny go for ten years."

Charlotte glanced over at the conclave of Greeks. "Do you
think they're going to be able to come up with the bail money?"

"I think so," said Patty. "If they don't, this arrest is going
to kill my father. It may end up killing him anyway."

After meeting with Patty, Charlotte headed out to the
Montclair Art Museum. She was probably chasing a chimera,
but she wanted to look at the painting that had caused the second
episode of cocaine-induced paranoia. If it *was* true that someone was after Randy, the clue to that person's identity must lie
with Verre's diner paintings. Only the paintings had induced
a sense of fear so overwhelming that it had caused Randy
temporarily to lose his mind.

She had no trouble finding Montclair, which was only about
twenty minutes from Paterson—a gracious suburb with big
old houses and beautiful tree-lined streets. The museum was
located on one of these streets in a Beaux Arts-style building
set in a small park, the Metropolitan Museum of Art in miniature. Her inquiry of a guard led her to the museum's library,
in a two-story colonial house adjacent to the park, where a
helpful librarian, after a few minutes of rummaging around,
produced a slide from among the clutter of bookshelves and
filing cabinets in the house's former dining room.

"Ordinarily you'd have to look at this through a viewer,
but we have the projector set up today," said the librarian, a
cheerful middle-aged woman with an Eastern European accent.
"Come this way."

Charlotte followed her into a reading room in what had formerly been the living room, where a projection screen had been
set up in front of the fireplace.

"This painting is from this year's show on Emerging New Jersey Artists," she said as she slid the slide into the carousel and then turned on the projector. "We hold it every year to highlight new artists who we think are particularly worthy of recognition. There we are," she said, as the slide appeared on the screen. "Is this the one you were interested in?"

"Yes," Charlotte replied.

The painting, titled "Falls View Diner with Banana Cream Pie," was a frontal view of a window of the diner, which was wet and fogged-over from the rain. On the opposite side of the window, a man with a ginger-colored beard sat at a booth eating a slice of banana cream pie. Behind him, two other men sat at the counter, watching John work the grill.

Again, Charlotte had the feeling that the artist had painted the diner on a specific night, in this case, a cold, misty night. It was almost as if he had had his nose pressed right up against the window.

As she studied the painting, she suddenly realized the connection among the three paintings. They were all of the identical scene! The painting in the Koreman show had been a long shot: the exterior of the diner, with the people too far away to be recognizable. This was a medium shot: the people could be seen in more detail, but the menu board, for instance, still wasn't readable. And the painting in the Paterson Museum show was a close-up.

The artist had been zooming in, and what he was zooming in on, she now realized, was the two men at the counter.

In this painting, she could tell little about them: the figures were blurred by the fog and distorted by the rain. One had dark hair and wore a navy blue jacket, the other had lighter hair, and wore a light-colored sweater. As in the other two paintings, they sat a stool's distance away from one another.

The painting in the Paterson museum show had been clearer, but she couldn't remember any of the details. She had only looked at it for an instant before being distracted by Randy.

"Would you like to see our file on the artist?" asked the librarian.

"Yes, I would," she said.

The librarian returned in a moment with a manila folder.

"There's not much," she said, handing Charlotte the file. "He must be young."

But he wasn't young, Charlotte found, as she studied the contents. His résumé stated that he was born in Peoria in 1938, which would make him fifty-one, and educated at the University of Illinois. His address was 24 Mill Street, the same address that Mary Catherine had given her, and his gallery was the Koreman. His only previous exhibit was at the Koreman.

The librarian, who had disappeared, now returned with a catalog in her hand. "I found something else," she said.

It turned out to be the catalog from the Koreman show, which told Charlotte nothing more than what she already knew. She would definitely have to track down Verre. Had he known Randy? she wondered. And if so, what was their relationship? Could Verre have been the person who was harassing him? But first she would have to take another look at the painting in the Paterson museum show.

When the librarian returned, Charlotte asked her to make a copy of a reproduction of "Falls View Diner with Banana Cream Pie" from an article about the show in the file.

She left a moment later with a color Xerox copy, marveling at the wonders of modern technology.

The return trip was much shorter, so eager was she to see the painting. She was now convinced that it held the clue to Randy's murder. "Every diner has a story," Tom was always saying. She now realized that Verre had been telling one of the Falls View's stories, and that she had to find out what that story was. At the museum, she parked the car, and fairly ran into the building. After paying her entrance fee, pausing only to reflect that a dollar fifty was a lot less than she paid in New York, she turned left past the White Manna toward the gallery area. And there it was: as clear as day. If she hadn't been distracted by Randy's bizarre behavior that night, she probably would have noticed it then.

One of the two men sitting at the counter was Randy.

Though you couldn't see his face—the view was from the rear—it was unmistakably him: the same short, well-built physique; the same long, blond hair tied back in a ponytail; the same black high-top sneakers. Now her question was, Who was the other man? She looked again at the calendar, which was last year's. It was from the Passiac Valley Water Commission, and featured a photograph of the Great Falls wreathed in ice. If the crossing off had been kept up to date, the date was April seventeenth. On reflection, she decided that there were just two people who might know who the other person was. The first was the bearded man eating the banana cream pie in the painting from the Montclair show. And since she didn't know who he was, she would have to go with the second: the grill man, John Andriopoulis.

Heading back to the lobby, she inquired about a pay phone, and was directed to a phone booth in the parking lot. After dialing information to get the number—as usual, there was no phone book—she called Patty.

Yes, her father had just been released on bail, she said. But he wasn't at the diner right now. He'd taken a little walk. She thought he was probably headed up to the observation bridge. "I told him about you," she added.

From the museum, Charlotte walked up Spruce Street to the Falls. At the head of Spruce Street, she entered the gate in a wire mesh fence, and followed a gravel path across the grounds of the hydroelectric plant that powered the city's street lamps. The path led to a caged-in footbridge over the intake reservoir for the hydro plant, and then across a grassy knoll overlooking the Falls basin. Crossing the grassy area, she found herself standing at the edge of the precipice, with only a few scrub trees growing in the crevices of the cliff face between her and the swirling water seventy-seven feet below. The sheer, coal-black basalt wall of the opposite side of the chasm was facing her, and the hulking brick structure of the hydroelectric plant, from whose turbines the spent waters emerged far below, was tucked into the cliff to her right. At her feet were the rusted remains of a wire mesh fence. Like the antique-reproduction street lamps whose globes had been put out, and the cast-iron park benches whose wooden-slatted seats had been smashed, the fence was another civic improvement that had fallen victim to urban blight.

From here, Charlotte could see the observation bridge spanning the gorge behind the trees to her left, and beyond the bridge, the white cascade of the Falls thundering into the chasm. There would be no rainbows today: the sky was overcast, and it looked like rain. A lone man was standing on the bridge, smoking a cigarette and looking out at the Falls. Turning, Charlotte headed back across the grass and rejoined the path, which passed through the grove of trees before emerging onto the bridge.

As Charlotte approached, John acknowledged her arrival with a nod, and then resumed his study of the Falls. Charlotte quietly joined him at the railing. The view was directly into the cleft of the inverted V of the chasm. The Falls poured over the wall of the chasm to her left. This was the first time she had seen the Falls up close, or at least the first time in forty-odd years, and they were as impressive as she remembered. Above, a quiet lake, and then, the heavy water cascading into the narrow opening, and reverberating with a roar that reminded her of the sound of the traffic on the George Washington Bridge at rush hour. Confined by the narrow canyon, the spray had nowhere to go but upward, and swirled around them like the smoke from a burning building, coating their clothing with a fine mist, and filling the air with the swampy smell of river water. From this close, the sense wasn't of grandeur or beauty, but of raw power. Below, the water surged and eddied around the sharp rocks before making its way down the rock-studded chute and emerging from the mouth of the gorge to quietly meander on downstream.

In responding to Patty's call for help, Charlotte felt a little like that water: plunging boldly over the precipice, heedless of the sharp rocks below that could cut her to bits, the currents that could drag her under, the whirlpools that could spin her senseless. But she knew that plunging over the precipice was what she had to do in order to reach that quiet place where the gorge released its contents into the order and quiet of the river below.

The man standing next to her was a different man from the big, warm-hearted energetic presence whom she had met less than a week before. He seemed diminished not only in spirit, but in size. He hadn't shaved, and the silver-gray stubble on his chin matched the waxen pallor of his cheeks. Deep furrows of misery were etched into his forehead, and his eyes were ringed with red. A shining orb of brightness had collapsed into a black hole of despair.

For a while, she stood there as John smoked, his left arm with its "Helen" tattoo bringing the cigarette rhythmically up to his lips, and then back down again. Then he spoke: "Is this the first time you've been here?" he asked. He had to speak loudly to be heard above the roar.

"In forty years," she replied, yelling.

"Do you know about Omanni?"

She shook her head.

"That's the Indian name for the Great Spirit of the Falls. When the water's low, he's easy to make out." He pointed to a rock formation that jutted out from between the dense sheets of water. "That's his profile." Then he pointed to a goldfinch on the top. "The bird's on his head." His finger traced a line downward. "Below are his nose, mouth, and chin."

As Charlotte stared at the mass of rugged rock, Omanni's profile suddenly took shape. "Oh, I see him now," she said, delighted. He had a bold forehead, and an open mouth, with a trailing mustache of vivid green weeds. His arms were crossed firmly across his chest, giving the impression that he presided with magisterial authority over the thundering waters.

"The Indians used to make sacrifices to him," he said.

"Is that what you were thinking of doing?" asked Charlotte.

"No." He smiled wanly, for an instant the old John. "But maybe I should. I'm going to need all the help I can get."

"Maybe I can help you," she said. "But first I need to know the facts. Lieutenant Voorhees said that you disappeared for about forty-five minutes that night. Between eleven and eleven forty-five. I'd like to know first, why you left, and second, where you went."

"I came here. To have a smoke. I often come here to have a smoke. I was still upset about Nick selling the Falls View. I wanted to think about my future. Besides, I didn't have anything to do until we reopened at twelve. Carlos was going to clean up."

"Why didn't you just go home?" she asked.

"I didn't want Helen to see how upset I was. Now that I have bigger things to worry about, it doesn't seem like such a big deal"—he sighed, a deep, weary sigh—"but at the time it seemed like the end of my life."

"Did you leave before or after Randy?"

"After," he said. "At least, I think it was after. I went out the back. But I hadn't noticed him the last time I had been out front, which was only a couple of minutes before that. He had been sitting at the counter all night."

"But you didn't see him on your way up here?"

He shook his head.

"When you came up here, what route did you take? What I mean is, did you cross the street in front of the diner, or did you wait until you got to the head of the street to cross?"

"In front of the diner. That's the way I always go. Cross in front of the diner, and then walk up the other side. Habit, I guess. Since I live across the street, I cross there a dozen times a day."

If John had crossed to the other side of the street, the chances were that he hadn't seen Randy lying in the cane-brake, if indeed that was where he had been. But there was also the possibility that John was lying.

"I didn't see Randy, but I did see something unusual," John continued. "I doubt if it means anything, but it struck me at the time as kind of odd."

"I'm listening," she prompted.

"I was putting the soiled aprons out . . ."

"I was just about to ask you when you put the aprons out."

"I'm glad someone believes I *did* put them out. I put them out just before I left to come up here, a little before eleven. I always put them out on Sunday nights. Anyway, I was putting them out when a car drove around the building."

"Do you remember what kind of car it was?"

"A gray Mercedes, New York plates. I remember because it's not often that cars drive all the way around. It's a tight squeeze, and most people turn around in the parking lot. Then, as I was going out again—I had gone back to get a jacket—it came around again."

"Did you get a look at the driver?"

"Not then. But as I was heading across the street, I saw the car come around for a third time. This time, the driver parked and went inside. I thought he must have been looking for someone. He was an older man, tall, distinguished-looking, dressed in a suit and tie."

Arthur Lumkin, Charlotte thought. Come back to spy on Xantha. "Do you think you could identify him from a photograph?"

"I think so," he said. He looked over at her, his face for the first time showing a spark of hope. "Do you know who it was?"

"Let's just say that I'm very glad that you told me about this," she said. The last thing she wanted to be accused of was giving away privileged information. "Did you tell Voorhees about it?"

He nodded. "He didn't seem interested," he added with a shrug.

Charlotte was disgusted with Voorhees. Here was a clear lead that he hadn't even bothered to follow up. She suspected that he just wanted to close the case as quickly as possible, and move to Florida. "Could the driver have seen you putting out the aprons?"

"Yes. Easily. There's a fenced enclosure there, to keep the raccoons out of the garbage, but you can see through it. We usually keep the gate locked to keep people out—you'd be amazed at who'll come wandering in—but I had left it open because I was coming back."

"In other words, someone could have entered the enclosure while you were up here, and taken two of the aprons."

John nodded.

· 9 ·

CHARLOTTE GAZED OUT at the profile of Omanni. As she studied the sheets of water that hung like plaits of hair on either side of his face, she went over the facts in her mind. Voorhees had theorized that Randy had passed out at the east end of the parking lot, and had been dragged through the canebrake to the river. If the driver of the Mercedes had been Arthur Lumkin, and it seemed clear from John's description that it was, he might have seen Randy lying unconscious on his swing around the parking lot, come back for the aprons after John had left, tied Randy up, and thrown him in. Motive, means, and opportunity. There was also the matter of precedent, namely Victor Louria. Though the party guests would have been leaving, the end of the parking lot was far enough away from the building that Lumkin's activities would probably not have attracted notice. Also, he would only have had to drag the body a few feet into the bamboo not to risk being noticed at all. The stuff grew as high as a Kansas cornfield in July. But there were a couple of problems with this theory. The first was that Voorhees didn't know for sure that Randy's body had been tossed in the river at that spot. He only knew that the medical examiner had found bits of bamboo in the apron strings and in the backs of Randy's sneakers. Any of the party guests could have wandered into the canebrake to throw up, and any of them could have flattened the path to the river bank, perhaps to throw up some more. Second was the fact that somebody had been harassing Randy—somebody other than Arthur Lumkin, who, according to what Patty had said, was just an innocent neurotic with a mother fixation.

Turning back to John, she said, "Now I want to ask you what

you remember about the events of another evening, an evening last spring. But first I'll backtrack a little." After explaining about Randy's history of paranoia and about his reaction to Verre's painting, she said, "The date on the calendar on the diner wall in the painting was April seventeenth. Does that date mean anything to you?"

John shrugged. "It's over a year ago."

Reaching into her bag, she pulled out the catalog from the Koreman show and opened it to the page with the reproduction of "Falls View Diner on a Rainy Spring Night." Then she pulled out the photocopy of "Falls View Diner with Banana Cream Pie." She spread them out against the railing of the bridge. "Here are two other views of the same scene," she said. "Do they help your memory at all?"

John looked at them, and then exclaimed: "Yes. I remember that night now! That was the night the diner guy, Kenny Meeker, gave the concert in the parking lot." He pointed to "Falls View Diner with Banana Cream Pie." This scene is later on that night. That's Meeker eating the pie. Then he pointed to the van in "Falls View Diner on a Rainy Spring Night." "And this is his van in the parking lot."

"And these people?" Charlotte asked, pointing to the two men sitting on the stools in the background of "Banana Cream Pie."

"That's Randy Goslau on the left and Don Spiegel on the right."

Now we're getting somewhere, Charlotte thought. "Have you any recollection of what they were talking about?" Her heart was pounding: she felt like a daredevil about to go over the lip of the Falls.

"Yes, I do," he said quietly. "They were arguing about an article in an art magazine. Spiegel wanted Goslau to send a statement to the magazine, retracting what he—Goslau—had said about him. Spiegel had just come from a party in New York where everyone was talking about this article. He was pretty incensed."

Charlotte now remembered seeing a magazine on the counter in the close-up of the same scene in the museum show. "What was Randy's reaction?"

John thought for a minute, and then said: "I guess you'd

have to call it belligerent. He was pretty doped up. He was talking fast, waving his arms around. He kept bragging about what a great artist he was, but of course he always did that . . . That was also the night that Spiegel committed suicide."

"What!" Charlotte exclaimed.

John continued: "He jumped. Either from over there"—he waved at the cliff at the edge of the Falls—"or from the bridge here." Taking a final drag on his cigarette, he tossed it over the railing.

Charlotte watched it go down. It seemed to fall in slow motion, being turned this way and that by the air currents created by the Falls. Once it hit the water, it spun violently around like laundry in a spin cycle before finally being swallowed up. "Why?" she asked simply.

"No one knew. He didn't appear to have any reason, but . . ." Andriopoulis shrugged as if to say, *Who knows why people do the things they do?* "Goslau said it was because he couldn't stand the shame of having it come out that it was really he who did his paintings."

Above the Falls, a mother mallard paddled around in the lake-like expanse of water, her six tiny ducklings following behind. As she looked out at them, Charlotte asked herself: *How would Verre have known about what went on at the diner that night, and why would he have wanted to paint it—not once, but three times?* Suddenly she gasped as the last duckling was sucked into the current and pulled over the edge of the Falls. It landed a few seconds later in a pool surrounded by sharp rocks, and disappeared under the surface of the water. A moment later, it popped back up, and was carried downstream by the current.

John had seen the incident too. "What's she going to do now?" he asked, referring to the mother mallard.

As they watched in fascination, the mother flew down to the duckling at the foot of the Falls and then back up to the rest of her brood. She repeated this several times, clearly confused and upset. Then, one by one, she nudged the others over the edge. Each disappeared under the water, only to pop back up again a moment later. When they had all made it safely over, the mother joined them at the debouchure of the gorge, and they paddled downstream happily together.

"Whew," said Charlotte, once all the ducklings were reunited with Mama. She realized that she had been holding her breath.

"And I thought I was in a predicament," John said. "She ought to go down in the history books right next to Leapin' Sam Patch."

"Who's he?" asked Charlotte.

"One of Paterson's historic figures. An Irish mill hand who took a dare to climb a tree and jump into the gorge. He landed right down there." He pointed to the same pool where the ducklings had landed. "It's the only place where you can land and survive. Anywhere else, he would have been smashed on the rocks. The drop speed is sixty-three miles per hour; somebody on the rescue squad once figured it out."

Charlotte stared down at the quiet little pool of yellow-brown stillness surrounded by the sharp-edged rocks and swirling waters.

"He went on to make a living at it. People would pay to see him jump. From Paterson, he went on to other falls. He was said to be the only person ever to have jumped into the Niagara River without a flotation device and survive. But he finally pressed his luck too far: he jumped off a cliff at a falls up around Rochester somewhere and never came up. They didn't recover his body until the next spring. It turned up in Lake Ontario, frozen in a block of ice."

Charlotte shuddered at the image.

"When I was a kid, we used to sing a jingle about him." He paused a minute to recall the words, and then proceeded to recite them:

Poor Sam Patch—a man once world renownded,
Much loved the water, and by it was drownded,
He sought for fame, and as he reached to pluck it,
He lost his balance, then kicked the bucket.

Charlotte was still staring at the pool of water, and wondering what it must have been like to land. Suddenly, she asked: "How do we know that Don Spiegel committed suicide?"

"He left a note in his typewriter. Also, there was the body. It came up four months later, right over there." He turned to point to the stretch of river behind them where it widened before emerging from the gorge. After pausing to light another cigarette, he continued: "I watched them haul it out. What was left of it. The head was almost gone; he must have landed head-first on a rock. There wasn't much skin left, either. Bodies decompose pretty rapidly in warm water, and it had been an unusually hot summer."

"How did they know it was Spiegel's, then—from the dental records?"

"No, the teeth were missing: some had been knocked out, the rest had fallen out when the soft tissue decomposed. They couldn't identify the body from fingerprints, either. They'd been nibbled away by fish. From what I understand, they identified it through the bones. Don't ask me how."

Not very accurately, she suspected. *"*How old was he?"

"I don't know for sure. Between forty-five and fifty, I'd guess."

"Height and weight?"

"Five foot ten, a hundred and seventy-five pounds."

Average, she thought. "Any distinguishing features?"

He shook his head.

In other words, thought Charlotte as she headed back to her car, the bashed-up, badly decomposed body that the rescue squad had pulled out of the river was the body of a Caucasian male of about Spiegel's age and height. It might have been any one of the winos or crackheads who made their home in the vacant mills of the historic district. A glimmer of a hypothesis was beginning to form at the back of her brain: that Spiegel had faked his own suicide and then taken on the identity of Ed Verre. Which then led to the question of why he had done so, if indeed he had. First on her agenda was proving that he had. Toward that end, she got back into her car, and headed back to the Montclair Art Museum. (What was it that she had said to herself about driving cross-country and back again?) As a prominent New Jersey artist, Spiegel must have exhibited there at one time or another. Maybe the museum even had some of his paintings in its collection.

"Oh, yes," said the librarian in response to Charlotte's request for information. "We have a lot on him." Getting up from her desk, she disappeared among the stacks.

Though the librarian had been surprised to see Charlotte back
so soon, she had asked no questions about why she wanted the
information, made no demand for credentials, required no payment. Her only aim was to provide smiling, efficient, speedy
service. Charlotte had always ranked librarians up there with
diner waitresses and attentive nurses among the unsung saints,
and the museum's excellent librarian only served to confirm
her already high opinion. She returned a few minutes later with
a thick file folder, two books—one on photorealists and one on
Spiegel, and half-a-dozen catalogs from Spiegel's various
shows. "If you need anything else, just let me know," she
said.

Charlotte found what she was looking for right away: Donald
Edgar Spiegel, born in South Bend in 1938, educated at Indiana
University. Same year as Verre, neighboring state. She also
took note of the fact that Edgar, the shortened form of which
was Ed, was Spiegel's middle name. From there, the *curricu-
lum vitae* went on with page after page of listings: exhibitions,
awards, articles, and so on. But no photo.

Going over to the librarian's desk, Charlotte asked if they
had one.

"No, I'm sorry," she replied. "We don't keep photo files.
But there might be one in one of the books or articles about
him."

But there wasn't, in either the books or the catalogs. After
asking the librarian to make copies of a couple of the pages of
biographical information, Charlotte thanked her and left. Then
she got back into her car and headed back into the city.

Before she confronted Verre, there was someone else she
wanted to see.

Morris and Evelyn Finder lived in a rent-controlled, one-
bedroom apartment in the Village, which was crammed to the
rafters with the fruits of a lifetime of art collecting. All the
available wall space had long ago been taken up by paintings,
and there were now paintings under the bed, behind the doors,
and on top of the kitchen cupboards. The living space, modest
to begin with, was now reduced to a place for the bed, a narrow
path to the bathroom, and a small area in the kitchen with a
tiny table and two chairs. All the living was done at this table,

where the Finders entertained, read, watched TV, and ate, though Morris had once told Charlotte that they rarely ate at home anymore because there was no room to cook. "Not that I ever liked to cook in the first place," Evelyn had added.

"I know what you mean," Charlotte had replied. She was not much of a cook herself, and tended to eat most of her meals out as well.

But despite its modesty, the atmosphere of the apartment was rich with the sense of the Finders' devotion to art, far richer in this regard than, say, the Lumkins' luxurious uptown penthouse. After visiting the Finders—as she often had when she was still living with Jack—Charlotte always felt as if she had come away from the mountain retreat of a Confucian scholar or the cell of a medieval monk. One never felt confined there, because the apartment's ambiance was that of a great institution—the Institution of Art. Nor did the conversation ever degenerate into the mundane: garbage removal, neighborhood restaurants, or the real estate market. One had the feeling of being in the storeroom of a great museum, and indeed, the Finders had been courted by the directors of museums around the country, who had visions of their institutions becoming the ultimate repositories of the Finders' collection.

It was to the tiny kitchen table that Morris and Evelyn now escorted her. They had just returned from their regular Saturday morning gallery rounds.

"Would you like some tea?" asked Evelyn. She was a petite woman with short gray hair and oval, black-framed eyeglasses. She was stylishly dressed in a black cotton-knit suit accented by a colorful scarf.

"Yes, thank you," said Charlotte, taking a seat at the table, which was piled high with catalogs. She could use a cup of tea; by now, it was nearly two, and her energies were flagging.

"What painting is it that you wanted to see?" asked Morris as Evelyn assembled the tea things. He wore a plaid jacket, tan chinos, and white running shoes—not stylish, but ideal for pounding the city's sidewalks.

"The one by Ed Verre that was in the show at the Koreman Gallery," she replied. "It's called 'Falls View Diner on a Rainy Spring Night.' "

"Where's that one, Evie?" asked Morris.

"In the rack next to the hall closet."

As Morris went to fetch the painting, Evelyn carried the tea tray to the table. The tea was served in glasses, Russian-style. "Go ahead," she urged, passing Charlotte her glass. "Drink it before it cools off."

Charlotte took a sip of the brew. It was an herb tea of some kind, but with a delicious fruit flavor, not weedy-tasting as many herb blends were. "It's delicious," she said. "What's that floating around in it?"

"Cherry preserves," Evelyn replied, joining her at the table. "To sweeten it. That's how they serve it in the old country. Or so Morris says. I wouldn't know. The closest I ever got to the old country was the Russian Tea Room."

Morris had returned with the painting, which he propped up against the refrigerator. "There we are," he said. " 'Falls View Diner on a Rainy Spring Night.' " He stood to one side, his arms folded over his chest.

"Thank you," Charlotte said. "Actually, there's another painting that I'd like to see too. Would you mind?"

"Not at all," he said agreeably. "Which one?"

"Anything recent by Donald Spiegel."

Morris' gray eyes widened in surprise, and Evelyn set down her glass of tea and stared across the table at Charlotte.

Once Morris had regained his composure, he said: "We don't have anything recent by Don Spiegel. He priced us out of the market a long time ago. But we do have a painting of his that might interest you."

Evelyn looked up at him. " 'Herald Square'?" she asked.

He nodded.

"It's in the bathroom," she said.

Morris' reappeared a moment later with the Spiegel, which he leaned up against the refrigerator next to the Verre.

It was a view of Herald Square, looking east, with Macy's in the foreground and the Empire State Building in the background. As in the Verre painting, it was a rainy night scene, and the lights of the city were reflected in Macy's wet plate-glass windows.

"Is this the kind of painting you were looking for?" asked Morris, fixing her with a questioning gaze that told her he also suspected, or possibly even knew for sure, that Spiegel and Verre were one and the same.

"Yes," she said. She looked at the painting again, and then back up at Morris. "So you suspected it too," she said.

"I suspected the moment I saw it." He nodded at the painting of the Falls View. "A painter of that calibre comes along once in a lifetime. Besides that, the coincidence was too great to ignore."

Evelyn chimed in: "Don Spiegel commited suicide in April; Ed Verre appeared out of nowhere the following January."

"When I got the Verre home, and could compare, I was certain," Morris continued. "Spiegel's brushwork is distinctive—it's very sure. He never blends colors, never goes over anything. That's his genius, the sureness and quickness of his brushwork."

Charlotte remembered that Diana Nelson had also talked about Spiegel's distinctive brushwork.

"Evelyn, where's the magnifying glass?" asked Morris.

"In the basket," she said. She got up and handed it to him.

Holding the magnifying glass up to the canvas, Morris gestured for Charlotte to come over. "See," he said, "there's no attempt to clean up the stroke. He leaves it ragged and coarse, which makes the effects he achieves all the more remarkable."

He was right, she thought as she compared Spiegel's brush stroke to Verre's. The brushwork was exactly the same: sharp and bold, but with coarse, jagged edges that let you know it was the hand of the painter and not an airbrush that had applied the paint to the canvas.

"It's Spiegel's brushwork that gives his work its confidence and lack of pretense. Now I'll show you a painting by another photorealist. A lot of them use an airbrush, of course, but among those who use a bristle brush, this artist is probably the most comparable to Spiegel."

"The question is, do you know where the painting is?" teased Charlotte.

"No," Morris replied, with a lopsided grin. "But Evie does. I'd be lost without her." He looked down at his wife. " 'Jim's Super Service?' " he asked.

"Under the dining table," she replied.

After pulling the painting out from under the table, Morris returned with it to the kitchen and set it down next to the Spiegel. It was a painting of a pickup truck parked in front of a convenience store. "Jim's Super Service" was painted on the door.

"This is by a West Coast photorealist," he said. He handed Charlotte the magnifying glass: "As you can see, the artist tries to obliterate the brush marks; everything is smooth. I think the worked-over feeling gives it a tediousness that Spiegel manages to avoid."

After taking a look, Charlotte handed the glass back. "It looks as if you've lived up to your name again, Morris," she said. "By finding Don Spiegel, or should I say, re-finding him."

"I couldn't find anything without Evie," he joked.

"Have you told anyone?" she asked.

Morris shook his gnomish head. "Why should we? We've been buying Spiegels for ten thousand dollars. Some day it's bound to come out that Verre and Spiegel are the same person, and then our Verre/Spiegels will be worth ten times that. Not that the value matters to us."

"We enjoy them no matter how much they're worth," said Evelyn.

Morris gazed down at Charlotte. He was leaning against the counter, his arms folded across his chest. "How did *you* figure it out?"

That was a good question. The answer had to do with Leapin' Sam Patch and ducklings and a quiet pool of yellow-brown water. But rather than go into all that, she fudged it by saying that she had noticed the similarities in the paintings in the museum show.

"Very perspicacious of you, my dear Charlotte. To me, the similarities weren't readily apparent. It was studying the brushwork that convinced me. The brushwork, and a couple of other things."

"Like what?" she asked.

"First the name, which is something a *shiksa* like you"—his gray eyes twinkled—"would never have caught on to. Spiegel means glass in Yiddish, or, for that matter, in standard German; and Verre means glass in French."

Of course! thought Charlotte. She was far from fluent in either German or French, but she had developed a passing acquaintance with both of those languages during the years she'd spent at a posh Connecticut finishing school.

"You're right," she said. "But I did catch on to the use of his middle name. He also moved his home state. Spiegel was born in South Bend in 1938 and studied at Indiana University, and Verre was born in Peoria in 1938 and studied at the University of Illinois."

"I guess people who change their identities figure it's best to stay as close to the truth as possible." Morris commented. He turned back to the paintings. "Then there's the matter of the initials. Spiegel always signed his paintings with his initials, which were hidden somewhere in the painting."

"Like Alfred Hitchock in his movies," said Evelyn.

"Here they are, here," Morris said, pointing to the backward reflection of the letters DS. Then he turned to the Verre, which bore the prominent "Verre" signature in the lower right corner. "I wasn't sure about the initials in this painting. There is a DS here"—he pointed to the license plate of the truck—"but it could be just a coincidence. Excuse me," he said. "I just have to get another painting."

"Also under the dining table," said Evelyn.

He returned a moment later with "Falls View Diner with Banana Cream Pie," which he set down in front of the other Verre.

"I didn't realize that you owned this one too," Charlotte said.

"We've bought all of them, including the one that's now in the Paterson Museum show. In this painting, the truck is gone," he said. "But the initials are still there. This time they're on this sign." He pointed to the initials at the bottom of a sign advertising a $2.99 breakfast special that hung on the inside of the window, just above the booth where Meeker was sitting. "Again, the initials are in reverse."

"Were Spiegel's initials in the painting in the Paterson Museum show?"

"Yes. That's why we went to the opening. To see if we could find them. It took us longer than we thought. They're on a candy bar in the display case under the counter. If you go back to the museum, you should take a look. Among all the usual candies—Milky Ways, M & M's, Mounds Bars, Lifesavers—is something called a DS Crunch."

"A DS Crunch," Charlotte repeated, leaning back in her chair, and taking a sip of her tea. "Have you ever met Verre?" she inquired.

Evelyn replied: "We've tried to set up a meeting, but we haven't had any success. His phone's unlisted, and he doesn't answer our letters. We hear he's a recluse, but we think it's more than that. We think he's avoiding us because he knows we're on to him. Why else would we have snapped up his every painting as if it were a diamond in the rough?"

Morris straightened up suddenly. "I just remembered one other painting that I want to show you. Where's the self-portrait?" he asked.

"Behind the couch in the living room," Evelyn replied.

He returned a moment later with yet another canvas, which he propped up in front of "Herald Square." "This one's called 'Self-Portrait with Two Reflections.' It's the only self-portrait Spiegel ever did."

The painting was a close-up of the smoked plate-glass window of a city tailor shop, showing the reflection of a man standing on the sidewalk across the street. He was reflected twice: once in the plate glass itself, and once in a mirror that hung above the counter inside the shop: a shadowy figure with dark hair, wearing jeans and a white shirt.

The painting reminded Charlotte of the chandeliers in the Hall of Mirrors of the palace at Versailles: reflection after reflection, stretching off into infinity. But in this case, the viewer was unable to see the original, and even the reflections were a reproduction of the real thing. It struck her that Verre was also a reflection, and how elusive that reflection was.

"If you were to ask me," Morris continued, "I would tell you that this is the self-portrait of a man who craves anonymity. Yet it is also the self-portrait of an artist who led the most public of lives. Evie and I have been to Don's studio at the Gryphon Mill many times. There were always people around; he was never alone. That kind of life can be death to an artist's creativity."

Charlotte nodded, beginning to sense what he was getting at.

"Plus there was the fact that he was locked into his style.

How is an artist to break away from a style that has become an artistic dead end for him when the paintings that he produces in that style sell for a million dollars before he's even set brush to canvas?"

"Tell her your theory, dear," Evelyn prompted.

"I think he faked his suicide in order to start over artistically, just as an author takes on a pseudonym. He often told us that he was happiest before he became a big success, when he still had the latitude to experiment."

"I see what you're saying," Charlotte commented, "and I would agree if what he's done as Ed Verre represented a new direction. But as far as I can see, he's just gone back to his earlier subject matter—diners—and is painting them in the same way as his cityscapes."

"Yes," Morris said. He raised a knuckle to his chin and gazed out the window, which overlooked an air shaft. "That puzzles me too. If shedding the trappings of success was the reason for the new identity, I don't understand why he hasn't taken off in a new direction."

"Maybe he hasn't gotten around to it yet," Evelyn offered. "Maybe he's going over the old ground one last time. After all, he's only been Ed Verre for what . . . nine months?"

"Maybe," Morris agreed. Then he looked at Charlotte. "I suppose we'll be competing with Jack Lundstrom now for the works of Ed Verre. Not that we mind," he added, looking at Evelyn for confirmation. "We were lucky to have the field to ourselves as long as we did."

Of course, Charlotte thought. As far as the Finders were concerned, she would have had a reason for her visit, and her being Jack's representative would make the most sense to them. She saw no reason for telling them otherwise.

"Not necessarily," she said.

She arrived home at about four, and went right to her library. She wanted to sit down and have a nice little think, to say nothing of a nice little drink. After fixing herself a Manhattan, she flopped down on the oversized sofa, and put her feet up. Vivian's tape recorder was still sitting there, but it had lost its threatening aura. She now had more important things to think about than her memories of the past. Specifically, what had happened on the night of Randy's murder. She now had two new important pieces of information. The first was that Arthur Lumkin had returned to the diner after making his call to Australia, which meant that he could have tied Randy up and thrown him in the river. He had been to the diner at least once before when Randy had found him hiding in his car. And if he and Xantha had sometimes dropped in at the mill, as Diana said they had, he had probably been to the diner more than once. The diner was the hangout for Paterson's art community, and although it was hardly the kind of restaurant usually frequented by someone like Lumkin—Lutèce would be more his style—there was nowhere else in the neighborhood to get a cup of coffee unless you wanted to try a Spanish *cantina*. He might already have known that the soiled aprons were kept in the enclosure out back, or he might have seen John putting them out when he drove around. In any case, his presence at the diner later that night qualified him for a slot at the top of the list of suspects.

The second new piece of information had to do with why Randy had gone off the deep end, which may or may not have had anything to do with his murder. She suspected that he had recognized that it was Spiegel who did the painting of the Falls View. If Morris had, why shouldn't he? As Spiegel's assistant, he had been intimately acquainted with his work. She thought back to the scene at the gallery. Had Randy's comments, "I see them" and "This time I'm certain I see them," referred to Spiegel's initials? Which led to the next question: what was it about the prospect of Spiegel's being alive that had been so frightening? Could it have been losing the paintings that Spiegel had given him? If Spiegel was alive, he could retract the gift agreement. But the prospect of losing the paintings didn't seem to warrant Randy's extreme reaction, or his sense of paranoia. Maybe the reaction had just been a cocaine-inspired fear of ghosts. Then again, maybe the painting really had been done by Verre, who had reproduced Spiegel's technique and concealed Spiegel's initials for some obscure reason of his own.

Looking at the tape recorder sitting on the coffee table, Charlotte was suddenly reminded of the Broadway play, *Angel Street*, in which she had starred in the early forties. It had later been made into a movie, *Gaslight*, starring Ingrid Bergman. The fact that she'd had to turn down the movie role because she'd been committed to another project was one of the major disappointments of her career. Apart from starring in the role she'd made famous on Broadway, she had missed her only chance to have played opposite Charles Boyer. It was probably a good thing; chances were that she would have fallen for him, and he'd been happily married. She bemoaned the dearth of sophisticated stars like Boyer in today's movies. By comparison, today's heroes struck her as overgrown sixteen-year-olds. But all that was beside the point. The point was that in *Gaslight*, the husband tries to drive the wife slowly mad. Had somebody—Spiegel or Verre,—been trying to do the same to Randy? And if so, why? Taking a long swig of her drink, she resolved not to think about it anymore for the moment. To do so was like trying to tell what was glass and what was reflection in one of Spiegel's paintings. From studying the Spiegels on Jack's walls, she had learned that in order to do this it was necessary to fix on a single point and determine whether it was reality or illusion, and then extrapolate from there. Even then, you often got it all wrong and had to start over again.

The same was true in a murder investigation. You had to take one point and follow it up. You couldn't allow yourself to be thrown off track by chasing after every lead. Since she had no idea how to pursue the Arthur Lumkin lead, she decided to follow up on the Verre lead instead. In order to tell if he was reality or illusion, she would have to compare his likeness directly to Spiegel's. And for that, she needed a photograph of Spiegel. His self-portrait told her little: a vague reflection showing a man of average height and weight with dark hair. How should she go about getting a picture? she asked herself, and decided to start by checking with Tom. Now that he was back, she wanted to fill him in anyway. With his connections at the New York newspapers, he might be able to dig up a photo. There must have been a photo with Spiegel's obituary. For that matter, it might be handy to get copies of the obituaries, too. The next step would be to pay a visit to Spiegel's ex-wife, Louise. She might also be able to provide a photo, and Charlotte wanted to talk with her anyway. Maybe Louise could give her a better sense of what this man of glass was all about.

· IO ·

BACK FROM HIS trip and eager to get in on the investigation, Tom picked Charlotte up at ten the next morning. He had suggested that she use him as an entrée to Louise Spiegel. When Charlotte had called Louise to make the appointment, she'd said that Tom was interested in doing an article about her ex-husband. Tom's journalistic pursuits came in handy as excuses for asking people questions that they might not ordinarily want to answer. As they headed out to Paterson in the Buick, eliciting admiring glances from passing motorists, Charlotte filled Tom in on what she had discovered, namely that Lumkin had returned to the diner on the night that Randy was killed, and that Verrc and Spiegel were probably one and the same.

At the mere mention of the words "new identity," Tom launched into a long discourse on the methods for creating one, starting with taking the name of a dead baby from a gravestone, the old grade B movie trick. Tom's experience in writing about true crime had left him with extensive knowledge of such arcane matters.

"Wild man Plummer," said Charlotte, as Tom, having expounded on the various ways of obtaining a phony birth certificate, moved on to the subject of altering one's fingerprints with acid . . .

He laughed.

In Mack Sennett days, every Keystone Kops story conference had had its wild man, an average Joe who was hired to sit at the conference table and toss out words at random—monkey, ambulance, chopsticks. The idea was to get the juices of creativity flowing among the writers. The Mack Sennett wild man was a Hollywood legend. That Tom was Charlotte's wild man was their private joke.

"No, seriously," Tom said. "The United States is the world's easiest country in which to forge a new identity. You know why?" Pulling out his wallet, he flipped it open to his driver's license. "This little document here. Which is used all over the country as a means of identification, but was never intended for that purpose."

They had gotten off at the exit for the historic district, and were now waiting at the stoplight in front of the museum.

"By the way, where are we going?" Tom asked.

"The Manor District, on the east side," she replied. She was studying the map that lay open on her lap. "Turn right here."

They were just turning onto Market Street when a cluster of people on the sidewalk in front of the Ivanhoe Gallery caught Charlotte's eye. A banner hanging from the building read, in gold letters on a purple ground: "Fine Arts Auction Today."

"Look. There's an art auction at the Ivanhoe." She checked her watch. "We're early," she said. "Our appointment isn't for forty-five minutes." They had allowed the usual amount of time, forgetting that the traffic on a Sunday morning would be light.

Tom looked around, saw the sign, and then met Charlotte's eye. Without a word, he pulled into the museum parking lot. "It's a wise man who knows when he's beaten," he said.

"You mean you can't say that in Latin?" Charlotte teased.

Tom shot her a dirty look.

Then they got out and headed up the street to the gallery. A sandwich board on the sidewalk in front of the gallery read "Going Out of Business. Everything Must Go." Next to the sandwich board stood a rack holding a collection of auction catalogs. Charlotte and Tom each took one.

"Hello again," said Diana, who stood at the head of the access ramp that covered a section of the steps. She waved a hand at the auctiongoers gathered on the patio below. "I finally decided that I couldn't make a go of it. A spur of the moment decision."

"What are you going to do now?" asked Tom.

"I think I'm moving to Paris," she said with a radiant smile.

"I'm selling everything, my inventory as well as the works from my personal collection."

The Diana of today was a different woman from the Diana of earlier in the week. She looked stunning in a sleeveless dress of red stretch fabric, which she wore with dangling jet earrings that emphasized the slender elegance of her long, white neck.

"Not bad," said Tom, speaking about more than just Paris.

Diana addressed Charlotte: "If you're still interested in Louise Sicca's 'Lemon Meringue,' it's for sale. Most of the ceramic pieces in the show were on consignment from the artist, but that particular one belonged to me."

"There you go," said Tom, giving Charlotte an encouraging nudge.

Diana opened the catalog, and then handed it to Charlotte. "Here it is," she said, pointing to the entry with a fingernail whose polish exactly matched the red of her dress. "Lot Number Fourteen."

As Diana turned to chat with some new arrivals, Tom and Charlotte descended the steps, and found two empty seats among the folding chairs that had been set up on the patio facing the spillway with its rushing waters. The auction had attracted a good-sized crowd.

No sooner had they taken their seats than Diana mounted the podium. After a few words about her regrets at leaving Paterson, she introduced the auctioneer, who was from a New York gallery. Then she stepped down and took a seat next to Jason Armentrout.

"I guess you were right about the Pernod," said Tom, directing his gaze to the couple, who were chatting intimately.

"Unfortunately for you."

"*Aliquando bonus dormitat Homerus*," he said. "Sometimes even the good Homer sleeps, or, you can't win 'em all."

"I'm sorry I challenged you," said Charlotte.

The first lot, called "Pine Barrens," was an abstract landscape of trees at the edge of a pond. The roots descended into a black pool edged with deep purple, from which a hint of light shined upward. Charlotte loved it, but she was saving her money for "Lemon Meringue."

The bidding for "Pine Barrens," which went for fifteen thousand, set the pace. It was fast and high, perhaps because of the New York auctioneer. A charming art nouveau poster of a couple in evening dress went for five thousand, a brooding oil of a mountain for ten.

"Look!" said Charlotte, as Number Four went on the block.

It was a painting of a diner, not as folk-arty as Randy's or as glitteringly precise as Verre/Spiegel's, but with a certain charm. Charlotte had the feeling that she'd seen it before, but she couldn't recall where or when. Paintings of diners were everywhere these days.

"Are you going to bid?" she asked Tom. "The price is low." The catalog listed it as unsigned and undated, and gave the estimated value as fifteen hundred dollars, reflecting its lack of provenance.

"I think so," Tom replied, his eyes gleaming with excitement.

As the bidding opened, Tom's arm flew up. His offer of five hundred was acknowledged by the auctioneer, and the bidding was on. There were a lot of bidders, but as the price went up everyone except Tom and Jason dropped out. Jason finally won the picture for twelve hundred.

"I'm just as glad," said Tom as the auctioneer's assistant set the next painting on an easel. "I thought it was going too high."

When "Lemon Meringue" finally came up for bid, Charlotte was primed. To her surprise, there were few bidders. She supposed that material illusionism had a limited audience. She ended up buying it for seven hundred.

"Diana was selling it for two thousand," said Tom as the gavel came down. "You got a deal."

Charlotte was pleased. As Diana had said, magical things were always happening in Paterson.

They stayed for a couple of more lots, and then left. A few minutes later, they were heading through downtown Paterson, top down and radio blasting. If it had been salsa on the radio instead of sixties rock and roll, they would have fit right in. The mood of the city was buoyant: it was a glorious day, and the sidewalks were crowded with shoppers. Though downtown Paterson must once have looked like that of any other older

American city, the influx of Latino immigrants had given the aging district the atmosphere of a South American open-air market. Much of the merchandise was displayed on the sidewalks. Huge bottles of pig's ears and knuckles, sweatshirts emblazoned with photographs of Malcolm X, plaster statuettes of the Virgin Mary: it was all to be found on the sidewalks of downtown Paterson. Driving through the hustle and bustle, they continued on for a few more blocks, and suddenly found themselves in a neighborhood of perfectly groomed lawns and charming houses that was separated from the urban blight by only a stoplight and an invisible line that somehow managed to keep the inner city at bay.

The address they were looking for was on Park Avenue, and they found it, fittingly enough, overlooking a beautiful park. The house was quite large, and in the English cottage style, one of the most charming on a street lined with pretentious English Tudors and Spanish colonials.

Louise was just emerging from a carriage house at the back as they pulled into the driveway. "I like your car," she said.

She was a tall, slightly plump woman with long, rangy limbs. In general type, she resembled Bernice, they were both large women with full faces, but where Bernice's features were sharply drawn, Louise's were soft. She must have been beautiful once, in an earthy kind of way. Charlotte could easily imagine how she must have looked in the sixties. Her long, full black hair; round, tanned, full-cheeked face; and rich, caramel-colored eyes were made to go with peasant blouses and Mother Hubbard skirts. But the face was now lined and careworn and the long black hair, now streaked with silver, looked out of place on a woman her age, even tied back in a ponytail.

"Thank you," Tom replied. After slamming the door shut, he ran a loving hand over the polished surface of the front fender. "She's my pride and joy."

Louise joined them at the car. "Forgive my appearance," she said. She wore a soiled white apron over a pair of sweat pants and an oversized man's pin-striped oxford-cloth shirt. "I've been working. I'm a ceramic artist." Then she held out her hand. "Louise Spiegel," she said.

Once introductions had been dispensed with, along with

the Charlotte-Graham-the-movie-star explanations that always went along with them, Louise led them toward her studio in the carriage house. Her recent works were displayed on shelves just inside the door: a dish of hard candies, a linzertorte, and a tray of cupcakes—all glitteringly, appetizingly real.

Charlotte immediately recognized them as being by the same artist as her recently acquired purchase. "I just bought your 'Lemon Meringue' at the Ivanhoe auction," she said. "I didn't realize that you were also Louise Spiegel. I'm delighted to meet you."

"You did!" said Louise, clearly pleased. "I'm glad you like my work. Diana's done well for me. I'm going to be sorry to see her leave. I'll never be a Don Spiegel," she went on, referring to the ostensible reason for their visit, "but I like what I do."

Charlotte was surprised at her self-deprecatory tone, but it offered insight into the problems with the marriage: a woman who lived in the shadow of her husband. Of course she would never be a Don Spiegel, but she could be a Louise Sicca and seemed to be doing very well at it.

"I think you're being overly modest," she said. "I find your work fascinating, though I couldn't begin to tell you why." She touched a finger to the raspberry filling of the linzertorte; it was hard and cool. "What is it?" she asked. "That your eyes tell you one thing and your sense of touch another?"

"Yes. In art critic parlance, it's the conflict between the visual and the tactile clues. Or between expectation and reality. The result is a disturbance in your sense of reality. There's a lot of mystery in it; it's like a magic trick. That's why I like to call it material illusionism."

"I just thought of why I like your work so much," said Charlotte.

"Why's that?"

"It reminds me of my profession. This is a piece of clay pretending to be a torte. If you look at it as the role [the linzertorte], it divulges that it isn't real; and if you look at it as the actor [a piece of clay], it oozes raspberries."

Louise smiled, and her face lit up. She had good teeth, large and white and even. "I never thought of my sculptures as playing a role before. But that's certainly what they do."

"How did you decide on food as a subject?" Charlotte asked.

"I used to do tiny ceramic rooms, complete with furniture," she replied. "Then one day I did a kitchen, and I got hooked on kitchens, complete with utensils, serving dishes, food. It finally dawned on me that it wasn't the kitchen so much as the food that I liked doing."

"After that, it was just food?"

Louise nodded. "Just desserts, now. Please, have a seat," she said, gesturing to a small living area made up of castoff furniture.

As they took their seats, Louise busied herself in a kitchenette, from which she emerged a few minutes later carrying a tray laden with coffee cups and a linzertorte. "One advantage of using food as your subject is that you get to eat it afterward."

"It looks almost as good as your artwork, but not quite," Charlotte said as Louise cut the torte, and transferred the pieces to the plates.

"Now," Louise said as she passed the pastry and the cups of coffee. "What is it that you wanted to know about Don?"

Tom pulled out a reporter's notebook. "Maybe you could start with how you met," he said, not wanting to jump right into it. "I gather you've known him longer than anyone else he associated with."

"I've known him . . . I guess that's not the right tense, is it?" She started over: "Better to say, I first met him in college—Indiana University. We were both art students there. After college, we went to graduate school together at the Rhode Island School of Design."

"When were you married?"

"Just after graduate school." Tears welled in her eyes, and she wiped them away with a clay-stained hand, leaving a streak of gray on her freckled cheek. "I'm sorry," she said. "It's just that I miss him so much. I feel like a piece of me is missing, a leg or an arm or something." She gazed out the mullioned window at the lawn, which was shaded by tall trees, and bordered by hydrangeas, whose flower heads nodded in the soft September breeze.

"Then you were close, despite the fact that you were divorced," said Tom.

"We weren't divorced. We were just separated." She took a deep breath. "Yes, we were close. He came here every day: to see me, to see Julius. We just couldn't live together. Or rather, I couldn't live with him."

"Why not?" Charlotte asked.

"Have you heard about the mill?"

"A little," she said.

"It was a zoo. There were people hanging around there twenty-four hours a day. I didn't leave Don because I didn't love him, but because I couldn't stand his life. I felt as if everything revolved around him. I didn't have any time for myself, for my art, for Julie. Most nights I cooked dinner for a dozen people: artists, musicians, the plumber who came in to fix the faucet—you name it. If they were there, Don made them feel welcome to stay until he went to bed, or even later than that. It wasn't good for Julie, either; it isn't good for a child to be exposed to a life like that. I just couldn't stand it anymore. The constant partying, the endless cooking and cleaning up, the lack of privacy, the way people took advantage of Don . . ."

"Like Randy?" interjected Charlotte.

"I would rank him as leech number one, yes. Don was so generous to him: helping him along, introducing him to collectors like the Lumkins. And then Randy turns around and stabs him in the back."

"The *Artnews* article," said Tom.

She nodded. "It sounds terrible to say, but I've often wished that it was Randy who died first. Things were fine before he came along. We had a nice quiet life together, the three of us. Randy introduced Don to that Bohemian life, and Don went along with it. I never really understood the appeal for Don, because he wasn't an extroverted person. We would have a dozen people for dinner, and he wouldn't talk to any of them. He just wanted them around, to validate his status as a big-time artist or something."

She was interrupted by the slamming of the screen door. A boy entered, carrying a knapsack. He was a short, slight boy of thirteen or fourteen, with a triangular face, dark skin and eyes, and an engaging puckish expression.

"Hi, Mom," he said, coming over to give her a kiss.

Louise introduced Tom and Charlotte. "My son, Julius," she said. "Mr. Plummer and Miss Graham are doing an article on Daddy."

"Neat," said Julius. Then he turned to his mother, and said: "Ma, Terry and Jack are going over to West Side Park to play ball. Jack's mom is going to drive them. Can I go too?"

Louise said yes and the boy disappeared as quickly as he had come.

"Where was I? Oh, the mill. It only got worse after I moved out. That was eight years ago. Whenever I called—it didn't matter what hour of day or night it was—I could hear glasses tinkling and the murmur of conversation in the background. I never knew who was going to answer the phone."

"Did that life style have anything to do with your husband's suicide?"

"I don't know. I have no idea why he killed himself," she said bluntly. She paused for a moment to collect herself. "It was an act that was totally out of character. There's not an hour of the day that I don't wonder if there was something I could have done."

"Like what?" asked Tom, gently.

"Sometimes I think that I shouldn't have moved out, that I should have been more firm and kicked the others out."

"Did the note reveal any motive?"

She shook her head. "It was vague. The 'I can't go on' sort of thing."

"What about Bernice's lawsuit?" he asked. "Did you approve?"

"No, I did not," she responded firmly. "First of all, the paintings are legally Randy's. Don signed them over to him. Whether Don meant to retract the agreement before he died or not is moot: he hadn't done so at the time of his death. Second, to take up arms against a sleaze like Randy Goslau is to invite trouble, which is exactly what Bernice got."

"In the form of the threat to sue for palimony."

"Yes. Randy's lawyers made no claim that there was any sexual relationship, but that was the image that the threat was designed to create. Anyone who knew Don knows that it was ridiculous. He liked women. Another reason I moved out was his peccadilloes with the adoring female art students who hung around the mill."

"Groupies," said Tom.

"Exactly. I once heard somebody say that artists are the rock stars of the eighties. Which is a good analogy because artists have groupies too."

"But you stood to benefit from the lawsuit."

"Only indirectly. It's actually Julie who will benefit if the paintings are ruled to be part of the estate. Julie gets a percentage. But even if they are, it doesn't make any difference. We don't need the money. Don left us well provided for. As I said, he was a generous man, generous to a fault."

"Are you and Bernice on good terms?"

Louise raised her hand and tilted it from side to side. "*Mezza, mezza,*" she said. "I tried to talk her out of the lawsuit, but it was no go. Stopping her would have been like stopping a rhino in mid-charge."

Or a pit bull, thought Charlotte, reminded of Diana's description.

"What about the paintings? Do you have any idea where they are?"

"Not a clue," she said.

Tom folded up his notebook and put it away in his breast pocket. "Thank you," he said. "You've been a big help. I'd like to ask one more favor. Do you have a recent picture of your husband?"

Louise shook her head. "Not a recent picture," she said. Don had a thing about photographs. He was like those primitive people who believe that the camera steals your soul."

That explained why Tom's efforts to track down a photo had been fruitless, Charlotte thought. "That seems like an odd attitude for a photorealist," she said.

"I think he took that attitude *because* he was a photorealist. He was aware of the power of the camera. He used to quote an essay that described the camera as a kind of assassin."

"I saw his self-portrait," said Charlotte. "The Finders showed it to me. If the camera was an assassin in that case, it was an assassin who had a hell of a time fixing its subject in its sights."

Louise smiled. "That's Don. A reflection in a sheet of plate glass: cool, objective, dispassionate. I lived with him for sixteen years, and I still don't feel as if I knew him."

"How about an old photo?" asked Tom. "From before he became a painter."

"That I have. Our wedding photo from 1965. But I'm reluctant to loan it to you because it's the only one I have."

"I understand," said Tom. "We could take it to a photocopier right now—you could even come with us—and have a copy made."

"That sounds okay," she said. "There's a copy shop a couple of blocks away that's open on weekends. I'll get it: it's in the house."

She returned a few minutes later with the photo, which pictured Louise just as Charlotte had imagined her, in a long gown of white Indian cotton with a garland of flowers on her brow. Don had the same puckish expression as his son. He wore a Nehru jacket, and his hair was down to his shoulders.

"Definitely a sixties wedding," said Tom as Louise handed him the photo.

"Definitely. Look at that jacket!" Louise studied the photograph. "The Italians—I'm Italian," she explained—"have an expression for a person who isn't really dead: someone who feigns death to get away from someone or something, or to get out of a sticky situation."

She spoke a word in Italian that Charlotte didn't catch.

"That's how I think of Don," she continued. "He's still so real to me. I know he's dead, but I can't believe it. I feel as if my feet are stuck in tar, as if I can't get on with my life until I come to terms with the fact that he's not going to be a part of it anymore."

I know that feeling, Charlotte thought.

"I had a dream about him just after he died. In the dream, he told me: 'I'm not dead. I just made a . . . ' "—she said the Italian word again—" 'I couldn't stand it at the mill anymore. I've gone to Round Hill for a while. Come and visit me'."

"Round Hill?" said Charlotte.

"It's our country house up in Dutchess County. You know, Julie and I actually went up to Round Hill after that. I really thought I might see him there. That's how alive he still is to me."

*   *   *

Their next stop was Ed Verre's apartment at 24 Mill Street. When Charlotte had called Martinez for directions, she had learned that it was located in the Essex Mill, an old silk mill that had been renovated and converted into housing for artists and musicians who could live there at reduced rents as long as they met the income qualifications. As a neophyte artist, Verre would have qualified, but Charlotte suspected that he wouldn't meet the income qualifications for long. If other collectors followed the Finders' suit, Verre's paintings would soon be bringing top prices.

But before they talked to Verre, Tom wanted to see the painting at the Paterson Museum again. Like Charlotte, he had only looked at it briefly before the incident with Randy. For that matter, Charlotte wanted to look at it again too, now that she suspected it had been painted by Spiegel.

"We can grab a couple of hamburgers there, too," Tom said in reference to the diner that was part of the exhibit.

"Is that the real reason you want to go back?" teased Charlotte.

"Part of it," he said. "I wouldn't want to miss a chance to taste one of Shorty's famous burgers again. Make that five or six of Shorty's famous burgers. There're pretty small."

Twenty minutes later, their stomachs filled with the delicious silver-dollar-sized gems that were smothered in chopped onions, they wandered over to take another look at "Falls View Diner at Two A.M."

"They're here," she said, pointing out the initials on the candy bar at the back of the display case. "DS Crunch." She also repeated for Tom what John had told her about the argument over the *ARTnews* article, and pointed out the magazine sitting on the counter.

"It's the same night in all three paintings, right?" asked Tom.

Charlotte nodded. "Long shot, medium shot, and close-up, as if the camera were on a dolly." Reaching into her bag, she pulled out the Koreman Gallery catalog, and opened it to "Falls View Diner on a Rainy Spring Night." "Here's the long shot," she said.

"That looks like Kenny Meeker's van," Tom said, pointing

out the old gray Ford Econoline van with Michigan license plates that was parked next to the semi. "He calls it his wheel estate."

"It is. John told me that he was there that night. On one of his cross-country diner trips." Reaching into her bag again, she pulled out the photocopy of "Falls View Diner with Banana Cream Pie." "And here he is eating the pie, or at least John said it was him."

"That's him, all right. The 'roads scholar,' as he calls himself. He likes puns. If you think I'm a sicko, you should meet Meeker. Talk about diner nuts: his diner log book has over twenty-five hundred entries."

For a moment, they compared the three pictures.

Charlotte was struck by the increasing mood of menace. The distance view had an innocent look, the middle view was darker, and the close-up was downright ominous. "I still don't get it," she said. "Why would Spiegel paint three scenes of that night?"

"Maybe Meeker would know," said Tom.

Of course! thought Charlotte. Why hadn't she thought of that. "Tom, you're a genius," she said. "From what John said, he was there for most of the evening—he had given an impromptu concert in the parking lot earlier on."

"Did John also tell you that he sleeps in his van?"

"No! That would mean he was there all night."

"It's a long shot, but it's worth a try. I could call him right now. I have his number. He works at home—some computer thing. So unless he's away on another road trip, he should be there."

"There's a phone booth outside," said Charlotte.

Charlotte stood by impatiently as Tom chatted with Meeker, whom he reached right away. After fifteen minutes, he hung up and emerged from the booth with an expression that spelled success.

"Sorry I took so long. He had to tell me about his latest diner finds. He remembered the argument, but listen to this. He said he had just settled down in the van for the night when he heard loud voices. When he looked out, he saw the two guys from inside arguing in the parking lot."

"I wonder why John didn't say anything about that."

"Meeker said he'd moved his van down to the far end of the parking lot, where it borders the river. John had wanted to reserve the spaces right in front for the early morning breakfast crowd. Anyway, Meeker said the argument degenerated into a fist fight."

Charlotte raised an eyebrow.

Tom continued: "When he looked out again, he saw the guy with the ponytail walking up the street. He never saw the other guy again."

"Could he hear what they were arguing about?"

"No. But he said it was the guy with the ponytail who seemed to be the angrier one—shouting the loudest, and so on—and that he seemed to be demanding something from the other guy that the other guy wouldn't accede to."

Had Spiegel threatened to fire Randy? Charlotte wondered. To kick him out of the mill? To cancel the gift of the paintings?

"That's it, except for his complaint about some dogs waking him at five A.M. with their barking."

Patty's dogs, she thought.

What Kenny Meeker had told Tom changed everything. Charlotte had been operating under the assumption that Spiegel had deliberately changed his identity for some reason of his own. But now a different picture was beginning to take shape in her mind, a picture that answered the question of who it was that had been out to get Randy. The picture was one of an angry, coke-crazed young man, lithe and fit, taking on a man fifteen years his senior. He knocks him out, and then panics. Believing that he's accidentally killed him, he throws him into the river. He then returns to the older man's studio and forges a suicide note on his typewriter. When a decomposed body is pulled out of the river four months later, everyone takes it for granted that it's the body of the older man. But in reality, the older man isn't dead, only unconscious. He survives the plunge into the river, and comes back with a new identity to plot his revenge. His goal is to drive the younger man out of his mind, and ultimately to take his life, as the younger man had once tried to take his. Like a cat toying with a mouse, he wants the delectation of torturing his victim until he has taken his full measure of pleasure before proceeding to kill him. She could imagine how a painter with a style as precise and orderly as Spiegel's would delight in the balance of his vengeance: Randy tries to kill him by throwing him in the river; he retaliates by throwing Randy in the river. One was a reflection of the other.

The Essex Mill was only a short distance from the museum. They could have walked had they known it was so close. In fact, though it was separated from Gryphon Mill by another restored mill, it was almost directly across the street, and located on the same raceway. Had Randy's body passed through the culvert, it might have been carried right under the Essex Mill. They parked in a lot across the street from an area on the river bank that looked like Dresden after the firebombing: burned-out shell after burned-out shell, with only the smokestacks left to tell where mills had once stood. The Essex Mill itself, however, had been beautifully restored, its charm only heightening the tragedy that was the wreckage of the other mills. Charlotte and Tom entered through an archway that opened onto a central courtyard, with a smooth green lawn in the center and planters filled with flowers around the perimeter. The only occupants were an old woman who sat in a wheelchair with her wrinkled face raised to the sun, and her black companion, who sat knitting on a nearby bench. The only noises were the hum of the air conditioners and the sweet strains of a tenor saxophone: a jazz musician practicing a riff.

Verre's apartment was in the north wing, on the top floor. As they rang the doorbell, Charlotte's heart was pounding. She was convinced that the key to Randy's murder lay with the identity of Ed Verre. They had to wait some time for him to come to the door, but they could hear noises from inside, indicating that someone was at home.

At last the door opened, and they were looking at Ed Verre.

· II ·

THE WHEELCHAIR THREW her at first. It was so unexpected.
As was the silver-gray hair, beard, and eyebrows; the heavy,
black horn-rimmed glasses; and the brown eyes. The eyes had
been a light color in the black-and-white wedding photo: a pale
blue or maybe a blue-gray. But when she looked again, she
could see the triangular face and puckish expression of young
Julius behind the beard and glasses, and . . . the ears. Remembering them from the photo, she realized now that they were
responsible in part for the puckish look. They were unusually
small, and pointed. One could grow a beard, put on eyeglasses,
and wear tinted contacts, but one could not—short of plastic
surgery—change the shape of one's ears. She remembered a
story she'd once heard about the woman who had claimed
to be the Grand Duchess Anastasia. She told a convincing
tale, but was eventually exposed as a fraud because her ears
didn't match those in a photograph of the real daughter of Czar
Nicholas.

"Mr. Spiegel?" she said. "May we come in?"

For a moment, he sat there in his wheelchair with one hand
on the door lever (Charlotte noticed that it was a lever rather
than a knob), staring up at them. Then he gestured with his
free arm for them to enter.

The room he ushered them into was small, with a kitchenette and bathroom off to one side and a small bedroom off
to the other. But its size was offset by the white walls and
high ceilings—they were probably twenty-five feet—whose
hand-cut beams appeared to have been part of the original
mill.

He followed them in in the wheelchair. "Please sit down," he said.

Tom chose a Barcelona chair and Charlotte sat on a black leather couch. Spiegel pulled up his wheelchair in a space that had obviously been reserved for that purpose.

"How did you find out?" he asked. He raised a hand in a dismissive gesture. "Not that I'm unhappy about it. I've been expecting someone to come knocking on my door for some time now. Hoping for it, in fact. I was getting tired of being Ed Verre."

Charlotte started to reply, and was interrupted.

"Wait," he said. "First, who are you, and second, can I get you a drink?"

"The answer to the first question is Charlotte Graham and Tom Plummer," Charlotte replied, "and the answer to the second is yes."

Spiegel smiled. After chatting for a moment with them about Charlotte's movie career, he took their orders—a beer for Tom and a sherry for Charlotte—and then wheeled himself into the kitchenette, whose counters were at wheelchair level, with recessed spaces for the knees.

As their host fixed the drinks, Charlotte took the opportunity to look around. The room was sparsely furnished, but the furniture, of the black-leather and chrome-tubing variety, was of good quality. A door at the back opened onto the studio: a large, bright room with enormous windows.

"Now," said Spiegel as he wheeled himself back, the drinks balanced on a tray in his lap, "back to my earlier question."

Acutely aware that Spiegel might be a murderer, Charlotte proceeded to tell the story, leaving out any reference to the investigation. After identifying herself as Jack's wife, she said that she had concluded from the paintings in the museum show that Verre and Spiegel were one and the same.

Then she told him about her visit to the Finders.

"Yes," Spiegel interjected, "I knew from the way they were snapping up my paintings that Morris and Evelyn knew. They kept trying to set up a meeting with me. Actually, I expected it to be they who came knocking on my door."

Charlotte nodded, and then continued: "But despite all that, I still had my doubts. I wasn't sure until I saw you."

"Why?" he asked.

"Your ears," she said, and then explained: "We got a copy of your wedding photo from Louise. I noticed your ears; they're very distinctive."

Spiegel touched a hand to one ear. "I always suspected that Louise knew, even if it was only subconsciously. I saw her once in the Question Mark Bar. She looked at me very oddly. Maybe it was my ears she was looking at."

"She told us that she couldn't really believe you were dead."

"I'll have to call her now. I've missed her and Julie very much. They're really the only ones I've missed. Help yourselves," he said as he set the drink tray down on the coffee table. He leaned back in his wheelchair. "Now I suppose you'd like to hear my story."

"Yes, we would," said Charlotte. "Tom is a journalist. He's been working on an article about Randy Goslau's dispute with your sister." Leaving it at that, she got up to remove her drink from the tray, and to pass Tom's to him.

"For who?" Spiegel asked.

Tom named a New York magazine.

Spiegel nodded. "What's one more article?" he said. "Especially if it sets the record straight." He went on: "I've been eager to tell my story, actually. It's been a burden carrying it around with me." Picking up his drink, which appeared to be a Scotch on the rocks, he took a sip, and began. "I met Randy ten or twelve years ago. At the time, my career was beginning to take off and my time was being consumed more and more by the business of being an artist. I found that I needed someone to help around the studio and to help with the business side of things. Randy seemed as if he would fit the bill, and he did— at first. He was eager to learn, and I encouraged him. When I learned about his mania for diners, I encouraged him to paint them. I nurtured his career, and he in turn freed up my time for painting. We became very close. He had a taste for the high life, which I didn't share, at first. But I grew to like it, having people around all the time. It drove Louise crazy; that was one reason why she moved out." He paused (perhaps thinking about her other reason for moving out), and then continued: "As you may already know, Randy was a cocaine user. Only recreationally at first, but he eventually became addicted. As the drug took hold, he became more irresponsible, more arrogant. He seemed to forget who was the boss and who was the employee. He began making outrageous demands—that I do this and that for him. Finally there was the *ARTnews* affair."

Tom nodded.

"So you know about that," Spiegel said. "I had been thinking about firing him, but I was reluctant to do so. He had been a good friend for so long. But the *ARTnews* affair was the last straw. I didn't even know about it until I went to an artists' reception in Soho one evening. Everybody there was asking me about it; a few, I think, believed it—those who didn't know me. Afterward, I went to a party and it was the same thing. When I got back to Paterson that night, I went up to the diner for some eggs, and Randy was there. I confronted him about it, hoping he would show some remorse, maybe even apologize. I was prepared to forgive him. But he was as arrogant as ever. He was spouting the 'If it weren't for me, you wouldn't be where you are' line. That's when I decided I couldn't put up with him anymore. On the way back to the mill—we were both on foot—I asked him to start moving his belongings out. He said he wouldn't, and I threatened to evict him. I was very angry; I felt betrayed. I also told him I was going to retract the gift agreement that gave him ownership upon my death of the paintings that I had loaned him over the years."

Charlotte noticed how his left hand gripped the arm of the wheelchair; the tension was all the more apparent by contrast with the limpness of his legs.

"That's when he started swinging," Spiegel continued. "We fought for a while—we were at the far end of the parking lot, where it comes right up against the river—but I was no match for him. He had been a wrestler in high school and college, and he was still very fit." He patted his rounded belly. "I was no fighter to begin with, and the years hadn't helped. The last thing I remember—apart from seeing stars, that is—is the right hook he landed to my jaw." He paused to take another swig of his Scotch, which he swallowed thoughtfully. Then he went on, speaking more slowly now: "The next thing I knew, I was in the river. Randy had thrown me in, thinking I was dead, I guess. It must have been the shock of being immersed in the cold water that brought me to. Before I had really figured out what was going on, the current had carried me under the Spruce Street Bridge, and then over the S.U.M. dam. The dam isn't high; most of it's under water. It's only a drop of eight feet or so, but the surprise of going over was enough to jolt me into the realization that I was headed for the Falls. I was terrified: I knew that if I went over, I would die."

"I had to force myself to think, but once my head was clear I realized what I had to do. I had to get over to the other side of the river to where there's a backwater that collects behind the remains of an old dam at the head of the gorge. If I stayed where I was, I'd go over the Falls. Thank God I'm a good swimmer, because the current was strong; it had been raining for several days. It took all my strength, but I finally got over—or so I thought. But at the far side, I was sucked into the current. It carried me over the top of a rock outcropping at the base of the dam that I spoke of, for about fifteen feet, and then dropped me over the lip of the Falls." He paused to ask if they wanted refills.

Charlotte and Tom shook their heads; they didn't want him to stop.

Spiegel took another sip of his drink, and continued: "I thought that was it, but as I went over I got caught in the crotch of a tree trunk that was wedged diagonally across the chasm at the head of the Falls. Its being there was a miracle, really. Though I've since noticed that a lot of tree trunks get stuck there in just the same way. It's where the chasm is the narrowest; it's only about eight feet wide at that point. I find myself going back to the Falls a lot—I'm drawn to the place, especially after a storm. Maybe it's because I'm still trying to make sense of it all. Anyway, I managed to shimmy down the tree, but there was nowhere to go from there. The lower end was still sixty feet or more above the water. Even if I had survived a jump—and there were lots of rocks below—I would have been up against two hundred and eighty feet of rock-filled chasm. The best I could hope for was to hang on until morning and pray that someone would rescue me, but I had injured my arm when I was going over the rocks—I later found out it was broken—and hanging on until morning was an impossibility.

"It was then that I noticed, just below me, a stone archway

that crowned the entrance to a tunnel. In all the times I had visited the Falls, I had never noticed that tunnel entrance before: it was always covered up by the spray, and by the vegetation growing between the rocks on the face of the old dam. Just below the archway was a steel reinforcing beam spanning the opening. There was nothing else for me to do but to try to jump down into the tunnel. I figured I could do it in two stages: first onto the steel beam, and from there into the tunnel itself. The first jump would be the hardest—the beam was less than a foot wide. But it wasn't that far, and I made it all right. From there, I could see into the tunnel. It was dark, but I could make out a wide ledge on the tunnel wall about fifteen feet below me. If I could land on that, I could get a better sense of where the floor of the tunnel was. I managed to jump down onto the ledge, but once I landed I realized that I was only halfway there. The floor of the tunnel was another twenty feet beneath me. I jumped for a third time, and this time I wasn't so lucky. I broke my leg. It just snapped; it sounded liked a dry twig breaking.

"I didn't know it at the time," he continued, "but the opening wasn't the entrance to a manmade tunnel, but rather a natural tunnel, actually a rock fissure that's a continuation of the chasm. It had been used as the tailrace for a nineteenth-century turbine that pumped water from the river into a holding reservoir. The water company had covered over the fissure, and built the dam to create an intake reservoir for the pump. Anyway, there I was in this pitch-black tunnel with a broken leg. Or so I thought. Though I couldn't feel anything in either of my legs, I thought it was just temporary. I didn't yet realize that I'd injured my spinal cord. At this point, my only option was to see where the tunnel led, which is what I did. I had to crawl, of course. Or rather, pull myself along with my good arm. I had—still have—a lot of arm strength as a result of lugging canvases around. Actually, I have even more arm strength now, from working out with dumbbells and on the parallel bars. It was hellish, crawling through that dank, dark tunnel. There were rats, too. I could hear them squeaking. All I could think of was a cave I once visited in California. When the first explorers went into it, they found old skeletons of Indians who had fallen into the opening and couldn't get out. I thought that's what would happen to me.

"I must have finally passed out, because when I came to, it was day. I could see the light at the end of the tunnel." He laughed bitterly at the irony. "I continued crawling, but it was less scary because of the light. I didn't know the purpose of the tunnel, but I figured it must have something to do with the buildings on the other side of the Falls: there are two of them—quaint old little brick structures. At one point, I came to a shaft, which I've since learned was the old turbine pit. Sure enough, when I came to the end of the tunnel, there were stairs leading upward to a trapdoor. As far as I was concerned, they were the stairs to heaven.

"I wanted to get out right away, of course, but there was no way I could at that point. I was exhausted, and my broken arm was very painful. Oddly enough, it didn't occur to me to wonder why my leg didn't hurt too. Also, the pressure was off now that I knew there was a way out. I fell asleep again, and when I woke up it was five o'clock. I still had my watch on"—he held up his wrist—"it's a waterproof one. Once I was awake, I started to think. Now that I knew I was going to live, I got mad—furious. How could that little shit have tried to kill me after all I did for him? I started thinking about revenge. That's when the idea occurred to me of taking on a new identity. I waited until nightfall, and then crawled out. It was much easier than I thought it would be. The trapdoor opened into the basement of what I now know is the old water company pump house. I had to break a window to get out—the door was padlocked—but I managed. Then I crawled to a park bench, and asked the first guy who came along—a dog walker—if he would call a cab for me from the phone booth up at the stadium. I told him I had a bum leg. He did, and within fifteen minutes, a cab came to pick me up. The cabbie helped me to the car. I had him take me to my mother's. I thought of going to Louise's, but I knew she'd never be able to keep the secret. And Bernice was too far: she lives in Manhattan. Besides, she wouldn't have done well in the Florence Nightingale role. I ended up staying at my mother's for four months. All that time, I was planning my revenge."

"Who set your broken bones?" asked Charlotte.

"My mother," he said. "She used to be an orthopedic nurse. Later on, she drove me to the Kessler Institute every day for physical therapy; it's in West Orange. She didn't approve of the new identity, but she went along with it. She'd do anything for me, God bless her. Establishing my new identity was much easier than I would have thought. Randy took care of the hardest part for me by forging the suicide note, and Bernice took care of the rest. With the two of them fighting tooth and nail over my work, who would have believed that I was actually *alive*? With my death established, it was just a matter of changing my appearance, and getting new papers. I let my hair grow out—I had been dyeing it, and grew a beard. I hadn't realized how white it had become. My mother joked that it had turned white overnight. Then I got the tinted contacts and the glasses. I had also lost a lot of weight, which I managed to keep off. I even tried changing my mannerisms and my way of speaking. I practiced with a video camera. I wasn't very good at that aspect, but I discovered that it didn't matter. People are really much more interested in themselves than they are in you, particularly if you're in a wheelchair. If you're in a wheelchair, people don't look closely at you. In that respect, you're like a homeless person."

"What about the papers part?" asked Tom.

"I forged the birth certificate. For someone with my background in graphics, it wasn't hard. The birth certificate was the key: once I had that, I could get a driver's license, credit cards, even a passport. The spinal cord injury helped me get this apartment. The city sets a certain number of these apartments aside for the handicapped. The fact that I was handicapped *and* an artist made me a shoe-in. I guess I'm subject to some kind of fraud action because my real income exceeds the limitation, but I doubt the city is going to prosecute. As an aside, this is a great place for a paraplegic to live. Because it's a national historic district, it has to be barrier-free. There are curb cuts and wheelchair ramps everywhere you go. It's not so easy in a lot of other places. I've had to go to Soho a couple of times on business, and I found it next to impossible to get around. You never see people in wheelchairs there. But"—he smiled—"I digress. To get back to my story: I resented the wheelchair at first. But then I realized that it was a metaphor for my new life. I was discovering how much I didn't need: money, reputation, the society of other artists, even the use of my legs. It was like that game that therapists play with their patients, encouraging them to imagine that they're dead so they can figure out what matters to them and what doesn't. I also realized how much of my earlier behavior had been reinforced by people who expected me to act in certain ways, and conversely, how liberating reinventing myself could be."

Charlotte was well aware of this aspect of taking on a new identity. It was one of the elements of acting that intrigued her, and one that tended to keep actors from getting mired down in life. She supposed that's why actors were often such good company; they continued to grow, discovering new attitudes, opinions, and sides of themselves with each new role. "What about your revenge?" she asked.

"It was a game for me—to torment Randy with the paintings. I liked the elegance of the idea: to use the skills that he claimed were his to get back at him. I thought of it in terms of the movie *Gaslight*. I was gaslighting him."

Tom nodded at Charlotte in acknowledgment of her astuteness. But it wasn't so surprising that she and Spiegel had hit on the same idea. The movie was a lesson in how to drive someone slowly mad.

Spiegel continued: "The paintings were my primary *modus operandi*, but I did other things too. I telephoned him at all hours of the night, the idea being to screw up his REM sleep. When he had his phone disconnected, I called him at the diner. I had someone tailing him 'round the clock, so I knew when he'd be there. I paid kids to bump into him on the street, to let the air out of his tires, to break into his car and turn on the lights so that the battery would go dead. Subtle stuff like that."

"What about bugging his phone?"

"That wasn't me. I think it must have been his imagination. Though I was pleased when I heard he'd called in a countersurveillance consultant. It meant that my scheme was getting to him. Childish, maybe, but it gave me enormous satisfaction. I think I would have gone mad without it. If I'd had any reservations initially, they were canceled by what he did after I 'died.' "

"The threat to sue for palimony, you mean?" Charlotte asked.

Spiegel nodded.

"Did Randy know it was you who was gaslighting him?"

"I don't know. Probably in his more lucid moments, but only subconsciously. In his less lucid moments everything I did contributed to his general paranoia. I hang out at the Question Mark Bar. It's right down the street: flat all the way, with curb cuts at all the intersections. I play pool there; it's one of the physical activities I can indulge in. Anyway, Randy used to come in sometimes, and I cultivated his friendship. It was part of the game for me."

"Was your ultimate aim to drive him so crazy that he would kill himself?" asked Charlotte.

"I never thought that much about my ultimate aim, as you put it. For me, the medium was the message. If I *had* wanted him to kill himself, it wasn't a conscious wish." He thought for a moment, and then shrugged. "But he was killing himself anyway, so it wouldn't have mattered, would it?"

"Would it have mattered if you had killed him directly?"

Spiegel looked up in surprise at the accusation. "I don't know. Killing him wasn't part of my game plan."

"Then you didn't kill him?" asked Charlotte.

"No," he said. "I didn't."

Spiegel claimed that he had been at the Question Mark Bar on the night that Randy was killed. It was an easy enough alibi to check—the Question Mark was right down the street from the Essex Mill—a straight run, as Spiegel had said. As the Nag's Head Bar, the Question Mark had been famous in Paterson history as the headquarters for the Wobblies during the 1913 Silk Strike. It was at the Nag's Head that Wobbly leaders had plotted the strike by twenty-four thousand workers that had closed three hundred silk mills for seven months, and dealt a crippling blow to the silk industry. This information was imparted to Charlotte by Tom, her expert on local history, as they headed toward the bar, which was located in a formerly Italian neighborhood—the home turf of Lou Costello. Judging from the signs, it was a neighborhood that was changing over to Hispanic. The store next to the Question Mark served its Italian clientele with "Pizzas to go" and its Hispanic clientele with "*Comidas criollas.*"

The door of the Question Mark stood open, and they walked in. It was a dingy, dimly lit gin mill, with a long, padded bar in the shape of a question mark covered in black leatherette, a map of Puerto Rico hanging on the wood-paneled wall, and a scattering of beat-up Formica tables. An elderly Hispanic man sat at the bar, and two others played cards at a table in the back.

The bartender was a thin Hispanic with a heavy accent. The name Ed Verre didn't ring a bell with him, but Tom's description of a man in a wheelchair with white hair and a white beard did.

"Oh, *sí*," he said, nodding. "He come in four, five nights a week. *Se artista.* During the day, the neighborhood people come here"—he waved an arm at the card players—"*por la noche, estan las artistas.*"

"Was he here last Saturday night?" he asked.

He thought for a moment, and then nodded: "*Sí.* He play *billar.*" He nodded at the pool table at the back. "He like play *billar.* He say is the only sport he can enjoy. Because of the"— he moved his hands at his sides as if he were rotating wheels— "*silla de ruedas.*"

"What time did he leave?" Tom asked.

"He stay until we close."

"What time was that?"

"Two-thirty."

At this point, they decided that they were obligated to pay a call on Voorhees. Spiegel's presence at the Question Mark was a good alibi: it would have taken him at least half an hour to make it up to the diner in the wheelchair, plus another half an hour to tie Randy up and toss him in, which would have put the time of death well past the hour that the medical examiner had set as the outside limit. Then there was the fact that all of this would have been difficult, if not downright impossible, for a paraplegic, and the fact that someone surely would have noticed. A man in a wheelchair was invisible unless he happened to be moving a body around in the wee hours of the morning. But whether or not Spiegel's alibi held up (Voorhees would probably want to question the patrons of the bar who had been there that night), the fact that he had come back from the dead hell-bent on revenge was highly pertinent to the case. He might not personally have killed Randy, but he might have been linked to his death. Then there was the question of the decomposed body that had been pulled out of the river. If it wasn't Spiegel's, whose was it? Voorhees would probably want to tie up that loose end, if nothing else.

For Charlotte, the fact that Spiegel appeared to have a solid alibi was a big disappointment. From the beginning, she had felt that Randy's murder was linked to his reaction to the painting. If that assumption was wrong, then she had to go back to Square One. And the only player on Square One at the moment was Arthur Lumkin. She made a mental note to show John the photo of Lumkin to make certain it was he who had driven around back. Apart from that, she had no idea how to proceed other than to revisit the scene of the crime, which was always a good idea when you were stuck. And since the scene of the crime—in the form of the raceway where Randy's body had been found—was only a block up the street, they decided to do that first.

Charlotte wanted to retrace the route the body had followed. She had been prompted by the many hours that she was spending in Paterson, as well as by Diana's and Jason's references to it, to re-read William Carlos Williams' book-length ode to the city, *Paterson*, which compared the city to a man. Since their visit to the Question Mark, a line from the poem—a kind of refrain—had been running through her head: "No ideas but in things." Though its meaning was obscure, she took it as urging the reader to consider those things—those incidents from the past—that give a city, and a life, its meaning. The incident from the past that they were dealing with here was Randy's death, and Charlotte couldn't help but feel that the clues lay in its particulars. Though Tom thought it was a waste of time, he indulged Charlotte in her whim, not out of any generosity of spirit but because the promise of two hot Texas wieners "all the way" lay at the end of their little expedition.

From the spot where the body had been found, they followed the path along the bank of the raceway at the edge of the rubble-strewn lot opposite the Gryphon Mill. They had company, a crew of prisoners in orange jumpsuits who were picking up the garbage. A sheriff's deputy stood guard over them with a rifle. Most of them were Hispanic, and Charlotte was surprised at how young they were. Just babies, really. One especially baby-faced prisoner was picking up cans on the other side of the raceway, from among some tall weeds. As she watched, Charlotte realized that the weeds were bamboo. So much for its only growing behind the diner. Perhaps that was the only place where it could be found along the river, but the raceway was thick with it. At the back of the Gryphon Mill, the raceway made a 90-degree turn past the little brick building that was used as a crack den—crack vials littered the doorway—and then continued past the rear of a giant mill that was still in use. It was a beautiful day, and Charlotte welcomed the walk. Graceful sycamores overhung the raceway. Queen Anne's lace bloomed at the edges of the path, and the blue, jewel-like flowers of pickerel weed brightened the waters of the canal. Even the presence of the prisoners and the garbage that had been tossed into the race—an old shopping cart, an open umbrella, countless bottles of cheap wine—couldn't spoil the lazy, pastoral mood. At Spruce Street, the raceway ran under the street and opened up on the other side into the pond at the foot of the Ivanhoe Wheelhouse spillway. The body must have come over this falls, Charlotte thought.

Crossing the street, they headed toward the Falls. The Upper Raceway was on their left, the river on their right. At the head of the Upper Raceway was an old gatehouse bearing a billboard for the Falls View on its roof that proclaimed: "Hot Texas Wieners since 1939." Just below the gatehouse was a concrete dam, on which a maintenance worker (identifiable as such by the DPW truck parked at the curb) stood, pulling on a long-handled lever. As he moved the lever from a 90- to a 45-degree position, the flow of water on the downstream side of the dam gradually increased. As Charlotte watched the water stream through the opening, she was struck by a thought: in order for Randy's body to have reached the bridge by the Gryphon Mill, it must have passed through this opening. But judging from the size of the area that was disturbed by the inflow of water, the opening couldn't be that big.

"Hello down there," she yelled to the DPW worker. "How big is the opening?" she asked, pointing down at the dam.

"Thirty-six inches square," he replied.

"Big enough for the body of a man to fit through?" she asked.

"If the valve was all the way open. But it never is." He gestured at the angle of the lever. "Halfway is the most we ever open it. The upper sections of the retaining walls are in bad shape; if we fill the raceways to the top, we get too much leakage."

"When was the last time the valve was opened all the way?"

He shrugged. "I don't know. Ten, twelve years. The last time I remember for sure was when President Ford came here in 1976 to dedicate the historic district. Now we just open it enough to flush out the junk."

"Thanks," said Charlotte.

"The city's applied for money to repair the walls, but . . ." He shrugged as if to say that nothing would ever come of it. "It's a shame. The water used to really race through here." He wrapped a chain around the lever, and locked it. "Now it's just a glorified ditch."

"Good work, Graham," said Tom as they continued on.

From the beginning, Charlotte had had the feeling that there was something not quite right about the theory that Randy's body had been tossed into the river behind the diner. She supposed that feeling had been behind her wanting to retrace the route the body had followed. Now that she knew the body had been tossed directly into the raceway, she knew what was at the root of that hunch: if the body had gone over the Ivanhoe Wheelhouse spillway, it would have been bashed up. There would have been lacerations and contusions, at the least. But Randy's corpse had looked pretty good, apart from the bloating and the turtle bites. It wasn't a body that had gone over a twenty-four foot spillway. She wondered why this hadn't occurred to her earlier. Why it hadn't occurred to the medical examiner was beyond her.

The diner was back to normal, with John working the grill and Helen behind the cash register, but an air of gloom hung over the place as a result of John's arrest. It seemed to have lost its spit and polish; the shine of the stainless steel seemed less bright, the glow of the mahoghany less warm.

They took a seat at the same booth in which they had sat the other day with Patty—down at the end, away from the crowd.

"What do you want to hear?" Charlotte asked Tom after they had placed their orders with the waitress, who must have been an Andriopoulis—she looked just like Patty. Her quarter was poised above the slot in the tabletop jukebox. "How about some Glenn Miller?"

Tom made a face, as she knew he would.

"I know, Chuck Berry," she said. She flipped through the selections. "Well, there's 'Sweet Little Sixteen'; 'Johnny B. Goode'; 'Go, Johnny, Go'; 'Maybellene', 'No Particular Place To Go.'"

Tom handed her some more quarters. "Here. Just play all of them."

After dropping the coins in the slot, Charlotte pressed the series of numbers. "I've always wondered how these things work," she said, as the opening refrain of "Sweet Little Sixteen" blared out of the speakers. "Are there a bunch of little records in there, or what?"

Tom smiled, and proceeded to explain the intricacies of the wallbox system. Then the waitress appeared with their orders—two hot Texas wiener platters—and they turned their attention back to the case.

"What I wonder about is this—" Tom said, as he sank his teeth into a wiener heaped with the special sauce. "If the body was thrown into the raceway instead of into the river, why did the murderer wrap it up in aprons that had come from the diner?"

"I've been wondering about that too. Anyone who knew the raceway system would realize that the body would be found. The flow isn't strong enough to carry a body out to the river. In fact, it petered out to a trickle just below the Essex Mill. Did you notice that?"

Tom nodded.

She continued: "I think it must have been a deliberate attempt to make it look as if the murderer had been at the diner."

"From the murderer's point of view, the more suspects, the better."

"Exactly. What I think happened was this: we know that Randy was probably unconscious when he was tossed in. I think he must have passed out on his way home. The murderer came across him, and took advantage of the situation."

"Then went back to the diner to get the aprons."

Charlotte nodded. "They were kept in a bin that John had put out back for the laundry service. Anybody could have taken them."

"But they would have to have known they were there."

"Yes, but anybody who frequented the diner a lot, which seems to include most of Paterson, might have seen the bin. Especially if they ever went out back to look at the river. Or drove around the building," she added, in reference to Arthur Lumkin.

"Now what?" he said. "Do we interview every wino and crackhead on the west side to see if anyone saw Randy that night?"

"That might not be such a bad idea."

· I2 ·

THEY WERE ON their dessert—lemon meringue pie for Charlotte and banana cream pie for Tom—when Patty slid onto the seat next to Tom. She was wearing her sequined Mickey Mouse jacket over a T-shirt and blue jeans.

"I'm off today," she said. "But I wanted to talk with you. I saw you come in from across the street." She nodded at the house across the way, whose picture windows—one up and one down—stared out at the diner. "Anything new?"

"We had one lead, but it looks as if it's going to turn out to be a dead end," Charlotte replied, referring to Verre/Spiegel. "But we did just run across something else," she added. She explained about Randy's body being thrown directly into the raceway.

"That's something, anyway. Everything helps. I just came back from the lawyers'. It looks like the value of the estate, exclusive of the paintings, is about four hundred thousand. With the paintings—and the lawyers say they'll go to us—it'll be eight million more."

"What are you talking about?" asked Charlotte.

"The estate lawyers. I thought Marty told you. I'm the heir to Randy's estate. That's one of the reasons he arrested Daddy."

"What!" said Charlotte.

"He figured that I—and, by extension, Daddy—stood to profit from Randy's death. He thought that Daddy was planning to use the money to buy out Uncle Nick. In other words, he killed Randy to save the Falls View. But why arrest Daddy? Why not arrest me?"

Charlotte set down her wiener and leaned her head against

the back of the seat. "This is a surprise, to say the least," she said. *Damn Voorhees for keeping them in the dark.*

"It was to me, too. The biggest surprise of my life. I still can't fathom it. It's hard for me to get my head around any amount that exceeds a day's worth of tips. At this point, it's actually Randy's postcard collection that I'm most excited about."

"You had no idea?" asked Charlotte.

"Not the slightest. It was like winning the lottery. But with some unpleasant complications." She glanced over at her father, who looked like Gene Krupa, so fast were his arms flying around, flipping hamburgers, scrambling eggs, heaping up mounds of home fries.

As they watched, his arms seemed to slow down, as if the speed of a film were being decelerated. Then they fell to his sides, and he crumpled to the floor. Then Helen screamed. "Oh my God! John's having a heart attack."

"Daddy!" cried Patty, rushing to his side.

Charlotte and Tom were right behind, as were a dozen other diner patrons. John lay on his side between the grill and the counter. The arm with the tattoo lay outstretched on the floor. Helen was crouched down next to him.

Charlotte didn't have to be a doctor to know that it didn't look good. John's skin was gray, and he wasn't breathing.

Patty took charge. "Carlos, call the ambulance!" she shouted to one of the cooks in the back. Then she crouched down next to her mother, and said: "Tom and Joe, help me turn him over on his back."

He was a heavy man, and it took Tom and two others to turn him over. Once he was on his back, Patty removed his glasses, which had been smashed in the fall, checked for a pulse, and then started CPR. She was cool and calm—she knew what she was doing—but her trembling lower lip revealed her fear.

"Don't die, Daddy," she chanted as she pressed, arms straight and elbows locked, against her father's sternum. It was a mantra that she repeated in time to the pumping action: "Don't die, Daddy. Don't die, Daddy. Don't die, Daddy."

They never did get around to seeing Voorhees. After John's heart attack they didn't feel like going back to the detective bureau. And after the stunt Voorhees had pulled about Randy's will, they weren't especially eager to rush right down there, anyway. Besides, Tom was about to depart on a promotion tour for his most recent book. After driving him to the airport, Charlotte dropped his car off at his garage, then had a light dinner at a café in his neighborhood and took a cab home. All she wanted to do was mix herself a drink, put her feet up, and think things over. Which is exactly what she did.

As she sipped her drink and munched potato chips, she reviewed the suspects in her mind. At this point, the front-runner was Arthur Lumkin. He had the strongest motive: jealousy. He had been on the scene, and he could have spotted the laundry bin when he drove around the back. Moreover, he might have followed Randy home in the expectation that Xantha would be meeting him there. Then there was Spiegel. Another strong motive, revenge; a good knowledge of the diner; and, unfortunately, an alibi—maybe. Hopefully Voorhees would let her know what he found when he checked it out. Then there was John. Though she hated to think ill of someone who at that very moment was fighting for his life, the news that Patty was Randy's heir cast a new light on him as a suspect. The diner was his life. He had worked there three hundred and sixty-odd days a year for fifty years. His occasional days off were spent—where else?—the diner. The prospect of losing it must have seemed worse than death; he had said as much himself. And though in most people's minds it was usually passions such as jealousy or revenge that provided the motive for murder, Charlotte knew that in actual fact it was more often just plain greed. In this case, not so much greed as the desire to preserve a business that represented a lifetime of hard work and devotion. John had admitted to being on the observation bridge that night. He could very well have seen Randy walking down the street—seen him, and maybe followed him home.

Then there was a host of other suspects, starting with Bernice Spiegel: greed again, as well as the desire to preserve her brother's reputation. With Randy out of the way, the palimony issue would be eliminated. There was also the possibility that she could have claimed the missing paintings for Spiegel's estate. The estate lawyers had told Patty that the paintings would go to her, but maybe they were wrong. Next was Louise Sicca: same motive as above, but diluted. Unlike Bernice, she didn't care about her husband's name. Nor did she appear to care about his money. Bernice and Louise were the major suspects on the "B" list. There were also two minor suspects. The first was Patty, who might have killed Randy for the same motive as her father. The second was Mary Catherine Koreman. For her, Randy's death not only eliminated an expensive middleman, it also opened up new business opportunities in the form of shaking down other galleries for the Lumkins' business.

In considering Bernice, Louise, and Mary Catherine as suspects, Charlotte wondered briefly if a woman would have been capable of wrapping Randy's body up in the aprons and tossing it into the raceway, and concluded that it would not only have been possible, but easy. Though he was muscular, Randy had been a small man—he couldn't have weighed more than a hundred and forty. Bernice, Louise, and Mary Catherine were all large women, reasonably fit and in good health. Bernice and Louise probably outweighed Randy by twenty or thirty pounds, and Mary Catherine by a good deal more. Charlotte remembered noticing how muscular Louise's forearms were, probably from pounding clay. And though Patty was petite, she would also have strong arms. Carrying trays laden with heavy Buffalo-ware was no easy feat.

She reached for another handful of potato chips, but the bowl was empty.

She was getting up for a refill when the phone rang. It was her stepdaughter, Marsha Rogers, nee Lundstrom. Though Charlotte no longer kept in touch with Jack, she did with his daughter. She and Marsha had similar interests, chief among them their interest in art, and Marsha often accompanied Charlotte to museum and gallery shows. Now that Marsha was married—she had married a paleontologist whom she'd met on a trip she and Charlotte had taken to China—she didn't spend as much time in New York, and they no longer palled around as much as they once had. But they did stay in touch.

Marsha was calling now to say hello. She had spent the earlier part of the summer on a dig in China, as she had for the past four years. The fact that her husband had discovered dinosaur fossils in China was a happy circumstance for a wife who happened to be a scholar of Tang dynasty poetry. While he dug for fossils, she translated antique manuscripts.

"How is your father?" asked Charlotte. She winced inwardly at the mention of a topic she would rather not have discussed, but which she felt compelled to bring up out of a sense of politesse that was probably overblown.

"At the moment, I'd have to say that he's steaming mad."

"Over what?" asked Charlotte, hoping it wasn't her.

"A Lipschitz," Marsha replied, referring to the sculptor whose abstract pieces had helped define cubism. "A small mother and child. He bought it a few years ago at a Madison Avenue Gallery."

"The one that was on the pedestal in the living room?"

"That's the one. Anyway, as you probably know, he was quite attached to it. The other night he gave a party, and one of the guests identified the piece as having been stolen from a warehouse in Hastings-on-Hudson where Lipschitz's sculptures are stored.

"How did this person know?"

"He was an art critic who had not only written a book on Lipschitz, but had also drawn up the *catalogue raisonné* of his works. He knew precisely which works had been stolen from the warehouse."

"Didn't the gallery Jack bought it from supply a provenance?" asked Charlotte. It was unusual for the kind of prestigious uptown galleries that Jack patronized to be anything less than on the up and up.

"Yes, they did. That's the interesting part. This is what the thieves had done: they had placed the piece in a house sale, not an everyday house sale, but a house sale at a mansion up on the Hudson—the kind of place that would have fine art, but not great art, if you know what I mean. They didn't identify it as a Lipschitz, of course. Then they bought it back for a fraction of its real worth. Now they had a receipt for an abstract sculpture of a mother and child purchased for five thousand, or whatever. They then offered the piece to Sotheby's. Sotheby's questioned the receipt, but the thieves had the catalog from the house sale to back it up. Sotheby's auctioned it off as a Lipschitz—it had been signed by the artist—and the Madison Avenue Gallery bought it."

Something about Marsha's story was sending signals to an alarm at the back of Charlotte's brain, but she didn't know what it was. "I hope the gallery is going to reimburse Jack," she said.

"Oh yes. He's not out any money, but he is out the sculpture."

As Marsha went on about Jack trying to buy the sculpture back from the Lipschitz estate, which owned the sculptures in the warehouse, the alarm in Charlotte's brain suddenly went off. She remembered where she had seen the painting of the diner that Tom had bid on at the Ivanhoe Gallery auction. "Excuse me," she said. "I don't mean to be rude. But you might have just helped me solve a very important problem. Would you mind if I called you back in a little while? I have to make a phone call."

After hanging up, she immediately called Voorhees' home number, which he had given her. He seemed surprised to hear from her, but was willing enough to listen to what she had to say. She could hear the tinkling of ice in a glass; it sounded as if he had spent the evening doing the same thing she had.

First she told him about Randy's attempt to murder Spiegel, and then about their discovery that Ed Verre was really Don Spiegel. Next she told him about John seeing Arthur Lumkin behind the diner. Finally, she told him about Spiegel's plan to "gaslight" Randy. She also asked him to check Verre/Spiegel's alibi, and reminded him to let her know what he had found out. "We only found out today that Patty Andriopoulis was Randy's heir," she complained. "It was a crucial bit of information that you just happened to leave out."

"I did?" he said, all innocence. "I must have forgotten."

"Well, next time tie a string around your finger," she snapped. Then she told him about their deduction that Randy's body must have been thrown in the raceway below the dam at the old gatehouse.

"I would say that you've been busy, Miss Graham," Voorhees said when she had finished. There was an unconcealed note of admiration in his voice.

"Now for the meaty part," she continued. "I know who stole the paintings. But this time you're going to be the one who has to wait to find out the details. Would tomorrow at ten be all right?"

"I'll be there with bells on," he said.

No sooner had Charlotte hung up the phone than it rang again. This time it was a woman with a heavy accent. Charlotte had trouble understanding the message at first. Then she finally got it: the caller was an Andriopoulis relative calling at Patty's behest to tell her that John Andriopoulis was dead. He had died in the coronary care unit at St. Joseph's earlier that evening. The funeral would be held in two days at St. George Greek Orthodox Church. The caller went on to say that the family appreciated Charlotte's efforts to clear John's name, and that they hoped she would be able to attend.

Charlotte wasn't surprised; John had looked like a goner. But she *was* surprised at how sad she felt about the death of a man she hardly knew. A lot of it was her own reading of a life that, to all outward appearances, had been one of unremitting drudgery. But she doubted that he had felt the same way. To him it had probably been a rich life, with close ties to family, church, and community. She felt as if she should go, but she also felt as if she would be doing so under false pretenses. She hadn't really been trying to clear John's name—she had just been trying to solve a murder.

Now she wondered if she ever would.

She arrived at Voorhees' office a little early. Though it was a foggy, rainy day, which usually slowed traffic down, it hadn't been as bad as she expected. The weather was due to the effects of a hurricane that was churning up the waters off the coast of the Carolinas. The National Weather Service had issued a hurricane watch for the storm, Hurricane Clyde, which was expected to start heading inland soon. She found Voorhees with his feet up on his desk, dictating into a tape recorder. She wondered what he was going to do about the investigation now that the suspect who had been charged with the murder was dead.

"Oh, Miss Graham," he said, returning his feet to the floor. "Come in." He nodded at the tape recorder. "I was just dictating some case notes," he explained. "Please have a seat." He pointed to a folding chair against the wall.

She nodded at the recorder. "Is there anything in your notes I should know about?" she asked sarcastically as she sat down.

"Touché," he replied, with a glimmer of a smile. "As a matter of fact, there is." He picked up a piece of paper and handed it to her. "You might be interested in taking a look at this."

It was a hand-drawn map of Randy's camp—actually two maps. The first one showed the general layout with the locations of each of the diners and the connecting pathways; the second one was a detailed floor plan of the Short Stop including everything from bidet to bird bath. The second map included a broken line indicating a sight line that ran from a nearby tree to the bed.

"Arthur Lumkin?" she said. As she spoke, she realized that they would never have the chance to show John the photo of Lumkin, and to determine for sure if it was he who had driven around the diner.

Voorhees nodded. "We found it in a desk in his apartment. Quite a place, by the way. A Park Avenue penthouse. Have you been there?"

"A few parties," she said.

He looked impressed. Charlotte imagined that the Lumkins' penthouse, with its opulent appointments and fabulous art must have been quite a switch from the tenements and burned-out mills that were the usual venue of Voorhees' investigations.

"We went in to talk with him last night, after you told us about John's seeing him at the diner. We had a search warrant. We also found another map—of Goslau's studio, with the number of steps from one room to the next all spelled out. Did you notice the sight line?"

Charlotte nodded.

"The map of the studio has one too. From the bluff overlooking the parking lot across the street. I find it hard to imagine a man of Lumkin's stature hiding in a tree with a pair of binoculars. Why do you think he would do something like this? You know him."

"Not that well. He never says much; it's always Xantha who does all the talking. I never understood why he put up with her affairs, but then, people do strange things in the name of love."

"So they do," he said with a rueful little smile.

"Did you find anything else?"

"A stack of bills from a private eye, along with transcripts of Xantha's telephone conversations with Goslau—some of them pretty spicy. He'd had Goslau's phone tapped. Also, some photos of her in bed with Goslau. Also pretty spicy."

Charlotte raised an eyebrow.

"Here's the map of the mill," he said, handing it over to her.

Charlotte looked at the drawing. "Maybe writing it all down gave him a feeling of control," she speculated. "Or maybe he's a voyeur who gets a kick out of seeing his wife in bed with another man."

"Or maybe he's a jealous husband who's obsessed with his wife's infidelity," he said. "Obsessed enough to kill."

"Maybe," she agreed. "I came across a piece on the gossip page of the *Post* that mentioned Xantha's leaving him for a young photorealist artist. It seems like more than just a coincidence that the piece ran the day before his wife's lover was murdered."

"I didn't know that. It looks like I'm not the only one who's been holding out." He looked at her, and smiled. "You're right: it does seem like more than just a coincidence."

They were interrupted by the arrival of Martinez with a woman whom Voorhees introduced as Agent Carolyn Healey of the art fraud squad of the FBI's New York division. Agent Healey was the least likely FBI agent Charlotte had ever met, though of the limited number of FBI agents of her acquaintance, none had really fit the image. Not only was she a woman, she was plump, middle-aged, and frumpy. With her round, rubicund face, wire-rimmed glasses, and Prince Valiant haircut (which looked as if someone had put a bowl over her head), she might have been a rural schoolteacher. But when they shook hands, the impression of schoolmarmish severity was immediately dissolved by her wide, sunny smile and honeyed Southern accent.

"Agent Healey has been working on the recovery of the missing paintings," Voorhees explained. "She's been working with art dealers and Interpol. The FBI is always called in to assist the local police on the theft of art worth over five thousand dollars because of the likelihood that it will be transported across state lines, which is a violation of Federal law."

Martinez, who had left the room, returned with another folding chair, which he placed next to Charlotte's for the FBI agent.

"Agent Healey is very eager to hear what you have to tell us," said Voorhees. "As am I and Martinez, here. We would be very pleased if you would enlighten us." Then he waved his arm stiffly as if he were Ed Sullivan introducing the next dog act, and the attention of the three law enforcement officers shifted to Charlotte.

"First, I'd like to see a list of the missing paintings, with descriptions," she said. "Do you have one available?"

Voorhees dug out two sheets from among the untidy heap of papers on his desk, and passed them to Martinez, who got up and handed them to Charlotte.

She, in turn, pulled out an auction catalog from her pocketbook. "This is the catalog for an auction that was held at the Ivanhoe Gallery last Thursday," she explained, handing the catalog to Healey. "The Ivanhoe is located on Spruce Street, just below the Falls. The owner is a Miss Diana Nelson. I call your attention to Lot Number Four: Diner, unsigned. Photorealist style. Oil: twenty-four by thirty-six."

Healey stopped taking notes to study the catalog.

"Now I'm going to tell you a story related to me by my stepdaughter, Marsha Rogers." She went on to repeat Marsha's story about the Lipschitz, to the bafflement of her audience. It was clear from their expressions that they thought she was off on a wild goose chase. Voorhees was wriggling with embarrassment at having called in the FBI agent to listen to such a wild tale. After pausing at the end of the story, Charlotte continued: "When I heard this story, I thought of the diner painting in the Ivanhoe auction. Though I didn't remember it until later, I had seen this painting several days before in the studio of the Paterson artist Jason Armentrout. Jason's usual subject matter is the world of go-go bars, and I remembered thinking then that a diner was an unusual choice of subject matter for him."

"Why were you visiting him?" asked Healey, pencil poised.

"I was there to ask him about the murder victim, Randy

Goslau. Lieutenant Voorhees had asked me to draw on my connections in the Paterson art world—such as they are—to look into Randy's death."

Healey raised an eyebrow at Voorhees, as if to say, *Do you mean to tell me that you're involving amateurs?* and Voorhees stared her down like an insolent fourth-grader caught breaking the rules.

"Jason was a friend of Randy's," Charlotte went on. "Or had been. They had had a falling out over a loan that Randy had never paid back. What I think happened is this: when Bernice sued Randy for the return of the paintings, he became worried that she would break into his studio and steal them. His studio was in the mill that had been owned by Spiegel, and was inherited by Bernice."

"So she would have keys," said Healey.

Charlotte nodded. "The fact that she had already tried to evict Randy demonstrated to him that she had few scruples when it came to protecting what she saw as her rightful inheritance. To prevent her from getting hold of the paintings, he asked his friend Jason to hide them in his studio."

"Address?" asked Healey, who now was sitting up at attention.

"I don't know. It's in the Columbia Bank building in downtown Paterson, to the right of City Hall."

"Martinez will get it for you," said Voorhees. He pointed the end of his pen at Martinez, who made a notation on a pad. "Do continue, Miss Graham," said Voorhees, now reassured that she wasn't going to make a fool out of him, that she might, in fact, even make him look good. He leaned back in his chair, and folded his hands across his belly.

"When Randy died, Jason realized that he was sitting on eight million dollars' worth of paintings that nobody knew were in his possession. Maybe he even thought he had a right to them because of the money Randy owed him."

"How did he know that nobody knew?" asked Voorhees.

"Maybe Randy told him that he wasn't telling anyone else. Or maybe he just waited, and when no one came forward to tell the police where the paintings were, he came to that conclusion. He decided to sell the paintings. But how to go about this? Any reputable gallery owner would question a painting without a provenance. That's where his diner paint-ing comes in."

"I see where we're headed now," said Healey.

"Then you've got better vision than I do," said Voorhees.

"I refer you to the ninth painting on the list of missing paintings: 'Diner. Oil. Twenty-four by thirty-six.' " Then she continued: "Jason makes a copy of this painting, and places it in the Ivanhoe auction. At the auction, he buys his own painting back for twelve hundred dollars. Now he has a bill of sale for a photorealist oil painting of a diner, twenty-four by thirty-six."

"I see now," said Voorhees, nodding.

"Then Jason disposes of his own painting and takes the Spiegel to a gallery along with the bill of sale. Ordinarily a gallery might have had a problem with an unsigned painting. But Spiegel never signed his paintings: his initials were always hidden in the painting, and they're often hard to find even for people who know they're there."

"Very clever," said Healey.

"More clever than I would have expected of Armentrout," she said.

"What do you mean?" the FBI agent asked.

"He didn't strike me as particularly bright. I think someone put him up to this. Maybe his girlfriend, Diana Nelson. But I suspect a bigger fish. I think what he or Diana did is put some feelers out in the art community as to who might be interested in buying a Spiegel with no provenance, the result being that someone came back with this suggestion for manu-facturing one."

"Do you know what his motive is?" the agent asked.

"I can guess. He's a Francophile: drinks Pernod, Smokes Gauloises, likes to think of himself as a latter-day Toulouse-Lautrec. He doesn't wear a black beret, but he might as well. Diana told me that she's moving to Paris, and I assume that he is too. I think he just wants to live the good life in Gay Paree, and he certainly can't afford to on what he makes from his painting."

"We can get a financial statement on him," said Voorhees. "See just how badly he needs the money."

"The same goes for Diana," Charlotte pointed out. "No

more limping along with a marginally profitable art gallery. With what they made from the sale of one Spiegel, they could live comfortably for a couple of years. Meanwhile, they could stick the other paintings in a vault and scout around Europe for a fence. When they ran out of money, they could simply sell another painting."

"It's easy to move art around," said Healey. "If you want to cross a border with several million dollars worth of drugs or diamonds, you're going to run into problems, but not with paintings. I've seen paintings change hands half a dozen times and go halfway around the world in a week." She addressed Charlotte: "Do you think he or Diana or both might have killed Goslau?"

"The thought has occurred to me. Especially now that we know the body was thrown directly into the raceway. The Ivanhoe is situated on the raceway, upstream from where the body was found. In fact, Diana told us that she once found Randy passed out in her doorway. Jason and Randy were supposedly friends, but people have been known to kill their friends in the name of money."

Charlotte paused while the FBI agent took notes.

"I guess that's it," she said once Healey had caught up.

Voorhees looked up at the clock, which read five of eleven. "I think it's time for a coffee break." He looked over at Martinez, who rose and went into an adjoining room.

After Martinez had left, Carolyn Healey turned to Charlotte. "Miss Graham, you said that your husband"—she consulted her notes—"Jack Lundstrom, I believe is his name, is a collector of contemporary art."

Charlotte nodded.

"Is he the level of collector who would buy a painting by an artist such as Donald Spiegel, a painting that would cost seven hundred and fifty thousand dollars or more?"

"Yes. In fact he has several Spiegels in his collection," she replied, wondering what Jack had to do with the price of bread.

Martinez returned carrying a tray laden with a coffeepot, sugar and cream, and matching cups and saucers. Voorhees had him well trained. He poured the coffee, and passed the cups around.

Healey sat quietly drinking her coffee for a moment. Then she set down her cup and said, "I agree with you that this scheme smacks of someone more sophisticated. A bigger fish, as you put it. I'd like to snag the bigger fish, and I'd like to use your husband as bait. Do you think he'd agree?"

Charlotte sat back. This was one development she hadn't expected.

The FBI agent continued. "If he did agree, he'd let it be known among the galleries he deals with regularly that he's in the market for a Spiegel painting of a diner. Then sit back and see who came forward."

"In other words, a sting," said Voorhees.

"Yes," said Healey.

"He was very angry about the stolen Lipschitz," Charlotte replied. "I think he would agree, yes. He would look on it as a worthy cause, as doing his part to see that art thieves are brought to justice." If he did agree, she thought with some apprehension, it would mean that she would have to see him and that they would have to come to some decision on the divorce issue.

But she was also tired of putting it off: it was time the issue was resolved. "I'll give him a call," she said.

· 13 ·

AFTER LEAVING VOORHEES' office, Charlotte headed back to the historic district. Before she went home to call Jack, she wanted to ask Spiegel about the missing paintings. If Jack agreed to go along with the plan, he'd need as much information as possible. Spiegel had known Randy better than anyone other than Patty. He should be able to tell her if her theory that Randy had given the paintings to Jason for safekeeping made sense. He might even be able to tell her where Jason had stored them. She also wanted to sound him out about Jason, whom he must have known pretty well. Was Jason capable of thinking up the scheme of which she suspected him, or was the idea more likely to have originated with someone else?

"Aha," Spiegel said as he answered the door. "Miss Charlotte Graham, the exposer of my real identity." He opened the door wide. "Won't you come in?" She had interrupted him at his work. He was wearing his painting clothes and holding a paintbrush between his teeth.

"I see that you're working," she said, after explaining that she had been drafted by Voorhees, because of her connection with Jack, to help track down the missing paintings. "Perhaps I should come back another time."

"No," he said. "We can talk while I work. I'm just putting the finishing touches on a painting. Follow me," he directed, rolling his wheelchair into the large, light-filled studio. After pulling over a chair for Charlotte, he transferred himself with the aid of crutches into a seat in front of an easel, which was mounted on an apparatus that was electronically controlled to move the seat up and down and from side to side.

"That's quite a rig," she said.

"Yeah," he agreed. "Fully automated. I may have little control over my body, but at least I can control my immediate surroundings. Everything in here is specially designed for the handicapped. Some of the features were already here; some I've added myself."

"I noticed," said Charlotte. "The door lever, the counters at wheelchair-height, the recessed space under the counters."

"The bathroom, too. That's the most important. I can roll my wheelchair right into the shower. The bathroom, and the Amigo."

"The Amigo?"

"That's the brand name. The technical name is a battery-powered three-wheeled platform mobility aid." He nodded at the motorized wheelchair that was parked in a corner, with another set of crutches tucked into a carrier on the back. "I can go anywhere with it: grass, sidewalks, carpeting—you name it. Four and half miles per hour, sixteen miles on a charge."

Charlotte stared at the Amigo. With it, she realized, Spiegel could have made it up to the diner for the aprons in much less time than she had figured, which did away with his alibi. Operating a motorized vehicle was a lot easier than rolling a manual wheelchair uphill. Moreover, he could have used the Amigo to drag the body from wherever he found it to the raceway.

"It's the world's greatest invention for the handicapped," Spiegel continued. "I use a wheelchair at home, but I use the Amigo everywhere else. The operating mechanism is a simple lever on the handlebars: you press one side for forward, and the other side for reverse. It's a lot simpler than this thing," he said, referring to his motorized easel.

In fact, Charlotte thought, the Amigo could explain the aprons. It would be easier to drag a body that was wrapped up than one that wasn't. As she mentally returned Spiegel to the top of her "A" list, she wondered: if the Amigo had been the instrument of Randy's death, why would Spiegel be telling her about it, and then decided that it might just be the arrogance of the murderer.

Spiegel pressed a button, and his chair moved up so that he could reach the top of the painting, which was a large oil depicting a man inside a cave, hunched over in torment.

Written across the top in Gothic lettering were the words: "Let the day perish wherein I was born." "This is my current work-in-progress," he said, as she sat down in the chair he had dragged over for her. "What do you think?"

Charlotte returned her attention to the painting. It was a realist painting, but not a photorealist painting, unless you could snap a shutter at the soul. In her opinion, the banality of the photorealists' subject matter was the weakness of the style. She understood the technical challenge of painting shiny surfaces, but the style lacked emotional appeal and importance.

"Well?" Spiegel prompted.

In this painting, Spiegel was applying photorealist techniques to important subject matter—not diners and storefronts, but personal myth and inspiration. In doing so, he was taking the style to new frontiers. "I think it's a masterpiece," she said finally. "The application of photorealist techniques to an inner reality."

"Exactly," he said, pleased that she understood. "It's a new direction for me. My new identity has also given me the chance to break new ground artistically. New York is filled with artists who repeat themselves *ad infinitum*. I didn't want to be one of them, but I couldn't break away. To have a waiting list for your paintings puts a damper on the need to take risks."

Morris Finder had been right. Spiegel had undergone an artistic rebirth, but it wasn't with the diner paintings; it was with these meticulous representations of the inner man.

Spiegel continued: "When I started out, all I cared about was sunshine and shadows. But as time went on, I found myself getting into reflections: what was bouncing off the glass. First from far away, then from up close. As I moved closer in, the surfaces kept bouncing me back out when what I really wanted to do was go through the glass, to see what was behind the glittering surface."

"To make your paintings subjective instead of objective."

He nodded. "William Blake said it best: 'As poetry admits not a letter that is insignificant, so painting admits not a grain of sand or a blade of grass insignificant—much less an insignificant blur or mark.' "

"What's it called?" she asked.

"This one is 'Job's Wrath,' after Blake. Being in that tunnel was my crisis of the soul. Like Job, I was angry at first at my fate, but then I came to realize that I had been denying what was most important to me—my art, my family, my soul." To her surprise, tears sprang to his eyes. "I had a spiritual disease, the cure for which was the renunciation of my former life."

"That's what the new identity was all about," she said.

He nodded. "I came to welcome even the paralysis. My inability to move my legs became a metaphor for my suffering: the outward and visible sign, so to speak." He nodded again at the painting. "This is the third in a series."

"You like doing things in series, don't you?" she said, thinking of the series of the Falls View.

"I guess I'm a systematist. Would you like to see the others?"

"Very much."

"The series is called the 'Path of Experience,' after Blake's *Job*," he said as he shifted himself back into the wheelchair. Then he rolled it over to a storage rack.

"May I help you?" she asked.

"It's not necessary, thanks. I've gotten quite good at this."

One by one, he slid three canvases out of their racks, and set them across his lap. Then he rolled himself over to another easel. "The only trouble is that I can't lift really large canvases," he said as he hoisted the first painting onto the easel. "But that's okay; I look on it as just another limitation that I have to work within."

"What's the 'Path of Experience'?" she asked.

"The five states established by Divine mercy to help the fallen man find his way to the true God. This painting represents the first state: Innocence. The title is 'The House of the Gryphon.' "

The painting showed the same man. This time he was sitting at a bountiful table, surrounded by his adoring family and friends. The setting was clearly the dining room at the mill. Written across the top were the words from the Bible: "When the Almighty was yet with me, When my children were about me."

Spiegel pointed to the gryphon—half eagle, half lion—that hovered above the assemblage: "The gryphon is an emblem of valor and magnanimity," he explained. Then he removed the painting from the easel, and put up the next one. "This painting represents the state of Experience. The title is 'The Palace of Delights.' "

The setting was the same room, but now it was the scene of an orgiastic party, with the same figure at the center. The Biblical quotation was: "Thy sons and thy daughters were eating and drinking wine in their eldest brother's house." The gryphon had disappeared, and now a cloven-hoofed Satan loomed over the gathering.

"The third painting you've seen, representing the state of Revolution when Job rebels against his woes, and now I'll show you the fourth. He lifted another painting onto the easel. "This is the Dark Night. The title is 'The Forest of the Night,' which is a metaphor for the false theories that block the path to enlightenment."

The painting showed a man cowering in a dark forest. Overhead loomed a beneficent angel of light. The quotation was: "Shall mortal man be more just than God? Shall a man be more pure than his Maker?"

"I haven't done the final state," he said as returned the painting to the rack. "I've managed to penetrate the surface of the glass, you see. But I have yet to come out on the other side." He rolled his wheelchair back over to the automated easel. "Now," he said, transferring himself back into the chair, "What can I do for you?"

"Do you know Jason Armentrout?" she asked. "I assumed, since he was a friend of Randy's, that you would know him as well."

"You assumed correctly. What do you want to know about him?"

Charlotte described the scheme that she suspected Jason of engineeering, and then said, "What I want your opinion on is this: Is Jason clever enough to have come up with this scheme on his own, or was he put up to it by someone a lot cleverer?"

"The latter," he said definitively. "Jason is a rich kid whose funds have dried up, and who can't make a living from painting: a *poseur*. He's too flaky to think up such a scheme himself. Maybe Diana"—he paused, and then shook his head—"but I don't think it was her either."

"That was the feeling I had too," she said. "But I'm glad to hear you confirm it. Which also means that you don't think Jason could have murdered Randy for the paintings."

"Not necessarily. You have to be clever to carry out a scheme of the kind you describe, but you don't have to be clever to throw somebody in a river, especially if he's already unconscious."

Charlotte noticed that he said *river* and not raceway, which could mean either that he was innocent or that he'd read the newspapers. Thinking over what he had said, she decided that he was right, which didn't mean that he wasn't trying to deflect suspicion from himself.

"What do you think?" he asked.

"I guess I'd have to agree," she said. "By the way," she added. "Do you care about the paintings? I'm just curious."

"Not a whit. They're ancient history to me now."

"Randy has left them to Patty Andriopoulis of the Falls View Andriopoulises. She's the heir to his estate. That is, if Bernice doesn't press you to get them back for her."

"They should go to Patty, if she's his heir," he said. "If they turn up, that is. Though I may have wanted to rescind it, I did sign an agreement saying that I gave the paintings to Randy."

"Bernice isn't going to be happy about that."

"Bernice isn't going to be happy, period. I'm going to have to call her today, before she hears about my resurrection through the grapevine. I have the feeling that she'll prefer me dead to alive. That way the real person doesn't get in the way of the reputation."

"One final question," said Charlotte.

Spiegel nodded.

"Do you have any idea where Jason might have stored them?"

Spiegel thought for a moment and then said, "As a matter of fact, I do. His studio is downtown in the former Columbia Bank building next to City Hall. Nine Colt Street."

Charlotte nodded. "I visited him there."

"Then you know the setup. Across the hall there's a utility room where he stores his canvases. It's filled with racks like those." He nodded at the storage racks against the wall. "I'll bet they're in there."

Charlotte smiled. "Thank you very much!" she said.

*   *   *

Back at home, Charlotte fixed herself another drink, and took a seat in her living room. She loved her little townhouse in Turtle Bay, with its mementoes of her fifty years on the screen. As her eyes swept the room, they alighted on a tape recorder that had appeared on an end table. This was getting ridiculous, she thought. She would have to have a talk with Vivian. The first one had appeared two weeks ago on her bed stand; the second one had appeared three days later on the kitchen counter; a third had appeared on a table in the library; and now, here was a fourth. They were multiplying like the pods in *Invasion of the Body Snatchers*. For a moment, she considered a policy of appeasement. If she spoke into one of them for a few moments—there must be some innocuous memories that she'd be willing to share with this sinister creature—would its shiny black plastic lose its threatening quality? Would it cease to reproduce at such a frightening rate? Would its commander in chief halt its relentless *drang nach Osten*? But ultimately she decided on a more hostile tactic. Getting up, she grasped it by its handle and then vigorously shoved it under the biggest armchair in the room. Then she resumed her seat, eyeing its resting place suspiciously. She had no doubt that it would reappear, if not here, then someplace else. Or worse, spawn dozens of tiny black plastic offspring among the dust bunnies in the womblike darkness underneath the armchair.

The tape recorder safely stuffed out of view, she took a long swig of her Manhattan. She had bought her townhouse years ago, when she had still been married to her first husband. It had been 1939. He had lived here by himself after she had gone to Hollywood. That was what had done them in: the separation. And her career. She had married him when she was eighteen. He had been her home town sweetheart. As diligently as he'd tried, he hadn't been able to cope with the sudden onset of her fame. One minute she had been the girl next door, the next she was a glamorous movie star. After the breakup, she had bought his share of the house from him. Looking back, she supposed he had really done quite well, considering how young he was. With the exception of her second husband, to whom she would probably still be married had he not died prematurely of a heart attack, none of her other husbands had done any better at being Mr. Charlotte Graham, and they had been well aware of what they were getting into. Including the most recent, Jack Lundstrom.

For a moment, a gorge of bitterness rose in her throat. To be dumped by a seventy-two-year-old Minneapolis businessman for a ladylike suburban widow whose sole function in life was to decorate houses and give parties! But the voice of reason quickly came to the rescue. What had she expected? Particularly when, after six cold, awful weeks in Minneapolis that had included half-a-dozen country club parties, a hospital charity ball, and—horror of horrors, a company snowmobile picnic— she had decamped to Manhattan, never to return. Jack wasn't the only one who should have known what he was getting into. Though she had known Jack made his primary residence in Minneapolis, she had made the mistake of acknowledging only the Jack who maintained an apartment at the Pierre, and who was well known as a collector of contemporary art. It came as something of a shock to find out that she had become the wife of a leader of the Minneapolis Old Guard with all the social trappings and expectations that went along with it.

If she couldn't claim to have loved Jack (after the initial infatuation, that is, and at her age she should have known better than to trust an infatuation), she had certainly liked him very much. He was amiable, charming, and considerate—an all-around boon companion—and she knew that he had felt much the same about her. She had vowed after her third marriage never to marry again, but Jack had been so different from the tin horn dictators and American man-boys, to borrow a phrase from Hemingway, that she was accustomed to from Hollywood. Their relationship had sputtered along on the basis of mutual regard for a number of years. She had stayed with him when he came to New York on business, and had even tagged along occasionally on his business trips abroad. He had accompanied her on a trip to China when she'd served as the advisor to a Chinese production of Arthur Miller's play *The Crucible*. But it was now time to call it quits.

She checked her watch. Nine here, eight in Minneapolis. He probably wouldn't be home. He was usually out every night of the week at some civic or charitable function. She had to grant Jack that, he was energetic. In fact, that had been part of her attraction to him: that of one energetic person to another, particularly at their age, when those who weren't already incapacitated by ill health tended to spend their time sizing up retirement villages and making arrangements for family trusts.

But he *was* home, according to the well-spoken woman who answered the phone. Charlotte couldn't help but picture her in terms of the upscale grandmothers on commercials for the telephone company, with wavy silver hair and a pink ultrasuede suit.

In a moment it was Jack himself on the phone.

"Hello, Jack," she said. "It's Charlotte." She realized that her heart was pounding as she waited for him to reply.

It was a long wait. At last he said, rather sharply: "Hello, Charlotte. And then: "What prompts you to call?"

She supposed some part of him was still angry with her for leaving Minneapolis. It must have been terribly humiliating for him to have her beat such a hasty retreat after having just been presented to Minneapolis society. (Such as it was, she thought cynically.)

"Nothing personal, Jack," she reassured him. "I'm calling on art business. I have a favor to ask of you. Marsha told me about your experience with the Lipschitz sculpture. I'm working with the police on a case now that has similar elements."

"Still interfering in police work?" he teased.

"It seems to find me," she replied, then went on to explain the details of the case and to tell him of her suspicion that someone other than Jason or Diana was involved. "The FBI is looking for a collector to lure them out," she said.

"Like me, for instance?" he asked.

"Like you, for instance. You're perfect. You already own some of Spiegel's paintings, you're far enough removed from New York to be above suspicion as a plant, and you've got the smarts and sophistication to pull something like this off."

"Do I get to wear a wire?" he joked.

"Oh, Jack," she said.

He went on to ask some questions of a more serious nature, but there was never any doubt in Charlotte's mind that he would do it. That was another of Jack's appeals: he was a good sport.

"Sure," he finally said. "When do we begin?"

"How soon can you get out here?"

"Tomorrow."

The funeral for John Andriopoulis was the next morning. Charlotte had skipped the visiting hours the previous evening at the funeral home, but had decided to attend the funeral. She was going to pick Jack up later that afternoon at Newark Airport anyway, and she might as well pay her last respects. She drove out from the city in the pouring rain, and arrived at the church a little early, which she was glad of, since it gave her time to check out the architecture. She had never been to a Greek Orthodox church before, and she was charmed by the interior—all rose and apricot and robin's egg blue, accented by gold leaf, like a Fabergé egg. By comparison with the severity of the Congregational church in which she had been raised, a church whose architecture reflected a masculine sense of order and intellect, the architecture of St. George's was delightfully feminine and emotional.

At her Yankee father's insistence, Charlotte had been raised a Congregationalist—the denomination of the Puritans. But her mother, of French extraction, had been raised a Catholic, and although she became a Protestant when she married Wilcox Graham, she had still practiced her faith, albeit covertly and intermittently, during the years that Charlotte was growing up. Charlotte remembered her mother swearing her and her sister to secrecy after ducking into a Catholic church for a Mass. After her mother and father had divorced, her mother was no longer obliged to worship in secret, but she no longer felt welcome in a church that condemned divorce, either. Charlotte herself had become an Episcopalian when she married her first husband, and she looked on that denomination as a happy compromise between the two religious strains of her childhood. But she must have absorbed some of her mother's Catholic sentiment, because she preferred her services high, and felt quite at home in the Catholic church. As far as the trappings of religiosity went, the Greek Orthodox church seemed to carry Catholicism one step further.

The funeral service itself was very much like a Catholic service, with some significant variations, one being that the bearded priest, wearing a black vestment, met the casket at the door and led it up the aisle to the altar. He carried a censer, which he waved over the casket, the clouds of incense symbolizing the rise of the departed's soul to the firmament of heaven. The other departure from the Catholic service was the fact that the coffin was opened once it reached the altar, giving the bereaved a final chance to pay their respects. And pay their respects they did, most of the mourners being from "the other side," as Patty called the old country, and not so Americanized that they were shy about making a spectacle of their grief. They sobbed and wailed and carried on over the casket, which was draped with flowers and decorated with a gilded icon of a sad-eyed St. George, the patron saint of the church, slaying a fire-spitting dragon. When Charlotte's opportunity came, she also went up to view the deceased. In death, John's face was a study in misery, the deep, longitudinal grooves that were carved in his cheeks a testament to a lifetime of hard work, and to the shadow that had been cast on his good name.

As she returned to her seat, Charlotte was surprised to see Voorhees among the mourners. In his light blue sports jacket, he stood out on the sea of black like a bell buoy on a dark ocean. She wondered why he was there. Was it strictly a professional interest, to see who had associated with the suspected murderer? Or was it because he felt remorse at having arrested the wrong man? The sight of him brought her thoughts back to the case. What should she do now? The inner voice that answered gave her the same reply that it had the last time: go back to Square One. Initially, she had interpreted Square One to mean the discovery of the body, but maybe, she thought now, she should go back to before that, to when the victim was still alive. It seemed to her that the life of the victim, as well as those of the major suspects, centered around the Gryphon Mill, but she had visited the mill only briefly, and then she had been distracted by Bernice's hysteria over the missing paintings. Now that Spiegel was at the top of her "A" list, she wanted to go back again, to get a feel for how he and Randy had lived.

The priest was now leading the casket back down the aisle. Patty's uncles, in black suits, served as the pallbearers. The women, in black veils, followed behind: Helen, Patty's sister, and Patty with little Johnny. Seeing these people only intensfied Charlotte's drive to find out who had killed Randy. The idea that an innocent man might have gone to his grave without being exonerated was bad enough, let alone the thought that the family might be left to suffer the disgrace of a deed he did not commit.

After the ceremony, she tracked Voorhees down in the clutch of mourners that had gathered in front of the church. He was standing under an umbrella at the side of the entrance portico, under which the mourners had taken shelter from the pouring rain.

"We meet again," he said, moving the umbrella over to accommodate her. They were about the same height.

She smiled faintly. She still wasn't sure how she felt about this man. He had the predatory air of the perennial skirt-chaser, but there was also something sad and vulnerable about him that elicited her sympathies. Maybe that was the idea, she thought cynically, having fallen for that with husband number three.

"I'd like to go back to the mill to take another look around," she said, getting right to the point. Subtlety had never been her strong suit. "Do you think I could arrange to do that now?" She had debated whether to tell Voorhees about the Amigo, and decided not to, for the moment.

"Are you going to the cemetery?" he asked.

She shook her head: "I have to pick Jack up at the airport at two, and I won't have time to do both. Are you?"

"Yes." He checked his watch. "Martinez should be at the Bureau. I'll tell you what. I'll call him on the radio and tell him that you're on your way. He can meet you there."

"Thank you very much," she said. He hadn't asked what she was looking for, which was just as well, since she didn't know.

"Don't touch anything," he warned her.

"Yes, Lieutenant," she replied.

· 14 ·

THE POLICE CRUISER was waiting outside the door of the mill when she pulled up ten minutes later. The rain had stopped, but the sun shone only dimly through thin clouds that raced toward the northwest. The National Weather Service was now predicting that the hurricane would hit Cape Hatteras with winds of ninety miles an hour sometime early that afternoon. A state of emergency had been declared for North Carolina. If the storm didn't head out to sea or veer inland, it would strike New York sometime around ten that night. Charlotte parked across the street, and joined Martinez on the sidewalk. After a perfunctory hello, he unlocked the door, and she followed him in. The building was one big room: a former dye factory. It was Paterson's dye factories that had established it as the world's silk capital, Tom had told her after her earlier visit to the mill. The water of the Passaic had a quality that made for particularly brilliant colors. The dyes had been mixed on the two long platforms that comprised the second story, and poured down through a gap in the middle into mixing vats on the first floor.

Passing quickly through the studio, Charlotte and Martinez headed toward the living quarters at the back. These were in a two-story addition, the downstairs housing a combination living room, kitchen, and dining room—the scene of the busy social life at the mill (she was reminded of Spiegel's paintings of this room, representing the states of Innocence and Experience)—and the upstairs housing Randy's studio apartment. Charlotte assumed that the police had searched Randy's apartment, but she wondered just how thoroughly they had gone over the downstairs, which was presumably where both Randy and Spiegel had spent most of their time.

It was no surprise that the place had been a hangout for artists, Charlotte thought as they entered the living area. It had great comfort and charm. At one end was the kind of kitchen that real estate agents referred to as a "cook's" kitchen, with a marble-topped island above which hung a collection of polished copper pots and pans, and around which were ranged half-a-dozen bar stools.

Martinez had found the light switch, and when he flipped it on, the room was flooded with light from the overhead track lighting.

To the left of the island was a long dining table which appeared to be made out of a single slab of wood, and which was surrounded by chrome-and-leather chairs, and topped by a centerpiece of ceramic fruit. Charlotte wondered if it was Louise's. At the opposite end was a living area with a U-shaped modular sofa of soft, fawn-colored leather, and a large glass coffee table. The floors were strewn with kilim rugs and the walls hung with a collection of folk art paintings. The choice of paintings was an odd one for a photorealist, Charlotte thought, but perhaps Spiegel had wanted to look at something different when he was relaxing.

Beyond the sofa, a wall of French doors opened onto the flagstone patio behind the mill superintendent's house. There was a wrought-iron table shaded by an umbrella, and a couple of chaise longues. The patio was planted with flowers and shaded by the old sycamores that lined the bank of the raceway on the opposite side of the stockade fence.

"Looks like it should be in a magazine, don't it?" said Martinez.

"Yes, it does," she agreed.

She decided that she would search this room first, and then Spiegel's studio. After that, she would take a look at the mill superintendent's house, and finally at Randy's studio.

"What are you looking for?" asked Martinez as Charlotte returned to the kitchen and started going through the cabinets.

"I'm not really sure," she said.

The cabinets were filled with gourmet gadgets of every

description. There was a pasta maker, an espresso machine, an ice-cream maker—you name it. Someone had been a gourmet cook, and since Louise hadn't lived here in years, she concluded it must have been Randy. Diana had said he did all the cooking.

"It was Randy who was the cook?" she asked, just to check.

"Yeah," Martinez replied. "Spiegel never cooked."

Just looking at the contents of the cupboard made Charlotte want to be a guest at the party. There were several different sets of china with glassware and tablecloths to match, wonderful ceramic casserole dishes. Even the dish towels were of the finest quality, she noticed as she went through a drawer stacked with crisply ironed linens.

It was then that she saw it: a large S in a circle, stamped in blue ink on a piece of heavy white cotton duck that had been shoved to the back of a drawer of dish towels. For a moment, she couldn't believe her eyes. It was the logo of the Supreme Linen Service, and it was stamped on an apron.

Reaching into the drawer, she pulled it out. Beneath it was another one. And then another. Three folded, crisply starched, white restaurant aprons, each bearing the same blue logo.

Martinez, who had wandered over to the living area to look at the paintings, had now come back: "The aprons!" he said.

"Yes," she replied. "The aprons."

Charlotte had thought at first that Randy had been thrown in the river by the diner. Then she had thought he'd been thrown in the raceway that ran past the Ivanhoe Mill. Now she suspected that he had been thrown in right here. As she pictured it, the scenario went like this: Randy passes out on the way back from the diner, somewhere near the mill. The murderer stumbles upon him, and takes advantage of the opportunity to kill him. There was also the possibility that the murderer encountered the unconscious man in his studio—had an appointment with him, perhaps. But the first possibility struck her as the more likely. As to the murderer's identity, only two of the suspects had access to the mill: Don Spiegel, who could have come across Randy on his way back from the Question Mark, and his sister. Possibly three, if Arthur Lumkin had gotten hold of a set of keys through Xantha. He must have gotten in at some point to do his floor plan. Seeking something with which to tie the victim up, the murderer then goes into the kitchen, and finds the aprons in a drawer. Quite by accident, perhaps. Maybe he was looking for rope or twine. Or maybe not by accident. The use of aprons with the same laundry stamp as those used at the diner might have been a deliberate ploy to create confusion. (Would Arthur Lumkin have known that the diner's aprons had the same stamp? she wondered. She doubted it. Ditto for Bernice, who didn't strike her as the diner type.) After wrapping the body up, the murderer then drags it (here the aprons would come in handy) or carries it to the edge of the raceway, and dumps it in, probably within only a couple of dozen feet of where it was found.

As Martinez looked on, she carefully refolded the aprons, and put them back, being careful not to touch the spots where the murderer might have left fingerprints. Then she told Martinez that she wanted to take another look outside. She wanted to get a sense of where the murderer might have come across Randy's unconscious body.

"Sure," he replied, adding, "Do you think the killer used the aprons from here?" It was the first observation she had heard him utter, so thoroughly had he been cowed by Voorhees.

"I think it's a good bet," she said.

After turning out the lights, they headed back out. Standing on the sidewalk in front, Charlotte studied the building. To the right was an alley leading to a loading dock at the rear. To the left was the alley between the mill and the mill superintendent's house, and to the left of that was the raceway where the body had been found. The alley on the right was a dead end. The wall of the loading bay abutted the wall of the adjoining building. But the other alley was a different story. On the left, it was bordered first by the yard of the mill superintendent's house, and then by the side of the house itself. On the right, it was bordered by the side of the mill where the entrance to Randy's apartment was.

She guessed that Randy had passed out near the entrance to this alley. She pictured the murderer coming across the body, and tying it up. But how would he have gotten it to the raceway? He could have dragged it out to the street and thrown it over the bridge, but he would have risked being seen. Then she thought of the fence. Was there a gate in it? she wondered.

As she stood there thinking, Martinez paced. At one point, he picked up an empty bottle of Courvoisier from the alley, and showed it to her. "The winos are drinking pretty classy stuff these days," he said, suddenly talkative. Then he threw it into a garbage can, one of a row of four of five, and wandered toward the back of the mill superintendent's house.

Following him, Charlotte emerged at the patio, a beautifully landscaped city garden, complete with a built-in fireplace and stone benches. It was bordered by a stockade fence that shut out the urban blight: the garbage-strewn lot next door, the crack house to the rear, and the parking lot for the giant mill in back of that.

Starting at the back of the mill superintendent's house, she followed the fence, looking for a gate. At the end of the patio she found it, concealed in the wet ivy like a secret door: a padlocked gate. Holding the ivy aside, she nodded at the padlock. "Do you suppose we have a key to this lock?" she asked.

Wordlessly, Martinez examined the lock, then picked out a key from the ring he held in his hand, and opened the gate.

The gate swung open onto the bank of the raceway, which was overgrown with bamboo. A path led to an old set of brownstone steps at the edge of the raceway. Standing at the top, Charlotte looked down at the murky water; she was less than twenty feet from the spot where Randy's body had been found.

The distance from the entrance of the alley to this point was probably less than fifty feet. The murderer would have had to drag the body down the alley, across the patio, and through the bamboo for a distance of eight or ten feet to the top of the stairs. From there, he could easily have rolled it down the steps and into the raceway.

It was a straight run—not even a need for a curb out.

It was no mystery to Charlotte why the police had missed the gate; if she hadn't been looking closely, she would have missed it herself. And it was concealed on the other side by the thicket of bamboo, as were the steps themselves, which explained why she hadn't noticed them when she and Tom had scouted the path on the other side. What *was* something of a mystery was why the police hadn't noticed that the bamboo had been trampled when they had canvassed the area after the discovery of Randy's body. Though it since would have grown back, the murderer would have had to flatten at least a few canes when he threw Randy in. If he was on an Amigo, he would have flattened a good deal more than that. On second thought, it wasn't a mystery at all. The police had found the flattened path through the bamboo at the diner first. It was the old Occam's razor story: the danger of formulating a theory and sticking to it, rather than keeping an open mind. If some poor soul hadn't tossed his cookies in the bamboo on that fateful night (the Di-Tabs ad popped into her mind; the nameless partygoer could have used some), they never would have been misled by the whole diner issue.

These were the thoughts that passed through Charlotte's mind as she drove up to the diner. She had left Martinez with instructions to report what they had found to Voorhees, and then taken off. There was something else she wanted to check before she left to pick up Jack. The diner parking lot was uncharacteristically empty for eleven o'clock, which was the start of the noontime rush. She found out why when she approached the door. A black-bordered sign read: "Closed due to a death in the family." Beneath that was another sign urging readers to open their hearts and their homes by adopting Poochie, a four-year-old Chihuahua-mix female: "Very friendly, good with cats." At the bottom was written: "See Patty, the waitress."

But the lights were on and she could see activity in the kitchen. Dirgelike Greek bouzouki music was coming over the sound system. It looked as if the kitchen help were getting ready for a memorial dinner. A lavish display of food had been set out on the counter. It reminded her of a Greek cruise-ship buffet.

Trying the door, she found it open (she remembered what John had said about there not being a key), and she went in.

Upon seeing her, Carlos, one of the short-order cooks, came out of the kitchen, and informed her that the diner was closed.

"I'm looking for Patty," she said.

"She hasn't come back from the cemetery yet," he replied. Charlotte had forgotten how long graveside services often took.

"We're getting ready for the funeral dinner," he explained. "But she's supposed to be coming back early to help." His glance shifted to the Andriopoulis house across the street, where a small red car was just pulling into the driveway. "In fact, here she is now."

Patty emerged, and headed across the street. As she approached, Carlos held the door for her. When she removed her black hat, Charlotte could see that her eyes were red from weeping. The clownish eyebrows looked out of place on her grief-stricken face.

"Miss Graham!" she said as she entered, surprised to see her.

"I just dropped by to ask a question," Charlotte explained. "It will only take a minute. The question is: did Randy ever ask you where your aprons come from? I found some aprons in the kitchen at the mill with the same laundry mark as those that are used here."

"I do recall him asking about our laundry service," she said. "Now that you mention it, I remember that he wore a diner-style apron when he cooked at the mill. I never saw the laundry mark . . . ."

"Thanks."

For a moment, Patty pondered the significance of Charlotte's question, and then said: "If you found aprons at the mill, it might mean that the aprons wrapped around the body didn't come from here."

"Exactly," Charlotte said.

As Charlotte drove to the airport, the news station on her car radio reported that Clyde had hit Cape Hatteras, causing millions of dollars worth of damage to the barrier islands, and was heading up the coast at a rate of fifty miles per hour. It was expected to strike later that night, bringing high winds and torrential rains. Though it was the south shore of Long Island that was expected to bear the brunt of the storm, residents of the greater New York area were being advised that the hurricane watch had been upgraded to a hurricane warning, and that they should take the proper precautions. Though it was the coastal areas that would be hardest hit, even inland residents were being advised to secure objects like garden chairs and garbage cans that might be dashed into a window by the wind. As she drove, Charlotte noticed that some homeowners were going to the extreme of taping their picture windows with masking tape. She wondered briefly if she should take in her trash cans and patio furniture, and then decided not to worry about it. In Charlotte's experience, hurricanes in the New York area were usually a non-event, at least for city-dwellers. The last real hurricane she could remember was the one in 1938, which had picked up her family's summer cottage on Long Island Sound and slid it a hundred yards down the beach. That was before hurricanes had names. Then there were a couple in the fifties that had been pretty severe: Carol and Hazel in 1954 and Diane a year or two later. But beyond those four, the hurricanes that had struck the area had been little more than severe rainstorms. Which wasn't to say they they weren't due for a bad one.

Though there was no evidence of the storm yet, the sky had turned an eerie yellow color, and the air had a sticky heaviness that was unusual for this time of year. The news announcer was predicting that the airports would be closed at around eight. It looked as if Jack's plane would get in just under the wire.

Jack was among the first off the plane. He always flew first class, not out of snobbery, but because the larger seats accommodated his size more comfortably. He was a big man: six foot four and well over two hundred pounds. That had been part of his attraction for Charlotte. Being no pint-size person herself, she had always gone for big men. All of her husbands had been well over six feet. She felt a pang of—what was it?—longing, she supposed, when she first saw him. There was something about him that was so comforting: his size, his geniality, his Midwestern honesty. He was square in the best sense of the word, dependable, with no surprises—like a big old easy chair that you could sink right down into. But then she caught herself. *Uh-uh*, she admonished herself, *you've tried that already, and it didn't work*. Jack was also like a dessert that looks tempting until you remember that you don't like it. She was reminded of what John had said about diner desserts that don't live up to their delectable appearances. If she had to put Jack in terms of a dessert, it would be a tapioca pudding. Or maybe, to give him a little more class, a blancmange. Your expectation was that it would have that same comforting creaminess that it had had in your childhood, but instead it turned out to be utterly tasteless.

Tapioca pudding! If he only knew what she was thinking, poor thing. Feeling guilty at her cruel thoughts, she welcomed him with a friendly hug.

"Guess what?" he said proudly as they headed off toward the parking lot after picking up his bags. "I called a few dealers after I spoke with you, and I've already got a nibble."

"Really!" she said. "From who?"

"The Koreman Gallery. I called Agent Healey right away, and we set up an appointment for tomorrow morning. You've been there with me," he reminded her. "It's the big gallery on West Broadway."

"I remember it well," she said.

On the ride back to Manhattan, Charlotte filled Jack in on the case, including the role of Mary Catherine Koreman. Though it was unlikely that she or her husband had actually killed Randy—they hadn't stayed around for the post-opening party—they could have been Jason and Diana's accomplices. And, although Charlotte hadn't thought of it before, it was quite likely that Jason, as Randy's friend, would also have had a key to the mill, which meant that he could have come across the aprons in the kitchen. But despite the involvement of Mary Catherine, Charlotte's thoughts kept returning to Spiegel. There was one thing about the Spiegel scenario that puzzled her: the aprons again. The aprons would have made it easier to drag the body, but they also would have been difficult to wrap around it. For a paraplegic, rope would have been easier, and Spiegel had lived at the mill; he would have known where to find a length of rope. Whereas the aprons . . . the aprons had the smell of someone who didn't know where to look and couldn't find anything else. Which would have been the case with Jason, she thought as she promoted him from the "B" list to the "A" list.

As she thought some more about Spiegel, another possibility occurred to her, the sheer audacity of which made her heart pound. It was the possibility that Spiegel wasn't really a paraplegic. If he had created a new identity, why couldn't he have created a disability as well? Especially if he had really spent some time in a wheelchair. Everything he said could have once been true: the spinal cord injury, the wheelchair as a metaphor for his new life—except that it wasn't true any longer. She remembered what he had said about his rehabilitation sessions at the Kessler Institute. She didn't know that much about physical disabilities, but she wondered why someone who was permanently paralyzed would need rehabilitation therapy. Wouldn't such therapy only benefit someone who had hopes of recovery?

Back home, she and Jack entered into the spirit of the approaching hurricane by mixing themselves some drinks—a Manhattan for her, a martini for him—and settling themselves in front of the television set to await the arrival of Clyde, who was now due to strike at about nine. It had started raining heavily when they hit the Holland Tunnel, and the rain now lashed at the windows. The traffic outside on Forty-ninth Street had dwindled to an occasional cab; motorists were apparently heeding the traffic advisory. Or perhaps the light traffic was due to the fact that offices had been advised to let their employees go early. After some footage of the devastated Outer Banks, the TV news reports shifted to Long Island, where evacuees from the rapidly advancing storm were taking refuge at shelters in schools and churches. The metropolitan airports had closed at four, making Jack's the last flight in from Minneapolis. Jack had been hopping up to check the reading of the barometer on the library wall regularly: at five, it stood at twenty-nine point four one and falling.

The rattle of the rain against the windows made her living room seem as cozy as a New England farmhouse kitchen during a nor'easter, and Charlotte relished the feeling. It wasn't often that you could feel cozy at home in New York, and it usually was during heavy snowstorms of which there had been precious few in recent years. When they finished their drinks, they would be going around the corner for a bite to eat at a neighborhood restaurant. Charlotte wondered briefly if it would be closed, but then dismissed the thought. They might have been taping windows in Clifton, but New Yorkers were undaunted by the likes of hurricane warnings, even if they weren't driving their cars (most of which belonged to out-of-towners anyway). For hors d'oeuvres, she had stuffed some celery sticks (a little brown around the edges, but Jack would never notice) with some cream cheese, and—for a "gourmet" touch—sprinkled them with paprika. It was all she could find in her refrigerator. Not only did she detest cooking, she was bad at it. Jack's daughter, Marsha, who was an excellent cook, was especially contemptuous of Charlotte's celery sticks, which she called "one step up from Cheese Whiz on Ritz crackers." Actually, Cheese Whiz on Ritz crackers was another one of Charlotte's specialties, though only when she was truly desperate.

As she watched Jack wolf down the celery sticks, Charlotte was pleased to realize that the warm and fuzzy feelings that his presence had momentarily elicited had now faded. Although she didn't mind having him as a cocktail guest (or maybe even an overnight guest, if the storm kept up), she was quite happy that there was no prospect of this enormous bear of a man ever again claiming her turf as his marital right. There, she had said it—she thought determinedly—if only to herself.

She could tell that he was uncomfortable. For a man who was always in command, he was uncharacteristically awkward.

He had listened patiently as she explained the ramifications of the case. He was particularly intrigued by the story of Spiegel's return from the dead, and asked a lot of questions about it. "I guess it's something we all think of at some point in our lives," he said. "The idea of being a fly on the wall of your own life. How did his wife react to his resurrection?" he asked.

"I don't know. I haven't seen her since then." She took a sip of her drink, and continued: "His appearance wasn't the only thing that changed. His whole life changed. He said that coming back from the dead taught him what was important in life. For instance, his painting style completely changed." She went on to describe the series of paintings based on Blake's *Job*."

"I'd like very much to see them," Jack said. Charlotte could see his acquisitive instincts come into play—the first to own a "new" Spiegel. "Don't you have a copy of Blake's *Job* here?" he asked, nodding at the library.

"I don't know," she replied. "Do I?" After fifty years of book-collecting, she was no longer sure what she had. Plus there were the books that had been contributed by her various husbands and lovers.

"I thought I remembered seeing it." Getting up, he wandered into the adjoining room. "Aha," he said, pulling a book off a shelf. "I may be over seventy, but my memory's still good." He returned to the living room, and handed her the book.

"I don't remember this," she said, turning it over in her hands. "It must have been Will's," she added, referring to her second husband, the only one besides Jack who displayed any interest in art.

Jack nodded curtly.

She had forgotten how resentful he was of her former husbands and how, during the course of their marriage, she had learned to avoid bringing them up in conversation. As a man who had been married to one woman for forty-odd years, he found her multiple marriages distasteful. Not having to tiptoe around that issue anymore, she observed to herself, was another benefit of being single again.

It was the catalog of an exhibition of Blake's illustrations of the *Book of Job* at the Tate Gallery in London. As she leafed through it, she described Spiegel's paintings to Jack, and showed him the corresponding illustrations from Blake. "Spiegel was only up to the fourth state," she said. "The Dark Night." As Jack studied Blake's illustration, Charlotte read the text.

As in Spiegel's painting, the inscription on Blake's work read: "Shall mortal Man be more just than God? Shall a man be more Pure than his Maker?" The explanation said that the God of Justice who appears to Job is revealed by his cloven hoof to be Satan. "This is Blake's most insistent doctrine," said the text, "that the true God is not the God of Justice, but the God of Forgiveness."

Suddenly, Charlotte remembered that the God in Spiegel's painting also had a cloven hoof, and she realized that his painting, like Blake's, was filled with symbols, and that what those symbols were saying was that the false God of Justice had also appeared to him. Could it be that the false God had appeared to him at the entrance to that narrow alley? she wondered. That the justice he was repenting of was Randy's murder?

A chill ran down her spine. It would be just like Spiegel to put the clues to the solution of the murder in a series of paintings. That was what he had done in the Falls View series, wasn't it? Maybe he was making his murder of Randy into an intellectual puzzle, just as he had his own death and resurrection. "A systematist," he had called himself. A master of cool, dispassionate precision.

"What is it?" Jack asked as he stood over her, looking at the book.

"Oh, nothing," she said.

Jack returned to his seat, and ate another celery stick. "What are these tape recorders all over the house for?" he asked. "There's one in the kitchen, one in the dining room, and now I see one here." He eyed the recorder on the end table, the one that Charlotte had previously shoved under the chair.

Talk about death and resurrection, Charlotte thought. "Vivian put them out. They're for my autobiography. I have a contract—not for the kiss and tell kind of autobiography," she reassured him, but for one in which I share my thoughts about life, that kind of thing."

"I can't see you doing a kiss and tell autobiography anyway," he said, not without a hint of suspicion. "But if you did, I might have to take some action to prevent you." He spoke jokingly, but she knew he was in earnest.

"No need to worry," she reassured him. "Vivian thinks that if she puts enough tape recorders around, I'll be prompted to start talking into one."

"And have you?"

"Not yet," she said. Then she took a breath, and added: "I have the feeling that I can't really start while I'm still in the middle of a chapter." She gazed at him with her clear, gray eyes. "If you know what I mean."

"I know what you mean." He paused, and then continued: "Charlotte, there's something I've been meaning to talk with you about. I admit that I've been dilatory about bringing it up, but I think it's time now . . . ."

· 15 ·

IN THE END, Clyde had veered off into the Atlantic, catching only the tip of Long Island in its embrace. The storm had hit at about eight, bringing torrential rains, and winds that gusted at seventy-five miles an hour. By ten, the wind had moderated, and a pallid moon ventured forth, providing the backlighting for the dramatic black clouds that raced across the sky. As the storm lashed the city, Charlotte and Jack had discussed the details of their impending divorce over a pleasant dinner at a deserted French restaurant. He wanted to marry the widow of his businessman friend. "We make a good couple," he had said, which only emphasized the fact that she and Jack had not. To her surprise, Charlotte wasn't jealous or regretful, only relieved. Her reaction reminded her of what a doctor had once told her when she was trying to decide on two alternatives for treatment: surgery or drugs, both equally efficacious, and both with their attendant drawbacks. "Throw a coin," he said. "Heads it's surgery, tails it's drugs. If it comes out heads, and your reaction is 'Oh, shit,' then you know you should have chosen drugs." She had fully expected her reaction to Jack's wanting a divorce to be "Oh, shit," and now felt free as a bird knowing that she had made the right decision. Or rather, that Jack had made it for her.

By morning, the only evidence that the storm had passed through was an occasional downed electric line, and the tree branches that littered the streets. It was still raining, not the heavy downpour of the day before, but a light drizzle that the weatherman predicted would cease by midday. After breakfast (unable to get a cab, Jack had wound up staying in Charlotte's guest room), she and Jack headed uptown for the meeting with Agent Healey. After that, they would be going down to Soho to see Mary Catherine. Charlotte planned to sit in. She wanted to be there, and there was no reason why she shouldn't. In fact, her presence enhanced Jack's credibility as a buyer. Mary Catherine had no idea that Charlotte had been working with the police, only that she had been interested on behalf of a friend of Randy's in his reaction to Verre's painting.

They arrived at the Koreman Gallery promptly at eleven. Much to his delight, Jack had been wired with a tiny microphone. His mission was to find out what Mary Catherine had to say about the provenance of the painting, as well as to induce her to produce the painting itself.

After being greeted by the sullen receptionist, they were escorted back to Mary Catherine's office, and offered some coffee. Then Mary Catherine appeared, wearing another hand-woven caftan and off-the-wall eyeglass frames, these of bright red to match the dress.

"How very nice to see you again," she said, extending her hand. Then she took a seat and asked innocently: "What can I do for you this morning?" as if her assistant hadn't already spoken with Jack.

"I'm looking for a Spiegel to add to my collection," Jack replied. "I have several of his more recent works, but I'd like one or two from his earlier period to round out my collection."

"Before he started doing cityscapes, you mean?" she asked.

"Yes. Something from the period when he was painting shiny surfaces—diners, airplanes, things like that. I'd like to get a sense in my collection of the artist's development."

"I think I might have just the painting for you." Turning, Mary Catherine signaled to a pale young man in an adjacent office. "Larry, can you bring out the Spiegel for Mr. Lundstrom, please?" she asked.

The young man disappeared into a storeroom, and reappeared a moment later with a painting protected by bubble wrap. After unwrapping it, he set it on an easel in a corner.

As Charlotte had anticipated, it was the same painting that Jason had copied and put up for sale at the Ivanhoe auction, and then bought back for twelve hundred dollars.

"The title is 'Hometown Diner,' and the date is 1967," said Mary Catherine. "The date and the initials are here." She pointed to a reflection in the window. "As you know, the date and initials are concealed in all of Spiegel's paintings."

Jack nodded. He went over to the painting, and appraised it with the cool eye of the prospective buyer who is reluctant to display too much enthusiasm for fear of being overcharged. It was a good piece of acting. "Can you tell me anything about its history?" he asked.

"A little. It was purchased at a gallery auction in Paterson after Spiegel's death by someone who was interested in diners. It had been in storage there for years. Neither the buyer nor the gallery knew it was an early Spiegel."

"Had it been forgotten?" asked Jack.

"Apparently so, or overlooked. Anyway, the buyer brought it here to be appraised, and when he found out it was a Spiegel, he decided to sell. All he had wanted was a painting of a diner, which he could buy elsewhere for a lot less money."

It was a plausible story, Charlotte thought, one designed to make Jack think he was getting a deal.

Jack turned the picture over, and studied the phony provenance taped to the back. "How much?" he asked.

"Five hundred thousand," said Mary Catherine.

Half of which would go to Jason and Diana, Charlotte guessed. Enough for them to lead *la vie en rose* for at least a couple of years.

"I'll give you four fifty," said Jack.

"Firm," was Mary Catherine's reply. "You can't buy a Spiegel anywhere for less than seven fifty. This is a bargain."

Jack appeared to consider the offer, and then said: "I'd like to buy it." Reaching into the breast pocket of his sports jacket, he removed his checkbook and placed it on Mary Catherine's desk. "Will a fifty-thousand-dollar deposit be all right?"

There was nothing like producing a checkbook to make a gallery owner's eyes glitter. "That would be just fine," she said.

"I'd like a new frame," he said. "Of my choice," he added.

You could depend on Jack to try to squeeze a little extra out of the deal, even when he knew it was just for show.

"Of course," said Mary Catherine, all smiles.

As she spoke, the door of the gallery opened, and out of the corner of her eye Charlotte could see Voorhees and Healey talking with the receptionist. After Healey had flashed her badge, they marched toward the back, and appeared a few seconds later at the office door.

"Good morning, Ms. Koreman," the FBI agent said. "I'm Agent Carolyn Healey of the Federal Bureau of Investigation, and this is Lieutenant Martin Voorhees of the Paterson police department. We'd like to talk with you for a minute."

Mary Catherine's round face blanched. Then a red flush started creeping up her neck, turning her face a shade almost as vivid as that of her dress. For a moment, she just sat there, speechless.

"I hope you don't mind if we sit down," said Agent Healey, taking a seat with Voorhees on the leather sofa against one wall.

"Not at all," said Mary Catherine in a tiny little voice.

"I wonder if you're aware of the fact that you've just sold Mr. Lundstrom a stolen painting," said Agent Healey.

As arranged, Charlotte and Jack met Voorhees and Healey a short time later at the Moondance Diner, where Charlotte had eaten on her earlier visit. Over "our best" coffee, delightfully seasoned with cinnamon, Healey told them what they had learned from Mary Catherine. All it had taken for her to spill the beans was the threat of a jail sentence. Not that there was much chance that she would actually go to jail. As Carolyn Healey explained, the Manhattan courts were so overwhelmed by rapists, muggers, armed robbers, and other denizens of the criminal underclass that the mere sight of an educated, well-dressed art thief was enough to make an entire courtroom breathe a collective sigh of relief. The result was that art thieves usually got off lightly, even when they were directly responsible for the theft, which wasn't the case here. Healey went on to say with some disgust that the light sentences were one reason for the dramatic increase in art thefts, which now rivaled the drug trade as the number one moneymaker for the underworld.

Mary Catherine had known the painting was stolen, but she

hadn't participated in the theft. She had, however, suggested the idea to Jason of putting his copy of the Spiegel painting in the auction, and then using the bill of sale as a provenance.

Having turned state's witness, Mary Catherine was now a participant in the sting. She was instructed to call Jason and Diana (she had said that they were both involved), and tell them that the painting had been sold.

They would be arrested and charged with the theft when they came to the gallery to pick up their money.

Though the question of who had stolen the painting had now been answered, there was still the question of who had murdered Randy. No matter what angle Charlotte looked at it from, she kept coming back to the aprons. "No ideas but in things," Williams had written, and the things that this case revolved around were two long, white restaurant aprons. That night, she dreamed about them: white aprons hung on a clothesline, white aprons sailing through a cloud-studded blue sky, white aprons swirling on a dance floor. The figure in her mental picture of the scene was clear: a man hurriedly going through the kitchen cabinets in search of something with which to tie up the body. But the face was a featureless blur.

The next morning, Vivian brought Charlotte her coffee and cinnamon toast in bed, along with the newspaper. The woman took care of her like an old-fashioned nanny: when she wasn't bullying her, she was spoiling her rotten. As Charlotte drank her coffee and ate her toast, she read about the damage inflicted by Clyde: five million dollars' worth of property damage in Montauk, and a record of twelve point nine inches of rain dumped on the metropolitan area over the course of twenty-four hours. Reading about the rainfall made her think of the Falls. Her walking-tour guidebook had said that they were most spectacular twenty-four to forty-eight hours after a storm. She had yet to see them in their glory: not only had the flow on her visits been less than usual because of the August drought, up to a quarter of that had been diverted to the hydrolectric plant. If the Falls were magnificent when the flow was reduced, what must they be like when it was heavy?

There was nothing like coffee in bed with the newspaper to

start the day off right, Charlotte thought as she finished. Setting the tray aside, she hopped out of bed and quickly dressed.

Then she headed out to Paterson.

At the Falls View, she took a seat in the usual booth and ordered the works: two eggs over easy, home fries, bacon, rye toast, orange juice, and coffee. Vivian's coffee and cinnamon toast had been great, but they weren't enough to hold her for the rest of the morning. Neither Patty nor her mother were there, and Charlotte missed them. To say nothing of John hunched over the grill, arms windmilling with his fancy grill work. Somehow the diner didn't hum along at quite the same even pitch without the Andriopoulis family. Her breakfast arrived instantaneously, and it was delicious. Bacon cooked to the perfect degree of crispness; home fries made from real potatoes, and not too greasy; eggs with yolks that weren't over-done or runny. Breakfast was such a simple meal, but so few restaurants got it right. As she ate, she planned her day. After breakfast, she would take a look at the Falls. Maybe take some pictures; she had brought her camera along. Then she would go over to Voorhees' office, and see if he had anything new. Not that he would tell her if he did, she thought.

No sooner had this thought occurred to her than she noticed Voorhees himself getting out of a car in the parking lot. He was wearing casual clothes—it must have been his day off— and he was accompanied by a pretty teenage girl: blond, with his own strong jaw.

A few minutes later he entered, and, spotting Charlotte, came over to say hello. He introduced the girl as his daughter, Demetra: "Demi, for short." The girl smiled sweetly, and shook Charlotte's hand in a very adult manner.

"I didn't know you hung out here," Charlotte said.

"Everyone from Paterson eats here," Voorhees said. "But not everyone from New York. What brings you here today?"

"The Falls. I thought I'd see them in all their glory."

"They should be something," he agreed.

"Would you like to join me for breakfast?" she asked.

"Thank you," said Voorhees. He directed his daughter to the seat opposite Charlotte and then slid in next to her.

For a few minutes, they chatted about a diving competition

in Atlantic City, where Voorhees and his daughter were headed. But once their food arrived, Voorhees left his daughter to
her pancakes and turned to business.

"Armentrout has a ticket for Paris," he said. "The FBI has
been keeping an eye on the airports in case he tried to leave.
He's scheduled to take off tomorrow morning. He's dropping
by the Koreman to pick up his money first."

"What about Diana?" asked Charlotte.

"She's not going, I guess. He only bought one ticket, and
the airlines don't have any record of a reservation in her name.
Maybe she's going later. If she doesn't show up with him,
we'll pick her up here later."

"But she told Tom and me that she was going. She's closed
the gallery."

Voorhees shrugged. "Maybe they had a falling out."

"Or maybe he's double-crossing her. Any new leads on the
murder?"

"Only that the M.E. had identified the body that he thought
was Spiegel's: a wino who had been missing since early last
spring."

"I have a new lead," said a voice. It was Patty. She was
serving the customers at the adjoining booth. "Sorry," she said.
"I couldn't help overhearing. Just give me a minute here."

Voorhees nodded a greeting, and then returned to his eggs,
clearly uncomfortable at the prospect of talking to John's
daughter.

A minute later, Patty sat down next to Charlotte. "First I want
to show you these," she said, pulling some photographs out of
her pocket. "They're pictures of my father's gravestone. They
made it over at Ippolito's." She nodded at the monumental
works across the street.

The photos showed a gravestone of dark gray polished
granite. Above the name John K. Andriopoulis and the dates
was an engraving of the Falls View, complete with "Open 24
Hours," and "Try Our Famous Hot Texas Wieners" written
under the name.

"John would have been very happy," said Charlotte. She
passed the photos to Voorhees, who gave them a cursory
glance and then gave them back. "What's your lead?" she
asked as Patty pocketed the photos.

Patty addressed Charlotte: "Remember when you stopped by on Tuesday? You asked me if Randy had ever inquired about the aprons?"

Charlotte nodded.

"I'm afraid I wasn't thinking very clearly at the time. There *was* someone else who inquired about the aprons: it was Jason Armentrout. He wanted to give some to Randy as a present. He thought Randy would like them because he was such a nut about diners."

"Patty, your order's ready," Carlos yelled from behind the counter.

"I'm coming," she shouted back.

The blurry face in Charlotte's mental picture now had features: a handsome, sharply angled face with vivid, deep set blue eyes, and graying hair pulled back into a ponytail.

She locked eyes with Voorhees.

He took a drag from his cigarette, and then stubbed it out in the red metal ashtray. "I don't think we'll wait until he gets to the airport to pick him up," he said as he gulped down the rest of his coffee.

"Are you leaving, Daddy?" asked Demi.

Voorhees leaned over to speak with his daughter: "I have to go to work now. I'll give Jenny's mother a call and ask her to pick you up here. Sorry I won't be able to be there for you, sweetie."

"That's all right, Dad," she said with a smile.

Patty nodded at her son, who was playing with some toy trucks in the last booth. "She can keep an eye on Johnny for me until her ride comes." She looked across the table at Demi. "Would you like that?"

Demi nodded. "I'd like it," she said.

"Thank you," Voorhees said to Patty. After wishing his daughter good luck, he kissed her goodbye, and then stood up to go.

Standing up herself, Patty scanned the detective's face anxiously. "Then it *was* important," she said.

"Yes, it was important," he said.

"Wait, Marty," said Patty, laying a hand on his arm. "I just want to tell you something. We got the autopsy report back. Daddy's coronary arteries were blocked, even the ones from the bypass surgery. He would have died anyway."

Voorhees looked at her with relief.

"But that doesn't mean that he should have gone to the grave without his good name," she added. "I want his name cleared."

"I hear you," said Voorhees. "*Philotimo.*"

"*Philotimo,*" said Patty.

Leaving her car in the parking lot, Charlotte joined Voorhees in the police cruiser. She hadn't asked if she could tag along; she had just done it, and he hadn't objected. If it weren't for her, he would never have known that the aprons were a present from Jason. He could hardly deny her the fruits of her own efforts. As they headed down Spruce Street, Voorhees radioed the dispatcher and instructed him to have Martinez ask Demi's friend's mother to pick her up at the diner. As Charlotte was listening to this exchange, she spotted a thin man with a ponytail approaching the gate in the wire-mesh fence at the beginning of the path leading to the grounds of the hydroelectric plant. As the car passed, she turned around for another look, and saw him enter.

"I think I just saw him!" she said.

"Saw who?"

"Jason Armentrout. Or somebody who looks like him. He just went in the gate to the grounds of the hydro plant."

Voorhees swung the car over to the side of the road, and parked. After radioing for a backup, he leaned over and removed a set of handcuffs and a gun from the glove compartment. Charlotte had no idea what kind of gun it was, but it looked menacing: it wasn't your everyday .38 calibre service revolver. He tucked the gun into a shoulder harness, and slipped the handcuffs into his jacket pocket. "I want you to stay out of the way. Do you understand?" he said.

"Yessir," she replied emphatically as they got out of the car.

By contrast with its desultory appearance of the preceding weeks, the raceway that paralleled the road now deserved its name: the water was over-flowing the dam behind the old gatehouse, and rushing downhill, barely contained by the retaining walls. Charlotte thought of all the debris—the shopping carts

and old umbrellas and broken washing machines—that would
be washed out into the river.

"Another couple of inches and the water would be over the
top," she said as she joined Voorhees on his side of the car.

"I've seen it that way," said Voorhees. "I've seen it flowing
right over the road: four or five feet deep."

The Falls also looked much different. Instead of individual
sheets of water separated by rock outcroppings, it was now a
solid white cascade, nearly three hundred feet long. The roar
was deafening, like the sound of an express train passing by
within a few feet, and the spray billowed high into the air.
They could smell the swampy odor from across the street.

"Let's go," said Voorhees. He adjusted his shoulder harness
and they set off.

The gravel lot just inside the gate of the hydroelectric plant
was empty. But once they reached the footbridge spanning the
intake reservoir, they saw Jason. He was heading toward a
woman who was standing on the observation bridge, taking pictures. Charlotte recognized her from her short-cropped
black hair and long, elegant neck.

As Diana lowered the camera to rewind the film, she spotted
Jason, and, with a wave and a smile, turned to join him.

Voorhees laid a restraining hand on Charlotte's arm, and
they stayed where they were, concealed behind the wire fencing that enclosed the footbridge.

For a moment, Jason and Diana talked. Then they started
heading back out toward the road. As they reached the knoll
at the edge of the chasm, Jason seemed to be bumping Diana
with his shoulder. At first, Charlotte thought it was accidental.
But then she realized it was deliberate. Diana must have too,
because she turned to confront Jason, her face confused and
angry. Seconds later, he had her in an elbow lock and was
pushing her toward the precipice.

"He's going to push her over!" Charlotte exclaimed.

"Fuck!" said Voorhees.

As Charlotte and Voorhees raced toward the couple from
one direction, a motorized wheelchair was racing toward them
from the other. It was Spiegel: a knight in shining armor on his
motorized charger, with a camera around his neck. He must
have been taking pictures on the other side of the chasm. With

one hand, he squeezed the lever that propelled the vehicle forward, and with the other, he brandished a crutch as if it were a jousting lance.

Charlotte and Voorhees were running, but it was Spiegel who reached Jason first. He slammed into him with the Amigo, and then tried to hit him over the head with the crutch. Releasing Diana, Jason turned to Spiegel, and wrenched the crutch out of his grip. Then he pulled out a gun and hit Spiegel over the back of the head with the butt. When Jason looked up, he was staring Voorhees in the face.

"Drop the gun," ordered Voorhees. He stood in a combat stance, with his legs spread apart and both hands gripping the handle of his revolver.

Jason complied.

Voorhees instructed Diana to move around to where Charlotte was standing, and then gestured to Jason with his gun. "Now, step away from in front of the wheelchair," he ordered. Removing one hand from his gun, he reached into his pocket for the handcuffs.

What happened next took only a few seconds, but each fraction of that time was engraved in Charlotte's memory as if it had lasted a hundred times as long. As Jason stepped away from in front of the Amigo, removing the barrier to its forward motion, the Amigo resumed its course. Spiegel's white head, now stained with blood where he'd been hit with the butt of the gun, was bent over the handlebars, and his hand was still squeezing the lever!

As they watched in horror, the Amigo raced toward the edge like a runaway horse. Turning away from Jason, Voorhees fired at the Amigo's motor, hoping to knock it out. But the Amigo raced on. For a second, it looked as if it might get hung up on the downed fencing at the edge of the precipice. It strained futilely, rocking to and fro with the effort of bucking the impediment to its forward course.

Then, just as Voorhees got off a second shot, it lurched forward, and disappeared into the swirling spray that boiled up from below. Diana screamed, but the sound was drowned by the roar of the Falls.

As Voorhees turned his attention back to Jason, Charlotte rushed over to the edge and peered over. There was nothing to be seen except the broken branches of the scrub trees that had found a root-hold in the wall of the cliff, and the foaming chartreuse waters below.

Acta est fabula, she thought. It was one of Tom's Latin phrases: the drama has been acted out.

Charlotte returned to Paterson the next day at Voorhees' invitation. He felt that he owed her a final accounting, he said. She had been excluded from the police's interrogation of Jason. Protocol, Voorhees had said, and she had understood. Her involvement was unofficial, and, she was sure, would not have been welcomed by the higher-ups, had they known about it, which she doubted they did. Voorhees was shrewd enough not to have talked about it, and Martinez was shrewd enough not to talk, period.

She would miss Paterson, she thought as the highway skirted Garrett Mountain. The city lay spread out to her right, encircled by the protective ring of the Passaic River: a rich tapestry of red-brick factories and mills that glowed with a warm, rosy patina in the late September sun, the church steeples and smokestacks reaching for the sky like the bell towers of a Tuscan hill town. It was a particularly human town, where old Italian ladies sold bouquets of black-eyed Susans, and the local eatery gave free meals to the homeless. More like a small town than a city, a small town where everybody knew everybody else, and where everybody knew somebody who had worked in the mills, or somebody who still did.

Once she had gotten off the highway, it took only a few minutes to reach the public safety complex. After parking her car, she walked up to the Bureau of Criminal Investigation on the second floor.

"Did your daughter get to her meet on time?" she asked once she was comfortably settled in Voorhees' office.

"Yeah," he replied. "I was sorry I couldn't make it. She took a first, which means that she qualifies for the nationals."

"And if she wins in the nationals?"

"She'll have a shot at the Olympics," he said. He smiled. "Little did I know what I was letting myself in for when I signed her up for diving lessons all those years ago."

"Congratulations," said Charlotte.

"Thanks. We'll see what happens. After years of training, a little injury could do her in. But meanwhile, she'll have had a good time. At least I hope she'll have had a good time."

"Demetra," said Charlotte. "That's a Greek name, isn't it?"

"You're asking because I knew the word *philotimo?*"

Charlotte nodded. "I thought you might be Greek," she said.

"Not me. I'm from old Paterson stock: Dutch, English, a little Irish. The Irish part worked in the mills. But my wife is Greek, so I know a little of the lingo. I've been in the doghouse with her relatives ever since I arrested John. I'm glad I'm going to be able to clear his name. Can I get you some coffee?"

"Thanks" said Charlotte. "Black is fine."

Voorhees disappeared into the adjoining room, and returned a moment later with two cups of coffee. He handed one to Charlotte, and sat down with the other in his swivel chair. Then he said, "I want to thank you. Without you, I never would have solved this case."

"I don't know about that," said Charlotte.

"It's true; the key was the aprons. I'm very grateful. I like the fact that I'll be finishing up my career with a closed case." He made a gesture of finality with his hands. "Nice and neat."

At Charlotte's questioning look, he explained. "I've put in for early retirement. We can put in at twenty years. I have another career to manage now." He nodded at the photo of Demi.

"It sounds as if it's going to be a full-time job."

"Close to it," he said. "My thanks to your husband, too," he said. "We're very grateful for his help. Will you be seeing him?"

"I doubt it. He's about to become my ex-husband," she added with a rueful smile, "but I do expect to be talking to him."

"I wish you'd pass along our thanks. I understand," he added. "I'm going through the same thing myself. My wife and I have been separated for sixteen years. She's been in a mental institution."

"Since your daughter was an infant!" said Charlotte.

He nodded. "I never wanted to divorce her—for Demi's sake. For a long time, I hoped she would get better. And she did sometimes, but then she'd go off again. But"—he shrugged—"there comes a time. Sixteen years is a long time to be lonely."

Charlotte berated herself for making a judgment about his being a ladies' man when he was just reaching out for some human warmth. She remembered his wry acknowledgment of her observation that people do strange things in the name of love. "I'm sorry," she said.

He shrugged again. "We recovered the paintings, by the way."

"Where were they?"

"The frames were exactly where Spiegel said they would be. In Armentrout's storage room. The canvases had been rolled up and stored in a vault right here in downtown Paterson. Armentrout told us where they were. He's angling for a light sentence."

"Did he confess to the murder?"

"Yes. After the party, he dropped Diana off and then continued on. He was passing the mill when he saw Goslau passed out on the sidewalk. He stopped with the idea of helping him, and then got the idea of throwing him in the raceway."

"So Diana wasn't involved."

"No. She didn't even know. But she was in on the scheme to sell the paintings. She just thought Jason was taking advantage of a situation in which Goslau was dead." He took a sip of coffee, and then said: "He used Goslau's key to get into the mill."

Charlotte slapped a palm to her forehead. "Of course!" she said. "And here I was wondering whether Randy would have given him one." She was reminded of Tom's Latin phrase: "Sometimes even the good Homer dozes."

Voorhees chuckled. "I can't say that I was too quick on the uptake on that one myself. Some detectives we are, huh? He couldn't find any rope—that's when he remembered giving Randy the aprons."

"I suppose he used Randy's keys to open the gate too."

Voorhees nodded. "Now, here's the interesting part: while

Armentrout was wrapping Goslau up, he started coming around. Whereupon Armentrout went back inside for the bottle of Courvoisier, and then poured it down Goslau's gullet."

"So that bottle hadn't been consumed by an upscale wino."

"Nope." As far as I'm concerned, that bottle of Courvoisier is the difference between taking advantage of a situation—if that's what you want to call throwing an unconscious cokehead in the drink—and premeditated murder."

"Motive?"

"Greed, as usual. It's always greed. Or almost always greed. You were right about his being in financial trouble. The trust fund had run out, and he was in debt up to his eyeballs. He'd been living off Diana, but they had exhausted her resources, too."

Just then, the phone rang.

"Excuse me," said Voorhees as he reached to answer it.

A second later he had hung up. "That was the chief of the rescue squad. They're about to start trying to retrieve Spiegel's body. They would have done it yesterday, but they thought it would be too dangerous for the divers. Are you interested in going over?"

Charlotte said she was, and they arrived shortly after the rescue squad, which had already lowered a rubber boat over the retaining wall at the Falls overlook. Joining the throng of spectators, they watched the divers search the area where Spiegel had landed.

It was tough work. Though the volume of water was less than the day before, it was still heavy and the divers kept getting dragged downstream by the current, and having to be pulled back.

"How deep is the water there?" asked Charlotte.

"About twenty-five feet. Deep enough so that the current shouldn't have carried the body very far."

"Especially if it's weighted down by a wheelchair."

Just then, one of the divers popped to the surface and pointed at the spot where he had just come up. The rescue workers in the boat tossed him a grappling hook, and then he dove back down again. It was the same spot that John had pointed out to her, the spot where the body they'd thought was Spiegel's had come up.

This time, the diver was down for quite a while. He finally came back up and signaled for the men on the boat to start reeling in the winch. They turned for several minutes before the bumper of the Amigo broke the water. Next came the steering mechanism, and finally the seat. Spiegel was still strapped in, his camera still around his neck.

Though the face was bloated from decomposition, there was no mistaking the white hair and the beard. "Guess it's Spiegel, all right," said Voorhees, turning away from the upsetting sight. "Let's go."

"Nice and neat," Voorhees had said. But it hadn't been nice and neat, not by a long shot, Charlotte thought as they left. Two innocent people were dead; almost three. John Andriopoulis would probably have died anyway, but that wasn't the case for Don Spiegel. She thought of the white, bloated body: how ironic that he had once escaped death at the Falls, only to succumb the second time. It seemed as if it was fated.

But that's how things often happened. She had heard on the news only that morning about a traffic reporter who had died in a helicopter crash after surviving a similar crash only the week before.

As she looked back, Charlotte noticed the rainbow. It spanned the mouth of the gorge, one end emerging from the mist directly above the spot where they had pulled Spiegel's body out. As she watched, the yellow-orange band dissolved into the mist, which carried it upward in copper-colored puffs. They reminded her of the puffs of incense that carried the soul of the departed to heaven.

Magical things were always happening in Paterson.

·16·

CHARLOTTE PAID A condolence call on Louise the next day. She had learned from Voorhees that Spiegel and his wife had reconciled before his death. He had been planning to give up his studio apartment in the Essex Mill and move back in with her and Julius.

His intentions became apparent as soon as Charlotte drew up to the house. The stairs leading up to the front door had already been covered over by a newly constructed wheelchair ramp. Charlotte walked up the ramp, and rang the doorbell.

Louise answered, and escorted Charlotte into a paneled living room filled with mission-style furniture that matched the period of the house. She looked well—far better than she had when Charlotte had seen her earlier that week.

"You were right about your husband not being dead," Charlotte said. "You must have powers of extrasensory perception."

She smiled, her nut-brown skin crinkling around the eyes. "I should have known when his mother didn't come to the funeral. She said it was because she was sick, but if he'd really been dead, she would have been there, even if they'd had to carry her in on a stretcher."

"I noticed the wheelchair ramp. Lieutenant Voorhees told me that your husband was planning to move back in with you."

"Yes," she said, "he was. The ramp was the least of it. We were also going to put in a new shower—one that he could wheel himself right into—and a studio for him. I'm going to go ahead with the studio anyway. I have hopes that Julius might want to use it some day."

"Does he show an apptitude for art?" asked Charlotte.

"Very much so. He's a very talented draftsman. But I don't want to push him." She laughed. "You know how teenagers are. If I encourage him to be an artist, he'll probably want to be a rocket scientist, and vice versa. But it will be there for him, if he wants it."

"I'm very sorry about your husband," Charlotte said. "It seems a terrible tragedy that he had to die just when things were starting to go well for him."

"That's what I thought, too—at first," she said. "But the more I think about it, the more I think that Don's life as Ed Verre was a precious gift. Some people go an entire lifetime without ever coming to terms with themselves, with their creativity, with their God."

"All of which happened to him in the last few months," Charlotte said.

Louise nodded. "To say nothing of coming to terms with me. I'm glad we had the extra time together, however brief it was. Did he shown you his 'Path of Experience' series?"

"Four of them," said Charlotte. "He hadn't finished the fifth one yet." She thought again of the fourth, the one that had prompted her to suspect him. The punishment that he was repenting of wasn't that he had killed Randy, but that he had tried to drive him crazy. "I thought they were brilliant."

"He finished the fifth one on the day of the hurricane. He was planning to expand the series to thirteen, which is the number in Blake's series. That's what he was doing at the Falls: taking photos for the next one. He was going to have a waterfall in it."

Charlotte remembered the camera around his neck, the camera that was still there when they pulled him out of the river.

Louise got up and went into another room. She returned a moment later carrying a canvas, which she leaned up against a wall. "This is it: 'The New Life,' " she said. "He worked on it all day Tuesday, all night too. He had a kind of epiphany out there in the hurricane."

The painting showed a beatific Job and his wife facing a brilliant light that was descending from heaven in the midst of a whirlwind of mystical ecstasy. It was the Lord answering Job out of the cyclone.

Charlotte thought of Spiegel's observation that although he
had managed to penetrate the glass, he had yet to come out on
the other side. In this painting, he had made it through. Then
she noticed the Biblical quotation written across the top of the
painting.

It was: "He bringeth down to the grave and bringeth up."

Charlotte was sitting at home a week later reading an old
issue of the *New York Post* that Vivian had left lying around.
Sipping her coffee, she turned to "Page Six," and found herself
looking at a photo of Xantha and Arthur Lumkin at a Metropolitan Museum of Art Costume Institute gala at the Grand
Ballroom at the Plaza. Xantha, dripping diamonds and dressed
in a gown that looked like an inverted mushroom, was standing
on tiptoe to plant a kiss on Arthur's cheek. Arthur, in white tie
and tails, was looking sideways at a young man with black
hair that curled down over his collar. A white-gloved waiter holding a silver tray of champagne flutes looked on. The
caption was: "Lovebird Xantha Price, the oh-so-trendy fashion designer, gives hubby, financier Arthur Lumkin, a pretty
peck on the cheek at the Costume Institute ball." Studying
the picture, Charlotte speculated on how to read it: the peck
might have meant that Arthur and Xantha had made up, but it
seemed more likely that the young man with the curly black
hair had replaced Randy in Xantha's affections. The "lovebird" might be a double entendre. In any case, it looked like
the gossip page's earlier prediction of a Lumkin-Price bust-up
was wrong, to say nothing of the claptrap about the new emer-
ald ring. Having been the subject of more than her share of
gossip-page speculation herself, she should have known better
than to believe it.

As she drank her coffee, Charlotte pictured Arthur drawing
up a floor plan of the curly haired young man's apartment, and
then, in a flight of fancy, she imagined a whole book of floor
plans. Maybe making floor plans of his wife's lovers' apartments satisfied Arthur's need for a hobby, the way building
model airplanes did for other men. And what of the photos
he had taken of Xantha and Randy in bed? she wondered.
Did he and Xantha stay up at night, munching on popcorn
and reminiscing about old times as they leafed through his

collection of photographs of Xantha with her lovers? There was a time when she would have dismissed such speculations as preposterous, but she had long ago realized that there was no limit to people's sexual eccentricities.

She was getting up to get a second cup of coffee when the phone rang. She knew immediately who it was. If it was Saturday morning, it must be Tom. Ready to hit the blue highways, which is what he called the secondary roads that were marked in blue on the road maps.

She picked up the phone. "I have a hankering for some hot Texas wieners—all the way," said the voice on the other end of the line. "I can pick you up in half an hour. Whaddya say?"

As he spoke, Charlotte realized that her neurotic urge to flee was gone; her heart no longer beat with excitement at the prospect of a road trip. She felt grounded and at peace for the first time in a long time.

But that didn't mean she didn't want to take a ride out to diner-hunting territory on a beautiful September morning.

"Sounds good to me," she said.

"Where are we going?" she asked as they headed across town toward the Lincoln Tunnel, that glorious underground artery that led seekers of the perfect diner to the happy hunting grounds of the Garden State on the other side of the Hudson.

"The Falls View," said Tom.

"Don't you want to try the hot Texas wieners somewhere else?" she asked. Tom had expressed an interest in trying the wieners at other diners in the Paterson area to see for himself if the Falls View's sauce was the best.

"Nope. I have a special reason for wanting to go there."

"What?" she asked.

"It's a surprise."

"Let me guess. A new Chuck Berry tune on the jukebox?" Tom shook his head. "A new flavor of Jell-O?" He shook his head again. "A new waitress? Someone with a beehive hairdo, named Rayette?"

"No," said Tom, shaking his head even more emphatically. "Something even more special than a waitress with a beehive hairdo."

"I've got it," she said. "A modification of the recipe for

the sauce; a change that requires a new review in *Diner Monthly*."

"Nope," he said. "Let's just say that you'll never guess."

They arrived half an hour later. Charlotte was starving for eggs and home fries, Tom for hot Texas wieners. That Tom would eat hot Texas wieners for breakfast seemed to be carrying his devotion to the Falls View's culinary specialty much too far, but Patty had told them that Texas hots were a popular breakfast item.

They took a seat in the only empty booth—the diner was packed, as usual—and were immediately greeted with a fresh pot of coffee by an elderly waitress with stiff white curls whose name tag identified her as Lillian.

"Well," said Charlotte, after Lillian had gone, "I'm waiting."

"Be patient," said Tom, as he flipped through the selection of tunes on the jukebox. Then he put in his fifty cents and picked three. As the opening refrain of "Reelin' and Rockin' " blared out (Tom had turned the volume control to high), they were joined by Patty.

Her big brown eyes were dancing as she slid into the booth next to Tom. "Have you told her?" she asked.

"Not yet," he said, stroking his mustache with smug self-satisfaction. Then he reached out his hand, and wriggled his fingers. "Give," he commanded.

Reaching into the pocket of her black apron, Patty withdrew a ring of keys and handed them to Tom, who held them up and dangled them in front of Charlotte's nose. "Would you like to take a little ride out to Blairstown?"

Charlotte's gaze shifted from Tom to Patty—who was grinning like a Cheshire cat—and then back again. "Plummer!" she said. "Have you gone and done what I think you've gone and done?"

"Yep," he said. "I've done it. I am about to be the proud new owner of a vacation diner park on the Beaver River in Warren County, New Jersey. Courtesy of the heir to the Randall Goslau estate, Miss Patricia Andriopoulis."

Charlotte leaned back in delight. Tom was the perfect owner for Randy's camp: he would carry on the tradition of diner worship. "Well," she said, a twinkle in her gray eyes, "I suppose that if you're not going to settle down with a woman, you might as well with a diner."

"A group of diners," said Tom. He threw out his arms. "A whole *harem* of diners. Anyway, who knows? Maybe some day I'll find a tenant for the Short Stop. Until then, you can stay there any time, Graham. No strings attached.

"Thanks," she said.

He turned to Patty. "The same goes for you. But only if you let me look at Randy's postcard collection."

"Any time," Patty said, who was still smiling. "I thought I'd better grab Tom's offer," she explained. "I figured that the market for a vacation retreat in the form of a collection of classic diners was pretty limited."

"I'd say you figured correctly," Charlotte agreed.

"I'm buying out Uncle Nick," Patty went on. She nodded in the direction of the Falls. "He bought the Torpedo Base, the old sub shop on the other side of the Falls. He's already demolished it. He's going to build a new restaurant there: The Acropolis."

"How original," said Tom sarcastically.

Patty ignored his comment. "Mom and I are going to run the Falls View. So that makes two of us who will be settling down with a diner."

"I guess I won't need to list the Falls View in the Diner Alert column, then," said Tom.

Patty shook her head. "No way," she said.

"Won't the Acropolis cut into your business?" asked Charlotte.

"Nah," said Patty. "Different kind of clientele. You won't be able to get eggs any time there." She continued: "I'm also going to build a new pound for the puppies." She nodded across the street to where a dozen or more dogs were crowded into the tiny, fenced-in enclosure.

"You're not thinking of leading a life of leisure, then," said Charlotte.

"I don't know how to lead a life of leisure. I've worked here since I was ten. I love to waitress. I love people, seeing the regulars come in. I love to serve them food. I'm a Capricorn—back to the earth. We're concerned with the basics: food, clothing, shelter."

"For people and for animals," observed Charlotte.

Patty grinned. "I couldn't go a day without a diner fix," she went on. "My life runs on diner time." She nodded at an old man sitting at the counter. "How would I know it was ten o'clock if I didn't see Roger Barry come in for his free cup of coffee?"

"Speaking of diner fixes, what about you, Plummer?" asked Charlotte. "What are you going to do with your new acquisition?"

"I don't know. Play some tunes, mix some milkshakes, turn the neon signs on and off. Fix that Red Robin sign: I can't wait to see the robin hop. But I don't really have to *do* anything. For me, a diner is like a work of fine art. I can enjoy myself by just looking at it."

"It would be a good place to work on your new book," suggested Charlotte.

"There you go," said Tom. "Maybe you'd like to work on your book there, too. There's plenty of room."

Charlotte didn't reply. Sometimes Tom could be as irritating as Vivian. "What about Mrs. Blakely?" she asked. She had told him about her visit with Randy's neighbor. "She's going to give you trouble about the neon signs."

"I'll charm her," said Tom. "Invite her over for some onion rings."

He was joking, but there was some truth to it, Charlotte thought. If anyone could charm the irascible Mrs. Blakely, it was Tom. "When are we going out there to look them over?" she asked.

"How about right now?"

It was after eight by the time Charlotte got home. They had stopped at the Sunrise Diner for a roast chicken dinner on the way back. Not that Tom hadn't wanted to cook on the grill at the C & E, but he hadn't stocked up yet on groceries, and didn't feel right about loading up the refrigerator until after the deal was closed. She was just settling down to review some scripts when the phone rang. It was Jack, calling to tell her that his lawyer would be sending her some papers to sign. "How long is this going to take, Jack?" she asked. He replied that he expected the divorce to be final by the summer. He would be getting married as soon as it was, he added. "By the way," she said as their conversation was coming to a close, "Lieutenant Voorhees asked me to pass along his thanks. The police have recovered all of the other Spiegel paintings."

"What's going to happen to them?"

"I don't know. Bernice Spiegel was claiming them, but that was when her brother was still thought to be dead. She could hardly claim now that her brother never intended to leave them to Randy when he told me, and probably others as well, that they did legally belong to him."

"He told you that?"

"Yes. He said that although he meant to retract the agreement, he hadn't done so at Randy's death, which meant, as far as he was concerned, that they still belonged to Randy, and hence to Randy's heir, who is Patty Andriopoulis." She had told Jack about Patty.

"What will Patty do with them, do you think?"

"I imagine she'll sell them. I can't imagine Patty as a collector of contemporary art. Why? Are you thinking of buying one?"

"Yes, as a matter of fact. I'd like to buy 'Hometown Diner.'" His voice carried a smile. "As a souvenir of my experience as an FBI operative."

"I'll let Patty know," she said.

After they had exchanged a few more words, she hung up. She thought back to the day they had met. It had been at the opening of a show at a Fifty-seventh Street gallery. She had been dragged along by a friend, who had introduced her to an old acquaintance from her home town of Minneapolis.

She had been bowled over by this big, open, honest man: such a pleasant contrast to the egocentric, self-absorbed, juvenile men she was accustomed to from Hollywood. He had sent her red roses the next day. All that romance had now been reduced to the cold exchange of legal papers.

As she sat down, her eye caught the black plastic case of the tape recorder sitting on the end table. Now that this most recent chapter in her life was coming to an end, it no longer looked as threatening as it once had. Getting up, she fixed herself another drink, and then sat back down.

Where shall I begin? she thought. Then she supplied the

answer: with the beginning of the end. With one hand she picked up the microphone, and with the other she pressed the "Record" button. Then she spoke:

"The last thing I expected when my friend Christina Dodd asked me to attend an opening party for a Paul Klee show was to meet my fourth husband . . . ."